FROZEN DETECTIVE

A Piper & Porter Mystery
from Hallmark Publishing

AMANDA FLOWER

Table of Contents

For
Reepicheep Thomas Flower-Seymour

Acknowledgments

THANKS TO ALL MY READERS who gave my first P.I. novel, *Dead-End Detective*, a try. I hope that you love *Frozen Detective* just as much.

Thank you as always to my agent, Nicole Resciniti. She is the best advocate a writer could have, and I'm so grateful to have her in my corner.

Thanks to everyone at Hallmark Publishing for picking up this series and being so supportive of Darby, Tate, and me. And special thanks to my editor, Stacey Donovan.

Love to my husband, David Seymour, for his unwavering support and patience while I was on deadline and we were in the middle of building a house during a pandemic, no less.

Finally, to my Heavenly Father, thank you for each opportunity to write that you place in my path.

"It is a capital mistake to theorize before one has data. Insensibly one begins to twist facts to suit theories, instead of theories to suit facts."—Arthur Conan Doyle, *A Scandal in Bohemia*

Chapter One

I SAT BEHIND MY DESK AT Piper and Porter Detective Agency and nodded while speaking soothingly into the phone. I don't know why I thought the nodding would calm the person on the other end of the call. "Yes, Mrs. McPherson, I can see why that would be upsetting, but I can't arrest your neighbor just because he arrives home on his motorcycle every night at midnight."

The truth was, I couldn't arrest anyone. I wasn't a police officer. But I knew Mrs. McPherson wouldn't believe that. Even if a police officer told her, she wouldn't believe it.

"You have to do something," the elderly woman said. "I have called the Herrington Police countless times, and they do nothing at all. There is no respect for quiet hours in this town. If I hadn't lived here all my life, I would pick up and move. Motorcycles should be outlawed, in any case. They are dangerous, loud, and no good comes of them."

"But—"

"There are no buts. This situation is intolerable. Mrs. Berger told me that you're the one to talk to if

I ever needed help. Should I tell her she is wrong? Should I tell her you are not the kind young woman she claimed you to be?"

Mrs. Berger was an eighty-something widow whose disgruntled cat constantly climbed the tallest tree in her yard, and, somehow, it had become my job to get Romy the cat down each time. It was a service I did for free. My only payment was cat scratches and Mrs. Berger's gratitude. Fortunately, it was the middle of winter, when Romy seldom went outside. It gave me a short break from my tree climbing.

"Do you want me to have to listen to that motor- cycle the rest of my life?" Mrs. McPherson continued.

"I don't—"

"I will die hearing the sound, and it will haunt me to my grave. Is that what you want?"

I yanked on a lock of my dark brown hair. Mrs. McPherson was making me resort to pulling my own hair, as I had told her the same thing at least fifteen different ways. But the last thing I wanted to do was anger every elderly citizen in the town of Herrington. They made up most of the business for my private detective work, and they gave me referrals, which is priceless in this business.

My business partner, Tate Porter, appeared in my doorway with a silly grin on his face. He made a ges- ture indicating that I should wrap up the call.

Tate was a very fit man from years in the service, and then traveling the world after he was discharged. He had dark curly hair that was on the longish side, a well-trimmed beard, and blue eyes which revealed flecks of green in the right light. At the moment, I couldn't see any green in his eyes. They were just clear blue and amused. What he found so amusing, I didn't know.

"Are you still there?" Mrs. McPherson's voice was sharp. "I will not be ignored. I'm a taxpayer!"

I had no idea what Mrs. McPherson being a taxpayer had to do with me. I didn't work for the government. I worked for myself.

Rather than argue that point with her, I said, "I'm so sorry, Mrs. McPherson, but I have to go. It seems there's some sort of emergency here in the office. My business partner is in desperate need of my help. He just can't do this job alone, you know?"

Tate rolled his eyes at the comment, and it was my turn to grin back.

"An emergency that's more important than bringing a quiet hour violator to justice?" She was aghast. "Believe me, I will be speaking to Mrs. Berger soon and will correct her on the reliability of your services. She may never let you around her cat again!" She hung up the phone.

Hmmm...if Mrs. McPherson tattling to Mrs. Berger could get me out of cat rescue duty, maybe it wasn't such a bad thing after all.

I rubbed the spot between my eyebrows where a headache was forming. "I don't know if I should be happy or sad you interrupted me. I'm glad the call is over, but now Mrs. McPherson is going to tell everyone who will listen what a terrible person I am."

"Aww." He grabbed one of the chairs in front of my desk and spun it around so that he could lean his forearms on the back. It was the way he always sat when he came into my office. "Who listens to Mrs. McPherson, anyway?"

"Her church Sunday School class, her book club, her gardening club, and Mrs. Berger." I ticked the names off on my fingers. "We don't need to be bad-mouthed. Cases are scarce, and whether we like it or not, the elderly set in Herrington is the most likely to request our services."

"Nah, Mrs. Berger would never listen to someone who says unkind things about you. You've saved her cat too many times from that tree." He leaned back in the chair and balanced on the two rear legs.

"Don't sit in the chair like that. You'll break it." I cringed. I sounded just like my librarian mother.

He dropped the chair back on all fours and chuckled, as if he recognized the sound in my voice, too. He propped his elbows onto the back of the chair.

"I hope you're right," I told him. "Because I can't lose the support of the Sunday School class, book club, gardening club, and Mrs. Berger. We need all the business we can get."

My Ragdoll cat, Gumshoe, waltzed into the room and jumped on the empty chair next to Tate. The fluffy cat circled the seat twice before settling in the middle of it. He rested his chin on his paws prettily and waited to be praised.

Tate looked down at the cat. "Such a production."

Not receiving the adoration that he desired, the cat closed his eyes and went to sleep. There wasn't much that ruffled Gumshoe's fur.

"So what's up?" I asked.

"I finished those background checks you gave me. They were all very boring upstanding citizens. I could really use something more exciting to do."

I shuffled through the files on my desk and removed two. "Exciting is not in season around here."

He accepted the files and tapped them on the back of the chair. "It never seems to be."

"It's the middle of winter. It's bound to be slow. Just be thankful we have some money coming in with those background checks. If we didn't have them, we might have trouble keeping the lights on."

"Things will turn around, Piper. You have to trust me on this."

I pressed my lips together. How could he possibly know? Tate was always telling me to trust him. Probably because I had my share of trust issues, but the phrase was beginning to grate on my nerves.

We had been partners in the detective agency for about three months. Before Tate came on board, I partnered with his aunt Samantha Porter for ten years. Tragically, she died in a car accident. She left her half of the business to her nephew, which is how I was working with him today. He'd surprised me when he said that he wanted to go into the business instead of selling off his half. After serving in the Army, including in Afghanistan, and then traveling the world with little more than a pack on his back, I never thought he would want to stay in our small town and be a private detective. But that's what he chose.

I was just about to argue with him when a woman called from the lobby. "Hello?"

I gave Tate a look and whispered, "Did you forget to lock the front door again?"

He shrugged. "Maybe."

I sighed and was just about to get up from my desk when a woman appeared in the doorway. She had striking features and silky black hair that just brushed her shoulders. Even with the snow and ice, she wore three-inch high heels under the hem of her black trench coat. If I ever saw anyone and thought, "That person is from New York City," it would be now. She looked like a direct transplant from the Upper East Side.

"May I help you?"

I stood up from my desk, and Tate tried to, but in his haste, got his leg caught in the chair. Both he and the chair fell over. Startled awake, Gumshoe bolted out of my office like his tail was on fire.

Tate scrambled to his feet. "I'm okay! I'm okay!" he cried, fully flustered.

The woman glanced at Tate. "You really do work here."

He nodded.

My head swiveled back and forth between them. "You two know each other?"

"CeCe and I go way back," Tate said.

CeCe? Why did that name ring a bell for me?

She narrowed her eyes. "I go by Cecily now. Cecily Madd."

"Right," Tate said. "I heard you changed your name when you moved to New York."

She frowned. "Cecily is my given name. CeCe is a childish nickname."

So she didn't like her old nickname. Got it. Yet I still had no idea what she was doing in my office and why Tate, who was usually so cool to the point of being downright annoying, was so flustered around her.

"Why are you here?" I asked.

She put one hand on her hip. "Isn't it obvious? I need a private detective."

Tate and I shared a look.

"Why don't you take a seat," I said. "And we can discuss it."

Cecily looked at the fur-covered chair Gumshoe had vacated with disdain. Tate noticed and jumped out his seat. "Have my chair."

She studied it for a moment, and then perched on the end. If she scooted one inch closer to my desk, she'd fall off the seat.

"How do you two know each other?" I asked.

"Ce—Cecily was in my high school class right here in Herrington," Tate said.

My eyes widened. That's why the name was familiar to me. I didn't know Cecily Madd, but I did know CeCe Tragger. Like CeCe and Tate, I grew up in Herrington, New York, a small town in the Finger Lakes region. Tate was three years older than I, so when he was a senior in high school, I was a freshman. CeCe had been in his class. The only reason I even took notice of her was because she was the prettiest girl in town. She was close to six feet tall, model-thin with that silky black hair, and had perfectly symmetrical features. No one was the least bit surprised that she went to New York City to pursue modeling after she graduated from high school. She would have gone earlier if she'd been allowed.

I folded my hands on my desktop. "It's been a very long time since you moved away from Herrington. What has brought you back?"

She folded her hands in her lap. "My husband and I are hosting a New Year's weekend at Garden Peak

Lodge for friends and clients. We reserved the lodge and the ski slope for the entire weekend for our private event. There will also be an opportunity for vendors and contractors to meet with my husband over the weekend to pitch ideas to him."

My eyes went wide. There were almost a dozen ski resorts in the Finger Lakes region, making the winters just as popular for vacations as the summers. Of those resorts, Garden Peak Lodge was the most expensive. Very few of the locals had ever seen the inside the lodge, myself included. The price to ski or even have lunch there was just out of the question. The townsfolk I knew who had been to the resort had worked there, and they all said the resort was just as fancy as advertised.

If Cecily and her husband had reserved the entire lodge, including the ski slope, I couldn't even guess what that cost. The resort was on Garden Peak Mountain, just on the edge of town. It was the closest resort to Herrington, which sits on the banks of Seneca Lake. Its skiing was supposed to be the very best in the area. Not that I knew from personal experience. I had never downhill skied before and had no desire to start.

"It promises to be a great event for our business," Cecily added.

"And what business is that?" I asked.

She pressed her hand to her chest. "My husband is Dr. Garret Madd. He's a famous dermatologist in New York City. He even has his own skincare line called MaddlyCare, which is worth fifty million dollars."

I stared at her. "Did you say *fifty million*?"

She nodded. "I'm surprised you haven't heard of my husband or his business. I thought everyone had heard of MaddlyCare. We are the premier skincare line in the country." She studied my face for a moment. "You really should try it. It would do wonders for your skin."

I shifted in my seat. "So what's the trouble you've run into that you might need a P.I. for?" I asked, determined to keep this conversation on track.

"I'm worried about my husband. I think his life might in danger. He's been receiving some very threatening and worrisome notes over the last several months. I want you to find the person writing the notes before it escalates out of control."

"It sounds like harassment to me," I said thoughtfully. "Even without all the details. If your husband is receiving direct threats, you should contact the police. They can help you get a restraining order and protection if they think there's a need for it. We can't do either of those things. We might be able to identify the person, but we can't keep them away from you or your husband."

"I know, but my husband forbids me from talking to the police. He's very high-profile in his industry and needs discretion. That's why hiring a private detective is appealing to me."

I felt myself grow more intrigued. Maybe it was boredom. Honestly, anything was going to beat Mrs. McPherson's case right now. "We are pretty far from New York City. Why not hire a P.I. from the city, if that's where you live?"

"We're here for the weekend, and this is where I want to find out who is behind these notes. I suspect the person writing them is on the guest list. I just don't know who it is."

"Why did you pick Garden Peak Lodge?" I asked. "With the success of your husband's business, I assume that you could have had your weekend anywhere in the world."

"Yes, but I wanted my husband to come here and see where I grew up. The lodge was my father's, and I inherited it from him. I have good people on staff and the lodge runs itself. Though I've considered becoming more involved."

"What makes you think someone on the guest list has written these notes?"

She tucked a stray hair behind her ear. A giant diamond stud sparkled in her earlobe. I had a feeling it was the real thing, too. "Based on the content."

This case did sound intriguing. "And what does Dr. Madd think?"

She pressed her lips together. "That someone is trying to capitalize on his fame and fortune. He's not putting much thought and worry into it. He's faced threats before, but this time it's different, because the threats are more specific. It's as if the person sat down and gave a lot of thought as to how he or she was going to hurt us." She opened her small leather purse and removed an envelope and held it out to me. "This is a note my husband received two days ago."

I took it from her hand. It read, *It will come to the point where you will have nowhere else to hide. You know what you did. If I have to spend the rest of my life hunting you, I will. This is your fate for ignoring my warnings.*

The note was typed in all caps on a piece of computer paper. The words were right-justified, which made the note appear off-center. I wondered if that was intentional, planned by the sender to unsettle Dr. Madd somehow. The other interesting detail was the word "point" was underlined. For whatever reason, the writer of the note wanted to put special emphasis on that word.

I handed the letter back to her. "That does sound like a serious threat, but it's not that specific. I'm not saying it's not valid and shouldn't get checked out. But truthfully, it's not a lot to go on."

"This is just the latest threat. I have others that are more specific."

"Then you should really give them to the police. Even if you hire a private investigator to assist in the investigation, the police need to be aware of the threats."

"I can't do that. My husband would be furious."

"Does your husband know you want to hire a P.I.?"

"No, and we need to keep it that way. I would like the two of you to come to the event and pose as a couple. Tate is an old friend from high school who I'm inviting to the weekend—that's all my husband knows."

I frowned. "Why do we have to pose as a couple?"

"It will appear less awkward that way to my husband." She paused. "I—I don't have many female friends, so it would surprise Garret if I still had a girlfriend from high school."

I wasn't sure I was buying that.

"Where are the rest of the notes?" I asked. "I'd like to see them before I make a decision."

"I don't have them with me. I'll let you see the rest when you start."

I frowned. "That's very unusual."

Cecily folded her arms. "It's the way it has to be. I'm not sharing the rest of the notes with you until you agree to the job. I need discretion. My husband and I are already staying at the lodge and our guests arrive tomorrow."

"Tomorrow is New Year's Eve," I pointed out.

"Yes, and the big New Year's Eve party to kick off the weekend is that night. I would like the two of you to check in to the lodge tomorrow as well."

"Why wait?" I asked. "If we checked in today, it would give us time to see the lay of the land and go over the other threatening notes. I don't want to go into that party not having seen them."

Cecily shook her head. "I don't want to give my husband any reason to suspect I'm up to something. Since none of the other guests are arriving until tomorrow, I don't want you there until then either."

I frowned and wondered what kind of marriage Dr. Madd and Cecily had that she had to keep it secret from her husband that she was trying to protect him. I didn't have a great track record when it came to relationships, though. I'd had only one serious boyfriend, with whom I'd broken up and got back together three times. We'd last broken up over a year ago, and I didn't plan to go back. Although, if I was being completely honest, I hadn't planned to get back with him the other times. either.

"Cecily, can you step outside for moment, so Tate and I can discuss this?" I asked.

She frowned but got up from the chair and walked out of the room.

Tate shut the door behind her. "I think we should take it," he said.

When I didn't say anything, he went on. "I know we can crack this case. It's a great opportunity and might lead to bigger and higher-paying clients. I mean, if that's what you want. If you want to stay stuck in petty crime..."

I scowled at him. Tate knew that expanding the business and putting it on firmer financial footing was my biggest goal for the New Year. This case might be the start we needed. That didn't change the fact that something didn't feel right here. It was a gut feeling, and for good or bad, my gut was usually right. I didn't like going into a case not knowing all the facts, and I didn't trust Cecily for holding so much back from the beginning.

"It's a no-brainer," Tate said. "We have to take the case."

I looked up at him. "Tate, we are equal partners in this business. You can take whatever case you want. You don't need my permission."

"True, but you're the only one with a P.I. license, for now, so you have to come with me, especially if this case is as big as I think it might be."

I thought of my New Year's Eve plans, which had been sitting on the couch with Gumshoe, drinking hard cider and eating Flamin' Hot Cheetos from the bag while watching the ball drop in Times Square on the TV. It was how I spent the previous New Year's Eve, since my ex-boyfriend and I had broken up right before Christmas.

I had a stack of background checks on my desk that I had been avoiding, and there was always work that could be done, no matter how boring.

"I can tell you're overthinking this like you always do." Tate interrupted my thoughts.

"I don't overthink things," I said in a huff, then wondered if that was true.

Tate gave me a look that said, *You're kidding, right?* "This case will get you out of the office and out of your funk."

"Funk? I'm not in a funk."

He gave me another look. "Piper, you're a perfect candidate for a light machine. Winter is not your time. You have been short-tempered. Frankly, it's getting a bit old. You need a change of pace."

He had a point. It wasn't uncommon for me to feel more anxious and depressed in the winter. I was a runner and ran every day that I possibly could. Even though I had winter running gear, it was harder to hit the roads when dealing with ice and snow, and to be honest, not nearly as fun, and I hated being cold. So yes, maybe Tate was right, and I wasn't myself in the middle of the winter.

There was a knock on the door and Cecily opened it. "I can pay three times your normal rate, plus accommodations."

My mouth fell open.

Tate grinned.

I tried to compose myself. "All right. We will take the case."

We spent the next half hour drawing up our contract, and Cecily signed it with a flourish before leaving the office.

After she was gone, Tate clapped his hands and pumped his fist in the air like a schoolboy headed for recess. "Pack your bags, Piper. We're hitting the slopes."

I had one more concern about the case. "Just because we're going to a ski resort doesn't mean we have to ski, does it?"

He cocked his head. "You've never been downhill skiing before?"

I shook my head.

He grinned. "This is going to be fun!" I noticed he didn't answer my question. "And pack a fancy dress for the party tomorrow night. It's black tie."

I stared down at my jeans and combat boots. "What on earth makes you think I own a fancy dress?"

"I don't. That's why you'd better get on it." He dashed out of the room before I could throw my pen at him.

Chapter Two

THE VERY LAST THING I wanted to do was buy a dress that I would wear once. I was much more a jeans and combat boots kind of woman. Luckily, I knew someone who would find great joy in finding me a dress, so I called her and gave her the assignment.

An hour after I asked her for help, my best friend Maelynn returned my call. "I have the perfect dress. Come down to the coffee shop and get it."

"That was fast."

"What can I say? I'm talented."

She certainly was that.

I grabbed my winter coat and left the agency. Tate had left a little while before me, presumably to go home and pack for the weekend at Garden Peak Lodge.

Maelynn's coffee shop, Floured Grounds, was on the same street, Lakeshore Avenue, as the detective agency. As I walked in the direction of the coffee shop, I looked around the street at the sparkling surface of Seneca Lake. Parts of the lake were open water, but closer to the edge there were frozen patches. It would have to grow a lot colder for the lake to completely freeze over. I know a lot of the ice fishermen in town were looking forward to it.

There were only a few hardy boats on the lake. Most of the boats in town were sitting on their dry docks, waiting for spring.

As usual, the front porch of Floured Grounds had an adorable seasonal display. As Christmas had only been a few days ago, Maelynn had a full Christmas tree decked out in red and green decorations, and a working electronic train set that ran around the bottom of the tree. There were twinkle lights everywhere too. No one loved holidays like Maelynn.

I went into the coffee shop, and it was mostly full of regulars. Just like for the agency, this was a slow time of year for Floured Grounds. The coffee shop made most of its money in warmer months off the legions of tourists who came to the Finger Lakes for bike trails, boating, and wine.

Maelynn was behind the coffee counter brewing an espresso. She was my age, thirty-one, a tall Black woman with curly hair and striking dark eyes. She grinned at me. "Give me one second."

I nodded and slid onto an empty stool. She finished making the drink and took it to a customer reading a book by the window. Then she came back and hopped on the stool next to me.

"Tell me everything. Did CeCe Tragger really hire you?"

"Shhhh," I whispered, looking around to see if anyone heard her. "I can't talk about an open case, you know that." I squinted at her. "And how do you know CeCe is Cecily Madd?"

She gave me a look. "I keep up with things, Darby. I don't live under a rock like you do."

I folded my arms. "I like my rock, thank you very much."

She sighed. "Well, you're going to tell me everything about the case when it's over. I mean, to spend the whole weekend at Garden Peak Lodge and go to a fancy New Year's Eve party—that's so not you."

She was right. It wasn't me, not at all.

"It's for a case, and I do appreciate you getting me a dress. Where is it?"

She hopped off the stool. "I'll go grab it." She ran into the back room.

A moment later she was back, holding a dress bag in one hand and a tote bag in the other. "I have a dress, shoes, and bag. As well as instructions on how you should do your hair and makeup. I put makeup and hair pins in there too. The works. I wish I'd had time to go shopping for something better, but I'm the only one at the coffee shop today. My barista is visiting her family in Texas for the holidays. I had to go shopping in my own closest, but I think I found the perfect choice for you."

"I'm sure this will be great. I had better get back home and pack." I stood up. "I'll tell you everything when the case is over. Which dress is it?

She cocked her head. "It's the cute black one."

I nodded, remembering the black dress that Mae-lynn had worn on Halloween. That would do very nicely. It was simple but elegant, especially since I wouldn't be wearing the witch's hat that she had paired with it.

Maelynn sighed. "You're going to look gorgeous in it."

That was yet to be determined, I thought.

The next day, I bounced in the passenger seat of Tate's pickup truck as it hit another rut in the steep road winding its way up the side of Garden Peak Mountain. I looked out the passenger window, and all I saw were the trees and snow-covered side of the mountain that seemed to fall in a sheer drop to the lake below. It was a wonder that the trees could grow on such a steep incline. Many of them looked as if they were holding onto the rocks with a single root.

Tate glanced at me. "Be careful. You might break my armrest. You're holding onto it so tightly."

I looked down at my hand. Sure enough, I had the armrest in a death grip. I pried my hand away and let it fall into my lap. "Sorry." My fingers ached from being clenched so long.

"You okay? I've never seen you this uptight about a case."

I shook my head. "It's not the case. It's the road, I guess. It's a lot steeper than I thought it would be, and the drive is a lot bumpier too."

"If you think this is steep, don't go to Nepal. Those peaks go straight up."

"Let me guess—you climbed Mount Everest?"

He shook his head. "Nope, but I did make it to base camp."

"Of course you did. I'd be more surprised if you said you didn't."

Not for the first time, I wondered about Tate's backstory. There was little evidence of Tate on the internet. Trust me, I had looked. Investigation was my job. In this day and age, when more and more people were showing more of themselves on social media, Tate was nowhere to be found. He could have built a following online, too. He was an attractive man, traveling around the globe. People would follow him and live vicariously through him. He was living the life many of them wanted but could never manage, due to family obligations, work, or cost. Yet as far as I could tell, he had no social media accounts.

At first, I hadn't been worried about not knowing his past. Samantha had trusted him, and I would too. Yet now that we had been in business together for several months and he hadn't told me any more of his story, I began to wonder.

Wondering was the curse of being a P.I. It was impossible to fully trust anyone. I didn't believe that Tate had outright lied to me, but I knew very well that he held things back. I tried not to pry. Despite his jovial demeanor, he'd had a sad life. He'd lost his parents when he was young and had been raised by Samantha. Then he'd lost his closest friend in the service. Tate Porter was haunted by something, that was certain. It might have been either one of those things, both, or something worse I didn't know about.

"Is something wrong, Piper?" Tate asked.

"No." I found I was gripping the armrest again. "Sorry. I'm just thinking about the case."

Tate looked like he was going to say something

more, but as we came around the curve in the mountain road, Garden Peak Lodge came into view.

It was a massive and imposing five-story building with a stone and log façade, a circular driveway, and a wide front lawn. The lodge was so big, in fact, that it had a map of the building and grounds on its website. At the moment, the lawn was covered with a foot of snow, but I could imagine how green and lush it was in the summer. A large digital sign read, *Welcome Dr. Madd and Guests!* and then it dissolved into *Happy New Year!*

Tate stopped his truck behind a stretch Hummer that I guessed cost more than my house. A man in a dark suit, accompanied by a giant Saint Bernard, came out of the lodge to greet the Hummer. Two young men followed behind him in bellhop uniforms. It was clear the man in the suit was in charge. I placed his age at just a bit over fifty. He had perfectly combed silver hair with an immaculate side part. Wire-rimmed glasses perched on the bridge of his nose, a straight spine, and a welcoming smile completed his look. The bellhops were half his age but mimicked his good posture. Posture seemed to be very important at Garden Peak Lodge.

The man in the suit opened the passenger door, and Cecily stepped out. She was beautiful as always in a wool suit and heels, with a leather winter coat draped over her shoulders.

The large dog waited patiently on the steps that led into the lodge. He was obedient, but from the way his feathered tail beat a staccato rhythm on the stone steps, it was clear he wanted to greet the newcomers.

The man retrieved her small black purse from

the car, and Cecily nodded in approval. He then ran around the other side of the car and opened it for a second person. A man with white hair and nothing less than glowing skin stepped out of the car. I recognized him from my research into the Madds last night as Dr. Garret Madd himself. He discreetly handed a bill to the man in the suit, who tucked it in his pocket without looking at it.

"Tate," Cecily Madd cried. "It's so nice to see you! It has been too long." She gave him a hug and acted like she hadn't seen Tate just the day before when she hired us. "I'm so glad you could come." Her voice was light and breathy, as if her excitement at seeing Tate was robbing her of air. "I just can't believe I'm seeing you again after all this time. It's been years." She studied him. "And you are even handsomer than you were in high school. It's a cruel twist of fate. Men become more attractive as time goes on, and women less so. As women age, they are in constant search of eternal youth." She smiled. "Which is not a bad thing for my husband's business. He sells the best to women over thirty, who finally realize there is no way to turn back time, just slow it down."

She glanced at me but didn't say so much as a hello. I didn't take this as a good sign.

Cecily waved at the man with white hair who had tipped the bellhop. "Garret, this is my friend Tate, the one I was telling you about. He and I went to school together right here in Herrington." She sighed. "Oh, isn't this quaint? Sometimes I long for the serenity of this little town. There is no serenity to be found in New York City."

Dr. Madd held out his hand to Tate. "When my

wife told me she wanted to host our annual New Year's Eve party in her hometown, I didn't hesitate. We've been married for nine years, and she's never brought me back home. I'm flattered that I finally get to see it."

Garden Peak Lodge wasn't exactly like the rest of Herrington. The town itself was quaint and touristy, especially in the summer when boats covered the large lake, but it wasn't as fancy as the lodge. Herrington was a weekend getaway from normal folks, not for people with Dr. Madd's bank accounts.

"We're glad you're here," Tate said. "I hope you will find time to go down to the village proper. It's a little sleepy this time of year, but very pretty. It looks like a Christmas card right now."

"We will plan to do that," the dermatologist said. He nodded to me. "And you are?"

"Darby Piper." I held out my hand for him to shake. He looked at it for a long moment, as if he was debating if that was what he wanted to do.

Finally, after a second too long with my hand suspended in the air, he shook it. His skin was extremely soft. I guessed that he used his own products.

Cecily smiled at me and said as if we hadn't already met, "I'm happy to meet you too. Tate has told me close to nothing about you, so we will have to use this weekend to become friends." Her dark eyes sparkled. "You're certainly not what I expected."

I straightened my spine to reach my full five-one height. It was no use; Cecily was model-tall and loomed over me. There was nothing I hated more than being loomed over.

"Dr. and Mrs. Madd," the man in the suit said.

"The ballroom is ready if you would like to look it over before this evening's festivities."

"I'll leave that to Cecily. She's the party planner between the two of us, and will know just what to do," Dr. Madd said. "I want to work on my speech a little bit more before tonight."

Cecily patted her husband's arm. "Sweetheart, I'm sure the speech is perfect. You have been working on it for over a week. What more can you say?"

"There is always more that can be done. Nothing is ever really finished, in my opinion."

Dr. Madd followed the two bellhops into the lodge.

His wife smiled at us. "Garret is such a perfectionist when it comes to his work. I suppose that's why he has been so successful. No one can beat his work ethic."

"Now that we're alone," I said. "Tate and I would like to see the other notes."

"I—I don't have them with me now, and to be honest, now is not a good time. You heard Herschel; I need to check the ballroom. I'm certain there will be dozens of adjustments for me to make. I have a vision for this party that I think I've been very clear on, but I'm not sure anyone else fully understands it." She sighed. "That's always the case when I throw a party for MaddlyCare."

"You could just give us the letters, and we can take it from there. Are they in your room?" I asked.

"No. I have them somewhere safe. I will show you after the party."

I cocked my head. "If you think the person threatening your husband will be at this party, we need as many clues as possible as to who that person is.

Those notes will go a long way towards helping us out."

"I can't do that right now." Cecily glanced at the lodge. "I don't have time before the party. It can wait until tomorrow morning. We have all weekend. Let's not rush into things." She hurried into the lodge after her husband.

After Cecily had disappeared inside the lodge, the man in the suit came up to us. The large dog trotted behind him. "Mr. Porter's party?" he asked.

Tate nodded.

"Oh, that's very good. All the other guests are already here. You're the last to arrive," he said in a slightly admonishing tone.

I glanced at my watch and saw we were thirty minutes early. Had there been a race to get to the lodge early that I didn't know about?

He placed a hand to his chest. "I'm Herschel Brighten, the general manager of this lodge. I've been at this post for over thirty-five years. If you have any questions or need anything at all, I will be the one to ask. I'm usually easy to find around the lodge. Tiny is always at my side." He let his hand rest on the massive dog's head.

Tiny? That was like naming a blue whale "Minnow."

Tate held his hand out to the large dog. Tiny shuffled over to him and gave his hand a good sniff. Tate passed the test, and Tiny licked his hand. Tate proceeded to scratch the dog behind the ears and on the top of his head.

Tiny sighed in happiness.

"I love Saint Bernards," Tate said. "I had one growing up, and it was like having a bear for a best friend. You won't find a more loyal canine."

A large drop of saliva fell from the dog's lower lip. He appeared to be friendly and kind, but a Saint Bernard was an odd choice for a place as pristine as Garden Peak Lodge.

Herschel smiled wide. "I've always thought the same. Tiny takes up most of the room in my office and on my bed, but I wouldn't have it any other way."

Tiny looked back at his master with a goofy doggy smile. I could see why Herschel wanted to have him around.

Herschel said, "And Ms. Piper, if you don't mind my saying so, you look so much like your mother. You have the same brown eyes and bright smile."

"You know my mother?"

"Yes, I know her very well," he said. "I go to the library any day I'm off and load up on books. She always has a stack ready for me and makes the best recommendations. Please tell her how much I appreciate that."

I smiled. My mother was the head librarian at Herrington Library and made a point of learning all of her regulars' favorite reads so she could share even more books with them. "I will. She loves that kind of feedback from library patrons."

He nodded. "I suppose that not all the feedback she gets is as kind. I most certainly know what that is like. Working in a service business, you just don't know how people are going to react to even the slightest change."

He glanced over his shoulder, and one of the two bellhops stood at the top of the stairs expectantly.

"I'm so sorry," Herschel said. "Sam is ready to take you to your rooms. They're adjoining suites. Other than the penthouse where Mrs. and Dr. Madd are staying, you have my very favorite rooms in the lodge."

"I'm sure it will be cozy. We can't wait to see them," Tate said.

The bellhop offered to take our bags to our rooms, and we followed him into the lobby. The interior of the lodge was enormous. Everywhere I looked, I saw polished wood: the floor, the ceiling, and the walls. It was broken up with a huge stone fireplace to the right that ran from the floor to the twenty-foot cathedral ceiling and wall of windows that overlooked the resort straight in front of us. Through the windows I could see a large patio, and beyond that, the ski slope.

The lodge was still decorated for the holidays. A fifteen-foot Christmas tree stood by the fireplace. It was decorated in silver and blue ornaments and a glass bead garland that wound around the branches from the very top all the way to the bottom. A blue velvet tree skirt lay under the bottom boughs, and the tree was topped with a silver star that reflected the light coming from the fire.

There were other touches of the holidays throughout the lobby. Bowls of pinecones and silver ornaments sat on side tables next to silver pillar candles. Garden Peak Lodge wasn't the kind of place where you would find Santa Claus's legs peeking out of the fireplace or an Elf on the Shelf.

A garland that matched the one wrapped around the tree traveled up the railing of the grand staircase as well. Everything was so lovely, decorated in silver and blue, and I couldn't help but find myself charmed by it all.

The bellhop caught me staring. "The original owner of this lodge wanted guests to walk out the doors in the morning and start skiing. There is a chair lift, of course, that brings them back up the mountain to the lodge after they go down the slope." He walked to the bay of elevators. "To the right, you'll find the entrance to the grand ballroom. That is where Mrs. Madd will be hosting the party tonight. It's sure to be spectacular. Down the short hallway to the left are the spa, fitness center, and pool."

I nodded. I guessed in a place like this, they had fitness equipment and spa treatments that I had never even heard of.

"Can we see the ballroom?" I asked.

The bellhop paled. "Oh no, Mrs. Madd gave strict orders that none of the guests can see the room until she has approved it."

That was interesting. I stored the detail that Cecily was a bit of a control freak in the back of my mind. It was as important to me to know the traits of my clients as it was to know those of the people I was investigating.

"We will see it soon enough," Tate said. "My girlfriend just really loves holiday decorations. She can't get enough of them. That's why she wants an early look at the ballroom."

"Oh." The bellhop visibly relaxed. "My girlfriend is like that too. May I show you the way to your rooms?"

Behind the bellhop's back, I made a face at Tate and he grinned. This boyfriend-girlfriend storyline was really starting to get on my nerves, and we'd just gotten here.

"Your rooms are on the third floor, and you are some of the lucky guests who have suites facing the slope."

We stepped off the elevator and he unlocked room 303 with a card key. "This is your suite, Mr. Porter. Miss Piper, you're next door in 305. It's identical to this one. As you can see, there is the door that adjoins the suites." The bellhop then handed me that key and a second one to Tate. He set Tate's bag in the room. "Was there anything else you need?"

"No, thank you," Tate said and tipped the man, who then said he'd take my bags next door.

Tate's suite was gorgeous, with a living room, bedroom, huge bathroom, and balcony with a clear view of the ski lift and the main slope. The furnishing was similar to the lobby. There was a lot of wood and a smaller stone fireplace. There was even a silver and blue-decorated Christmas tree in one corner of the living room. It was, of course, much smaller than the one in the lobby, but I thought it was an adorable touch. Maybe every guest in the lodge got their own Christmas tree.

Outside, the skiing looked busy today. I wondered how many of those skiers were guests of Dr. Madd's. Tate had said the Madds reserved the slope and lodge for the entire weekend, so perhaps all of them. The person making the threats against Dr. Madd could be skiing down the mountainside right now.

"What do you think?" Tate asked. "Pretty posh, right?" He fell onto the bed and let out a sigh. "Feels like a cloud."

"The lodge is very nice," I admitted. "But I can't help wondering why Cecily is so hesitant to share the other notes with us. All my warning bells are going off."

"She's just busy right now, Piper. Relax. Go check out your suite and enjoy yourself a little. She wants this case solved as much as we do. Stop worrying so much."

That was a lot easier said than done.

Chapter Three

I WENT TO MY SUITE, AS Tate had suggested, to get ready for the party. We wanted to be there early so we could see all the suspects, a.k.a the guests, as they arrived.

As the bellhop had said, my suite was identical to Tate's, down to the ornaments on the Christmas tree. I could imagine being curled up on that chair next to the tree with a hot mug of cocoa watching the ball drop on TV. I sighed. That was not to be. I went into the bedroom and pulled the dress bag from Maelynn out of the closet where the bellhop had hung it. I laid it on the bed and unzipped it.

This was not the simple dress I had been expecting.

I pulled out the black sequined frock with red crystal beaded fringe on the bottom. It was the perfect dress for Maelynn...but then again, she'd look gorgeous in a garbage bag. On me, the dress would look like a 1920s flapper costume for Halloween. All I needed was a feather for my hair.

It was not what I would have chosen. Frankly, I wondered if I could get by in the jeans and sweater that I'd packed for the night. I doubted it, especially after seeing Cecily. She wasn't a jeans kind of person, and I guessed she didn't want anyone around her to be one either.

I took the dress into the bathroom, which was bigger than most living rooms I had seen. Close to forty minutes later, I was as ready as I was going to be. I had followed Maelynn's directions as best I could about fixing my hair, twisting it into a braid that brushed my right shoulder. It didn't look nearly as good as it would have if she'd styled it, but it was passable.

I had also followed her step-by-step instructions on the makeup, and I thought it looked okay. I was the most nervous about the dress. I self-consciously smoothed it over my hips for the third time. Every time I moved, the tassels hit each other and made little wind chime sounds. This was not the dress to wear on a sting.

There was a knock on the door between our two rooms. I sighed and let Tate in.

"Darby—" He pulled up short. "Dang!"

I cocked my head. "Dang? Is that supposed to be a compliment?"

"It is. You're gorgeous."

To hide my red cheeks, I turned to pick up the tiny and impractical purse that Maelynn had lent me along with the dress. I couldn't fit much more in it than my phone. My handcuffs were certainly not coming along, but we weren't even close to the point of making a citizen's arrest. We didn't even know all the suspects or all the threats. It was not the best way to start an investigation.

"You're very handsome yourself," I said, and he was. He wore his hair smoothed back and a black tuxedo that was tailored just for him. What had Tate's life been like before, that he would own a tuxedo? How many events did the wandering globetrotter attend that needed a tuxedo?

He grinned. "Why, thank you." He did a little twirl and bowed.

I couldn't help but laugh. "Come on, Showboat. We have a case to solve."

"Showboat?" he chuckled. "Are you picking up 1920s vernacular, too?"

While Tate and I had been dressing, instructions for the night's proceedings had been slipped beneath the door to our rooms. They said that we were to enter the ballroom via the grand staircase on the second floor, unless there was some sort of disability that kept us from doing that.

Tate and I took the elevator to the second floor and found a short line of people waiting at the top of the stairs. It was a little after eight. The party started at eight-thirty, and I had expected us to be the first to arrive. Unfortunately, we weren't. A lodge staffer stood at the top of the steps and instructed each guest when it was their turn to greet the Madds.

Tate whistled under his breath. "*This* is a showboat affair."

I didn't respond. I was already on the case. Every person and face I saw, I analyzed. Did the person look angry, nervous, jumpy, or determined? Of course, having those feelings was no proof that the person was sending threats to Dr. Madd, but there was always a tell when someone was up to something. You just had to look for the signs.

The last person to go down the staircase before us was a man also wearing a tuxedo, like Tate's, but while Tate's fit him to a T, this man's tux was exceedingly large for him. He continually pulled on the sleeves to adjust the shoulders, which slipped from his thin frame over and over again. His hair was buzz cut and he wore glasses that amplified the narrowness of his face.

A man in tails at the door announced the gentleman in the baggy tuxedo as Frederick Hume. From my aerial view of the introduction, I noticed that Cecily wrinkled her nose when Frederick was announced, like she'd smelled something bad. I made a mental note to find out who Frederick was.

"You're next," the bellhop said in an oddly stiff voice.

Before we went down the grand staircase, Tate held out his arm to me. I didn't move.

"Come on. We're pretending we're in love, which means you have to at least pretend to like me. Get into character."

I looped my arm through his and plastered a smile on my face.

"Perfect. Just realistic enough. Only someone who really knows you would recognize the twitch in your eye."

I squeezed his arm. "Let's go. We have a case to solve, and I already have a suspect."

His eyes went wide as we walked down the stairs. "How can you have one before I do?"

I adopted his customary shrug. "Talented, I guess."

"That you are." There was a flash in his eye that seemed to hint at something more than friendly respect.

I looked away from him, as if I was suddenly interested in the gigantic crystal chandelier that hung over the staircase, because I felt a blush creep across my cheeks.

I mentally kicked myself. *Get it together, Piper. This is a job.*

The chandelier was intricate and the size of a small car. It sparkled above our heads as we made it to the main entrance of the ballroom. I couldn't help but wonder whose job it was to dust it. It had to be more than one person.

Tate and I joined a line of people entering the grand ballroom. At the door, Cecily and Dr. Madd greeted each guest in turn. Both of them were dressed to the nines, as my grandmother would have said. I assumed that the diamonds on Cecily's necklace and earrings were real and worth more money than I could even fathom.

I felt like I was waiting to be presented to the queen for my coming out season or some such thing. As we drew close to the Madds, laughter and music drifted in from the ballroom, along with delicious smells. My stomach growled. When we arrived at the lodge, there hadn't been enough time to eat before we had to get ready for the party. I had subsisted on a package of suspect saltine crackers I found pulverized in their wrapper at the bottom of my purse.

Even though I was starving and exceedingly uncomfortable with my outfit—the skirt was well above my knee, and I could only wonder how short it was on

Maelynn, who was five inches taller than myself—my head was on a constant swivel. I took care to subtly scrutinize every person we passed and commit the face to memory. It was impossible to know if Cecily was right, and the person making the threats against her husband was here. She'd insisted the person was here. I was also on the lookout for a man named Frederick Hume. He was definitely out of place in this room.

Even though it felt odd to be so dressed up, I was glad I was. Had I worn my jeans and sweater, I would've stuck out like a sore thumb. That was the very last thing a private eye wanted to do.

Cecily took one of my hands in both of hers by way of greeting. "It's so nice to see you both again. It's just a pleasure for us that you and Tate can be here."

Carefully, I removed my hand. "We're grateful to be invited. This is much better than our original New Year's Eve plans, so we thank you."

"Yeah, my plans consisted of eating Cheetos and watching the ball drop in New York City on the television," Tate said.

My head snapped in his direction. Was he for real? Or was he teasing me? How on earth did he know about my New Year's Eve plans?

Cecily laughed. "I hope you find this much more enjoyable."

"How could they not?" Dr. Madd said. "Thank you for coming. It's all my wife can talk about, you being here. I think she's more excited about your presence than mine." He chuckled as if that was the funniest thing he could ever say.

Cecily batted his arm. "Dear, you know that's not true." To Tate and me, "We will see you inside."

When we were in the ballroom, I released Tate's arm.

I was afraid that my jaw might have dropped when I stepped into the room. The space was gorgeous. There was a dark wood dance floor on one side of the room, and a large stage with a podium on the other. The tables were decorated in silver and blue, in keeping with the tree in the lobby and an identical tree in one corner of the ball room. Even from the doorway, I could tell the tables were set with real silverware and expensive china. I would have to be extra careful when I ate. I didn't want to be responsible for breaking any of those dishes.

"Let's split up and see what we can learn," Tate said.

"I have a feeling you'll have better luck with this crowd if you're unattached," I joked. I'd noticed some very beautiful women eyeing him.

"We'll meet up by the fireplace in forty-five minutes. That should be plenty of time to scope things out before the speeches begin."

"The fireplace?" I asked, and then I saw it. Sure enough, there was a stone fireplace at the far end of the ballroom as well. Garden Peak Lodge was really into foreboding fireplaces. "I see it. Sounds like a plan."

Tate headed to the bar and I went toward the stage. Throughout the room there were round tables, each with eight chairs. Closer to the side walls stood high-top tables where people could talk and drink.

I looked more closely at the large tables. There

were name cards at each place setting. Of course there were. I wouldn't have expected anything else from Cecily's party. In the sea of tables, I had no idea how I was supposed to find ours.

A waiter walked by with a tray of canapes, and I grabbed two golden pastry appetizers. Before I stuffed one in my mouth, I asked, "How do I know where I'm supposed to sit?"

"The seat master will help you. He's making his rounds now." He scurried away from me, out of fear that I might grab another appetizer, I thought. The truth was I had been planning to. I popped one of them into my mouth. The layers of phyllo pastry were wrapped around goat cheese; it was light, flaky, rich, and creamy all at the same time. I almost fainted, it tasted so good. I ate the second one and kicked myself for not grabbing a third.

"Are you having trouble finding your table, miss?" someone asked. I recognized the chirpy male voice immediately.

Startled, the goat cheese puff caught in my throat, and I started to choke. Benny B pounded me on the back, and I swallowed the puff. I stole a water glass from the nearby table and gulped down the water.

When I came up for air, I glanced around to see if anyone had noticed my less-than flattering episode. No one seemed to have any reaction at all. Apparently, in this crowd, if you were choking, you were on your own.

"What are you doing here?" I whispered in a hoarse voice.

"You and Mr. Porter are at table twelve. That is just to my right." Benny B smiled at me.

Instead of his usual track suit, he wore a hotel-issued tuxedo with tails and white gloves. His glasses slipped to the tip of his nose like they always did, and I could almost look him in the eye, since he was only a couple inches taller than I was.

"Benny."

He smiled. "Is there something else I can help you with?"

"Yes, you can help me by telling me why you're here, posing as lodge staff." I rubbed my throat; it was still sore.

"I work at this lodge. I have a staff I.D. card, a parking pass, the whole works."

"So you gave up being a paparazzo because the money was better in hospitality services?" My voice dripped with doubt.

Benny B was a paparazzo I had met while working on a high-profile case. He had been there with the hopes of following me, which would give him a story to sell to the tabloids. I wasn't going to let him use me like that again. Usually, he was never without his DSLR camera and its long zoom lens. I didn't see it anywhere around him now.

"Oh, I haven't given up being a celebrity photographer in the least. That's why I'm here, and I'm willing to bet you're here for the same reason." His eyes sparkled.

I shook my head. "I don't jump out of bushes to take compromising pictures of people to sell to the highest bidder."

"No, you jump out of bushes to take compromising pictures of people to give to your clients so they will pay you. You see, Darby Piper, you and I aren't that different from each other."

I ground my teeth. It unnerved me to think he might just be right.

"Now, did I apply for and take the job when I heard that Garret Madd of MaddlyCare was going to host a giant star-studded New Year's Eve party here? You bet. You know I'm not one to waste an opportunity, and this way, I get paid for the photos and from the lodge. I can't lose."

"I'm sure the lodge has a policy that you can't spy on the guests."

"They do, but I'm not afraid of you ratting me out about it, because then you'd be in trouble too. I hear that not even Garret Madd knows what your true occupation is. You are just here as Tate Porter's date, from what I gathered."

I clenched my jaw a little harder. My teeth were beginning to hurt. "Where's your camera?"

"It's safe. You know I take care of my pictures. As much as I would've loved to bring it here tonight, I think it would've blown my own cover. Cell phone cameras have come a long way in the last few years." He held up his phone and took a picture of my face. "This will work in a pinch."

"Stop that," I hissed.

"So tell me. Why are you here? If you're here, I know this story will be much better than a bunch of celebrities getting drunk on New Year's Eve. Tate Porter might, but I don't really see you moving in the same world as Cecily and Garret Madd."

I didn't argue with him on that last point because it was true. I didn't move in those circles. My circles weren't even in the same universe as Cecily and Dr. Madd.

"Tate is an old friend of Cecily's. She invited him to the party. I'm his guest. That's all there is to it," I said.

"Then why are you and Tate both walking around the room like you're doing reconnaissance to toss the place?"

"We're not. Considering our work, we're always looking for oddities in any and all situations. You can't just turn that inclination off."

He chuckled. "And I'm the King of England. I have my eye on you, Darby Piper—don't you forget that." He took his seating chart and waltzed away.

Like I could forget it.

Chapter Four

I RUBBED THE BRIDGE OF MY nose. I felt a headache brewing behind my eyes. If Benny B was here, this case had just gotten a lot more complicated.

Across the ballroom, a tall man walked the perimeter of the room with his hands behind his back as he looked toward the ceiling. I looked up. The ballroom ceiling had an intricately carved plaster design of pinecones and pine branches. I don't even know if I would have noticed it if the man hadn't been studying it so intently.

He was still looking up when he walked toward me. I had to say something to keep him from bumping into me. "Excuse me!"

He adjusted his glasses. "I'm so sorry. I just can't get over how beautiful this room is. I had never been in the ballroom before."

"It's my first time here as well," I said. "I was so grateful to be invited."

He studied me. "Do you work with MaddlyCare?"

"No, but my p—boyfriend is an old friend of Cecily's."

He nodded. "It seems everyone I've met so far

has a different reason for being here. They might be friends or staff or even people hoping to pitch ideas to the Madds. And then you have me."

"Why are you here?" I asked.

He gestured to the room. "Because of this place. It will be perfect."

I wrinkled my brow. "Perfect for what?"

"Wine tastings and sponsor parties. The ideas are endless."

"Do you hope to rent the lodge to do that?" I asked.

He looked at me. "No. I'm going to buy it."

"It's for sale?"

"Everything is for sale when you offer the right price. Everyone could use a little extra money."

"I wasn't under the impression that the Madds needed money. They're the owners of this place."

"Cecily Madd is, not her husband. It will be up to her if she sells. I'm confident that she will. It just makes more sense that this place belongs to someone local who can actually care for it long-term. This is the first time Cecily has even been back here to visit in ten years. How much control does she really have over what she never sees?"

"She trusts her staff."

He shook his head. "No one trusts their staff that much." He pulled a card out of his pocket and handed it to me.

I read it, "Stone Vineyards. Jeremy Stone, owner." It then listed the website, phone number, and address.

"I'm Jeremy, but everyone calls me Stone. I was happy to be invited to this weekend. I reached out to Cecily about purchasing this place a few months back. At the time, she said she wasn't interested in selling. But she gave me a call about a week ago and told me about this weekend. She said if I was willing to come up, she'd hear me out. That tells me she is ready to sell."

He held up his drink. "I think it's time to refresh this." He walked away.

I watched him go, thinking that was one of the odder conversations I'd had with someone while working, and I was a private investigator, so that was saying a lot.

I met Tate at the fireplace at the appointed time. He handed me a glass of wine. "Any luck?"

"I don't know if I would call it luck, but I found a new wrinkle."

He raised his brow.

"Benny B is here."

"What?" he hissed.

I nodded and took a sip of my wine. "He apparently heard about this party and applied for a job at the lodge so he could spy on the Madds and their famous friends."

Tate whistled under his breath. "He plays the long game. I can respect that."

"Whether you respect it doesn't matter. He could blow our cover. No one will talk to us about those threatening notes if they know that we're private detectives."

"I think it's in Benny B's best interests to keep our secret. If he reveals who we are, we'll do the same to him. People might stop talking to us, but they'll kick him out onto the street."

"That's a good point," I admitted. "I just wish we

had more information going into this evening. I have to question Cecily's motives for throwing us into this party without all the facts. If we'd seen the other threats, we might be able to narrow down the suspect list tonight. There must be a hundred people in here."

"There are one hundred and eighty-three guests. Plus, staff must be at least thirty more." He patted his label. "I got a guest list."

"From Cecily?" I asked.

"No, from the woman at the front desk. I told her that I was on Cecily's staff, which is not technically a lie. I think she was so starstruck by the celebrities at the party, she would've handed over all of the cash drawer money if I'd asked her."

"I doubt she would've done it for anyone else. You also used some of your Porter charm. I saw Samantha wield it like a weapon when she was on a case. Apparently, it's hereditary."

He chuckled. "It's not a bad gift to have, and you can be charming too when you set your mind to it."

I wanted to ask him what he meant by that, but was interrupted when someone struck a knife against a glass.

Tate and I looked across the ballroom. Most of the guests were seated at their tables.

"Please, everyone, take your seats," Herschel, the general manager, stood at the podium. He was in black tie attire like the other guests in the room. "For those of you who haven't met me yet, I'm Herschel Brighten, the general manager of Garden Peak Lodge. We cannot express how grateful we are to have Dr. Garret and Cecily Madd with us this weekend." He smiled at the couple. "The whole staff welcomes you and your guests." He gestured to the staff lined up by the entrance. They were all in uniform, except for the very last person in line. He wore baggy jeans and a geometric sweater. He was tan even in the middle of winter, and his hair was dark, but the tips were spiky and blond. He looked like a throwback from the 1990s. He was by far the most casually dressed person in the room.

"As you know, Cecily's father started this lodge decades ago," Herschel went on. "We are grateful that she has come back and brought so many friends. We look forward to the plans she has for the lodge in the future." Herschel smiled. "Now, we are going to receive a few words of welcome from our hosts."

"How do we know where to sit?" Tate asked as Cecily and Dr. Madd made their way to the stage.

"We're at table twelve," I said.

"How do you know that?"

"Benny B. It was the only bit of useful information that he gave me. He's in charge of the seating chart."

"So he knows where all the players are," Tate muttered.

"Exactly." Tate took my hand and started across the ballroom. I noticed his hand was dry and warm. I willed my hand not to sweat.

We found our name cards on table twelve. To my surprise, I was seated between Tate and Fredrick Hume, the man in the ill-fitting tuxedo. I smiled at him. "I'm Darby. It's nice to meet you."

He glanced at me. "Frederick."

Oh-kay.

"How long have you been friends with the Madds?" I asked as I set down my wine glass.

He looked me right in the eye. "I'm not *friends* with Dr. Madd and his wife. I'm a colleague. I also work in skincare."

"Do you have a line like Dr. Madd?" I smiled. "I'm always looking for new products to try." That was a lie. I had been using the same face wash since I was a teenager.

"No, I do not." He cleared his throat. "I do have a new product that I hope Dr. Madd will consider for his new eye cream line. You're a friend of his?" He now sounded interested in me.

"I'm friends with Cecily. I don't know her husband nearly as well." Of course, I didn't know Cecily much better than I knew Dr. Madd, but Frederick didn't need to know that.

"Oh," he said. "I know that Cecily has her husband's ear. Maybe you could give this to her?" He reached into his pocket and came up with a white tube that was roughly four inches long, printed with the words Miracle Smooth. He handed it to me. "The packaging isn't much, but it's simple and all I could afford. If I had the backing of MaddlyCare, they could package it any way they liked."

I opened my tiny purse and tucked the tube inside. "I'll give it to her."

His whole body relaxed. "Thank you. I didn't think I'd have an opportunity to pass it along to the Madds tonight." He cleared his throat. "What was your name again?"

"Darby. Darby Piper."

He nodded, as if this time he was committing my name to memory. He picked up his wine glass and swallowed a big gulp of it. Red wine stained his pale lips, and beads of sweat gathered on his forehead. Frederick Hume was nervous. Was he nervous because he was worried about the Madds buying his product, or nervous because he was behind the threatening notes?

"What would happen for you if MaddlyCare picked up your eye cream?" I asked.

He set his glass down. "Everything. I would finally be on the map as a cosmetic chemist. I know that I have an excellent product, but I don't have the means to get it in consumers' hands. When I received the invitation to this weekend, it took all I had to get here. I wasn't going to let anything get in my way." He held his wine glass so tightly that I thought it might shatter.

"Maybe take another sip of wine?" I suggested.

When I said that, he seemed to notice that he had a firm grip on the glass. He relaxed his fingers and took another sip. It was more measured this time. Finally, he let out a breath. "Just please give that eye cream to her."

"I will," I promised.

"Good evening, esteemed guests," Cecily Madd said from the microphone. "My husband and I are thrilled that so many of you can be here this weekend to ring in the New Year with us. I am personally touched that we can be here at my late father's lodge for this celebration. I know he would be so proud of Garret and me. It is our hope that this lodge can become a resource for MaddlyCare and its partners.

"MaddlyCare has had an incredible year, and it will just get better in the years to come. We invited you all here this weekend because we want to make that journey together. As most of you know, I met Garret when I went into his office with a problem with my skin. It is always important to have good skin, but as a model, it was my job. He treated me for six months, and where others had failed, he found the solution I needed. Over that time, we fell in love, but Garret, ever the professional, didn't ask me out on a date until I finished my treatment. It wasn't long until we realized what a dynamic duo we made. Garret would make the product, and I, as a client and model, could be the face of the company. That was nine years ago, and we haven't looked back. I could not ask for a more wonderful partner in business and in life." She held out her arm. "Dr. Garret Madd!"

The audience clapped. Frederick's eyes were glued to Cecily's face. I don't believe he even blinked during her entire speech. There was something off about the cosmetic chemist sitting next to me.

"Has anyone ever had a better introduction, or a more gorgeous wife?" Dr. Madd smiled and his white teeth sparkled under the overhead lights. "Now I know it's New Year's Eve, and we are here to party, so I am going to make this short. Thank you for being here tonight and this weekend. I have invited each and every one of you here for a reason. But there are a few I want to highlight. Kiera Bellworthy." He looked at a woman at the front of the room.

I couldn't see her face, but the crowd buzzed at the mention of her name.

Even though I couldn't see Kiera's face, I knew who she was. Maelynn thought I lived under a rock because I didn't have a social media presence and didn't keep up with pop culture. That was true on both accounts. Social media was a liability for a private detective, and I wasn't that interested in the latest trends. But Kiera Bellworthy was one of the highest paid actresses in Hollywood. Even I had heard of her.

"Kiera will be the new face of MaddlyCare moving forward." Dr. Madd clapped at his own announcement.

Behind Dr. Madd, Cecily's face flushed bright red.

"As you know," Dr. Madd went on, "my lovely wife has been the face of the line for years now, but we need a fresh, new face to appeal to the next generation of skincare clients. Kiera is just the person to do that. Kiera, why don't you stand up and wave to the people?"

Kiera stood up and waved. Her movements appeared reluctant, but that was understandable. It seemed to me that Dr. Madd was showing her off like some sort of trophy. When she turned to face the audience, I gasped. She really was gorgeous. She had perfect features and flawless dark skin. Her hair was styled in a pixie cut, which made her features stand out even more. There wasn't any doubt why Dr. Madd had picked her for this role. Anyone would be hard-pressed to find a more beautiful face.

She sat back down.

Dr. Madd beamed like he'd won some sort of prize. "Thank you, Kiera." He cleared his throat. "Tonight is a fun night, but tomorrow—even though it is a holiday—will be time to get to work. I know many of you are here for the opportunity to pitch your products or services to MaddlyCare. This is your one shot. Don't mess it up." He smiled. "But tonight, I want you all to enjoy this party and have the best New Year's Eve ever!" He held up his champagne glass. "To the New Year."

There was a tepid "To the New Year" from the audience.

The doctor stepped off the stage, and the band began to play again. The wait staff made the rounds with canapés, and the buffet and full bar opened.

Cecily Madd stood on stage with her arms crossed and glaring at her husband as if she wished him dead.

Chapter Five

$\mathscr{A}$T OUR TABLE, I TURNED to Frederick, but he held his hand over his mouth, jumped from his seat, and ran from the ballroom like he might be sick. Had Dr. Madd's speech made him ill?

"What's up with him?" Tate asked.

"He said he wanted to pitch his eye cream to Dr. Madd, and I think the speech psyched him out a bit," I said.

Tate got up from the table. "Let's dance." He took my hand.

"What? We have a case to solve."

"Yes, which is why we need to dance. We can't discuss it here." He pulled me from my seat and walked me to the dance floor. He placed my hands on his shoulders and his hands on my waist. "You should be good at this, right? You were a ballerina."

It was true. I had studied ballet all the way through high school with the hopes of being a professional dancer. Unfortunately, an injury had sidelined that dream. And even so, I wasn't a ballroom dancer. "Ballet and ballroom aren't the same thing."

"That's okay. All we're really doing is swaying."

I looked him in the eye. "And why are we sway-ing?"

"Because we have to talk about that speech where no one can hear us, but we can still see what's going on in the room."

I looked beyond his shoulder and realized he was right. I had a good vantage point of half the room. Tate, facing the opposite direction, had the other half.

"So, what did you think of that speech?" he asked.

"I think Cecily is not pleased with the idea of being replaced. Did you see her face?"

"She must have known it was coming."

I nodded. "That doesn't mean she likes the idea, though."

"Right."

"I also think there might be a lot of people here like Frederick who are wanting to pitch ideas to Dr. Madd for MaddlyCare, that are now a lot more nervous about it. He made it clear this was their one and only shot," I said.

"My thoughts exactly. With not much else to go on as of yet, it's a start."

"I spoke to Frederick before the speech and got a bit of his backstory, but I want to talk to him again if I can track him down. He ran out of here pretty fast," I said. "It's still an hour before midnight. Unless they left the party completely, presumably, he is somewhere near the ballroom."

Tate nodded.

"You should be the one to speak to Cecily since you have a history, and probably Kiera, too."

He raised his brow. "Kiera? Why should I talk to her?"

I cocked my head and looked up and him. "Because as you well know, Tate Porter, you are a handsome guy, and you look so dashing in that tux that even movie stars will fall at your feet."

He laughed.

Tate and I split up. The man I'd noticed earlier in the geometric sweater stood at the end of the buffet line with a scowl on his face. I wasn't sure if he was upset because he had to wait in line or because he didn't like the buffet selections that he could see.

He stood out so much in the crowd; I knew I had to speak to him. Besides, I was hungry. I joined the end of the line. He glanced over his shoulder at me, and I gave him my most winning smile. He turned back toward the buffet.

Okay, the smile didn't always work.

"It looks like they have some great stuff on the buffet," I ventured. "Is that lobster?"

He turned to me again. "It looks like it."

"Wow, I'm really glad I came this weekend. Although I've been nervous about it."

He didn't say anything.

"I have a couple of marketing ideas that I want to pitch to MaddlyCare. I work in marketing. Are you here pitching ideas too?"

"No."

"Oh, I think I saw you in line with the lodge employees. Do you work for the lodge?"

He looked at me. "The lodge works for me."

Before I could ask him what that meant, he reached the buffet and it was clear there would be no more talking.

I gathered my food from the buffet and took it

back to table number twelve, hoping that Frederick Hume had returned. Unfortunately, I had no such luck. I was the only one seated at the table and eating. Typically, I preferred to be alone, but being alone in a crowd like this felt a little bit like wearing a neon sign that said *Loner* on it.

But I was too hungry to care. I took a bite of potatoes that melted in my mouth. I had moved on to the steak when I spotted Tate across the ballroom near the fireplace. He wasn't having any trouble finding companionship. A small cluster of women surrounded him, and I noted that Kiera was there as well. Good; he was working on the case, not just socializing.

A pretty blonde in the group laughed at something Tate said and playfully smacked him on the chest. I couldn't help but notice that she left her hand there for a moment too long, and Tate didn't seem to mind in the least.

"You had better move fast, or one of those ladies is going to take your man," a voice I recognized said. Unlike Benny B's voice, this one put a smile on my face.

I jumped out of my seat. "Edwin Yule, what on earth are you doing here?"

"I should be asking you the same thing, but methinks you're on a case." His eyes sparkled. Edwin was a thin man with a perfectly manicured goatee and signature black glasses. He and his fiancé, Pierce March, owned and operated a popular health food store in Herrington.

"Shh, don't say that." I glanced around to see if anyone had heard him.

He clapped his hands. "So I'm right."

I frowned. "And why are you here?"

"Pierce and I were asked to be here to set up a table about healthy vitamins and minerals for Dr. Madd's guests. Our table doesn't go up until tomorrow. We'll be right outside the spa. CeCe invited us to the party." He sighed. "Oh, I should call her Cecily, shouldn't I? She will always be CeCe to me."

"Were you friends when she lived in Herrington?"

"That's flattering. I'm a few years older than she is. I was her babysitter, if you can believe that. Both her mother and stepfather worked, so I would meet her at the bus after school and play board games and eat junk food until one of her parents came home. It was the easiest job I ever had, and her mom always had the best snacks in the house. We kept in touch over the years, and I sent her an email when Pierce and I opened the store, hoping she would send her famous friends our way. That was years ago. I heard from her maybe two weeks back, telling us about this weekend and asking us to set up a table. I was overjoyed."

"What about this lodge? Did you know it was her father's?"

He clicked his tongue. "No! That was a real shock. She never talked about her father. She was close to her stepdad. Maybe she thought he was enough of a father to her." He shrugged.

It seemed that I would have to get the story about her father and the lodge from Cecily herself.

Edwin grabbed my arm. "I had to pinch myself. Did you see that Kiera Bellworthy is here? She is even more stunning in person than she is on the screen. I think if she buys anything from me, I will die."

"It seemed a surprise to most people in the room

that she's going to be the face of MaddlyCare," I mused.

He whistled. "Yeah, and not everyone is happy about it."

"Cecily?" I asked.

"You bet. Furious."

As if he'd beckoned her, Cecily Madd stomped across the dance floor and out the main door of the ballroom. It was about time that she told Tate and me what was really going on. "Edwin, I have to go." I stood up from the table.

"Yeah, I know. You're on a case," he said with a smile.

I hurried after Cecily as fast as the heels Maelynn had given me allowed. I was tempted to kick them off, but I was afraid that would draw too much attention. Outside in the lobby, Dr. Madd was standing by a door near the spa. A discreet sign by the door said it was the game room.

"How could you do this to me after everything I've done for you?" Cecily asked.

"My dear, you've known this was coming for months, after the board and I decided not to renew your contract to be the face of MaddlyCare."

"Yes, but I didn't know you were going to announce it tonight in front of all our guests. This is my lodge. Do you have any idea how embarrassing this is for me?"

"Cecily," he said, as if she was a misbehaving child. "This is business, and a party like this is the perfect place to make an announcement. Did you see how everyone reacted when I announced Kiera as the new face of the company? They loved it."

"A washed-up actress who can't control herself on the internet," Cecily grumbled.

"She's reinventing herself," he said through gritted teeth.

She pointed a long red fingernail at him. "I've been trying to protect you, and this is the thanks I get?"

"That's enough," Dr. Madd said to his wife. "This is a company event and I did what is best for the company." He turned and went into the game room.

Cecily stared at the door for half a second and then stormed in the direction of the spa and pool.

I was torn by which one to follow and wished Tate were there so we could split up.

In the end, I went into the game room. Perhaps I was expecting an arcade with pinball and Whac-A-Mole. It wasn't that kind of game room.

No, this was what I would call a lounge. Just like the rest of the lodge, the furnishings were plush, but while most of the lodge was dominated with nature-inspired décor, this room was much more masculine. The furniture was heavy, made of dark wood. The ceiling was broken up with thick beams. There were four game tables around the room and a pool table. Guests, mostly men I'd noticed at the Madds' party, were playing cards and pool.

I'd never felt more out of my element in my life.

"It's best just to take a seat and start playing," a woman's voice behind me said. By the time I'd turned my head, whoever had spoken had disappeared into the crowd.

"That was Heather Madd," a man at the closest game table said to me. "I would listen to her—she's the best strategist I've ever met. How else do you think she's been able to stay in the company after she and Garret divorced?"

I looked over my shoulder. "That was Dr. Madd's ex-wife?"

"Sure was," he said. "Here, take a seat. We have a space empty. Do you know how to play poker?"

It was probably the only worthwhile thing I learned from my one relationship. Other than the fact that I was attracted to men with commitment issues. I slid into the seat next to the man, who just might be the wealth of information I needed.

"You here to pitch ideas to Dr. Madd?"

I nodded. "You?"

"No. I'm just here for the free alcohol and chance to win some money, it would seem."

He was a big man, but his tuxedo fit him well. His dark hair lay perfectly in place, and his full beard was trimmed and neat. He had striking green eyes.

I smiled. "That was quite a speech that Dr. Madd gave. It seems like a big announcement about Kiera Bellworthy."

"Oh, that's not all the shockers he handed out tonight. Not by a long shot."

The dealer dealt a new hand. I glanced at my cards. There was no way I was winning this.

"What do you mean?" I asked.

"I'm Anderson Bray. I've been the distributor for MaddlyCare for the last six years. Our contract is up in a few weeks, and I came here this weekend expecting that we would sign the new paperwork as usual. Then, I come to find out that Garret already signed with another company and I'm left out in the cold."

"I'm sorry to hear that."

"Not as sorry as I am." He took a sip of his drink and traded in two cards.

When it was my turn, I gave the dealer four of my cards. My hand was that bad.

Anderson arched his brow. "Holding out for a full house?"

I shrugged. "Did Dr. Madd tell you privately about this?"

"Yes, not that it would've made a difference if he announced it to the whole room like he did about Kiera Bellworthy. I'm still losing my biggest client." He drank a bit more. "If you ask me, he's being completely disloyal to his partners in this business, and his wife. He's a perfect example of a man who can't get enough. Mark my words; he will file for divorce just as soon as he settles in with the new model."

"Settles in? You mean romantically?"

He shook his head. "No. Nothing like that. I just mean, as soon as Kiera's campaign is underway, what does he need Cecily for anymore? They fight constantly, and we are talking about all-out wars, not lovers' spats. With Kiera as the face of the company, he won't need Cecily anymore, and he won't have to put up with her tantrums either. She will become a liability that needs to be removed."

I wondered if Cecily had come to this same conclusion.

"Wouldn't that be bad for him?" I asked. "Cecily would, I assume, get half of everything he made while they were married. That is quite a bit, I gather. The financial loss might not be worth the divorce."

"Nope. She won't get anything more than an already agreed-upon lump sum. They had a prenup."

My mouth hung open. "How do you know that?"

He eyed me. "I have worked with Garret Madd for fifteen years. The one thing that man is not is private. He will tell anyone who listens every detail of his life." His voice grew louder.

I glanced over at Dr. Madd, who was playing cards two tables away. "Shh, he might hear you."

Anderson glared at Dr. Madd's back, but when he spoke, he did lower his voice. "I don't care. I don't have to play by his rules anymore. When he was getting married for the second time to Cecily, he made sure everyone knew he was getting a prenuptial agreement. I believe it was his way to reassure his partners that there wouldn't be a financial burden to his company like when he divorced his first wife."

"Are you ready to show your hand?" the dealer asked.

I looked down at my cards. The four he'd given me were winners. "A straight."

Anderson tossed his cards on the tabletop. "I'm not winning at anything tonight."

I excused myself from the table after that and went in search of Tate. In the short time we had been apart, I had two prime suspects to add to our list for the threatening notes: Anderson Bray and Heather Madd. Yet their motives were harder to pin down. Anderson claimed he hadn't known he was being dropped as the distributor for MaddlyCare until that night. Why would he have sent threatening notes? As for Heather Madd, I was still kicking myself that I hadn't gotten a better look at her. Even so, why would she be threatening her ex-husband after all this time, when it sounded like she'd gotten everything she wanted from the divorce?

I went back into the ballroom, and to my surprise, Tate was still in the same group of women, chatting away.

Tate looked relieved to see me. "Darby!"

"Tate," I said with a smile.

Tate squeezed out of the circle of women. "Ladies, it has been wonderful to chat with you, but duty calls."

"Who is she?" a willowy redhead in a tight black dress asked. She looked me up and down.

"This is Darby," Tate said with audible relief in his voice. "She's my date."

The redhead wrinkled her nose. "*She's* your date. I don't see her as being your type."

"She really is, but really, I must go." He grabbed my hand and pulled me away from the group of women and across the dance floor. "You didn't come a moment too soon. I was afraid I was never going to get away from them." His eyes were wide. "Do you know how many times she poked me in the chest? Her nails were like dragon claws. I'm sure they left a mark. When did poking a man in the chest become okay?"

I gently pulled my hand from his. "I thought you would enjoy the attention of so many beautiful women at one time."

"I'll tell you a little secret. Most men don't like that much attention."

"From across the room, you seemed happy to be there." I shifted my stance and tried to keep my voice even.

"Darby Piper, you're jealous." The sparkle was back in his eyes.

"That's ridiculous, and I actually came to find you because I discovered some very interesting things about MaddlyCare while you were chatting away."

"Everyone! Midnight is only five minutes away." Herschel was up at the podium again. "Grab your glass and your special someone, and be ready to ring in the New Year!"

I scanned the room and saw Cecily and Dr. Madd standing near the platform. By their body language, neither one of them was happy. "Did you get a chance to speak to Cecily?"

Tate shook his head. "This is the first time I've seen her since the speeches ended."

I glanced around. "She and Dr. Madd had an argument in the lobby." I promised to fill him in later.

Tate and I wove our way to our table to collect our drinks. Frederick Hume never reappeared from when he'd run out of the ballroom earlier that evening. I spotted Anderson Bray standing by the bar. He drank two shots in a row, glaring off into space. Kiera Bellworthy glowed on the stage next to Cecily and Dr. Madd. Cecily seemed to take care to stand as far away from the movie star as possible.

"It's time to start counting down," Herschel cried, as if it was the best moment in his entire life.

"Ten!" the crowd shouted.

"Nine!"

Anderson took another shot.

"Eight!"

"Seven!"

"Six!"

Tate took my hand in his. I looked down at it.

"Five!"

"Four!"

"Three!"

"Two!"

Tate pulled me close to him.

"One! Happy New Year!"

The DJ played "Auld Lang Syne" and confetti fell from the ceiling. Tate leaned in to kiss me. I ducked my head and awkwardly hugged him instead. I knew we were playing a part as a couple, but a kiss? That was something I couldn't do. It was far too dangerous.

"Happy New Year!" Dr. Madd cried, raising his champagne flute into the air. "Happy New Year!" He kissed his wife, and she pulled back from him as if he'd slapped her.

Chapter Six

HE LODGE GYM SMELLED LIKE chlorine due to the close proximity to the pool. My feet pounded on the treadmill. I stared at the screen. I was only halfway. This was the worst run in recent memory for me. I just wanted it to be over, but I was distracted by the events of the night before. Added onto that, I was getting a late start. I hadn't reached the lodge gym until seven that morning. Usually, I finished running at six-thirty. I reminded myself that it had been a long night and that today was a holiday, to boot. When it came to running, my guilty conscience worked overtime.

I increased my pace. I much preferred running outside, but with the ice and snow, it wasn't a safe option; the lodge was on the side of the mountain, and I didn't know the terrain.

But running on a treadmill was difficult. It felt mundane and pointless. I literally wasn't going anywhere. I always ran slower and watched the clock more closely to check when I could quit. Finally, I hit the three-mile mark in well over thirty minutes. Typically, I ran faster than that, but any runner would tell you she has bad runs now and again; it was just a matter of keeping at it, so you have a good one once again. I knew when I got back home and into my everyday routine, things would click together for me.

I wasn't sure if they would ever click together for this case. Cecily Madd was paying us a lot of money to find the person who'd sent her husband threatening notes, but as of yet, she had told us very little about those notes, such as their frequency and what the majority of them said. Both Tate and I had tried to speak to her last night at the party, but she had blown us off. She was angry at her husband, and I wondered if she was rethinking hiring us after his little speech.

Previously, Cecily had only said that she believed the person was close to her husband because he or she knew specific details about the doctor.

Yet, to contradict that, Anderson Bray had said the night before that Dr. Madd would share the details of his life with anyone willing to listen. One of them was mistaken...or lying.

I hopped off the treadmill and grabbed my water. I drank half the bottle before I lowered it from my mouth. The air inside the lodge was dry. Added to the high elevation, it was no wonder the three miles had been a struggle.

To be honest, I was surprised that I was the only one in the gym that morning. I knew the party had gone past four in the morning, but I had assumed there might be another earlybird fitness freak in the room working out alongside me. It was just as well; I didn't want an audience for such a terrible run.

Then I realized I wasn't completely alone. Through

the doorway that led to the weight room, I heard men speaking.

Lifting weights was not my jam. I did it at least twice a week because it made me a better runner, but grudgingly. Now I had the chance to use the stations in the next room. It was much fancier than my simple setup of dumbbells and resistance bands at home. I waffled. I just wanted to get back to the case. There were so many oddities that tickled the back of my mind, and I couldn't forget that Benny B was somewhere in the lodge watching and waiting. He would be watching me because he believed I could lead him to a story.

And I never had found Heather Madd, Garret's first wife, after hearing her voice as she exited the game room.

"You have to listen to me," one of the men on the other side of the wall said. "This is the only way we can make this work. If you want MaddlyCare to take you seriously, you have to listen to me. This is our one shot. We need this deal."

I stopped just to the right of the door. There was something in the man's tone that gave me pause. I was certain if I stepped into the weight room, they would stop talking, and I was very interested in what they had to say.

There was a giant thud, which I recognized as a set of dumbbells unceremoniously dropped on the padded floor. I winced, more for the floor than the dumbbells.

"He's a fool," a second man's voice said. This one sounded older and more gravelly. "If he won't take the deal, we have no choice but to find someone who will. Garret Madd isn't the only skincare guru on this planet. I refuse to grovel."

"But he's the one with the money who is actually giving us the time of day. We don't have the funds to boost a product like this. It would take a national campaign. One television commercial would set us back a million."

"Money? That's what this is always about. We will find the money. There is always another fool who's willing to write a check."

"Not if Dr. Madd talks," the first man hissed the words.

"He won't talk," The second voice snapped. "I'll make sure of that. If he tries, he'll be sorry. Sorrier than anyone you've ever known..."

I had to see who these two men were, but something outside the window caught my eye.

I glanced at the weight room, then I looked through the window again. Where I stood, I had a clear view down the slope, and it looked like someone was lying on the ground. Whoever it was must have fallen—and he wasn't getting up. I bit my lip. I had to make sure that person was okay.

I grabbed my mobile phone and ran into the hallway in my shorts and tank top. I was not dressed to go out on the slope. There was a small store to the right of the lobby that sold ski equipment and clothing. I ran inside.

The middle-aged merchant stood just outside the door with her mouth hanging open as she watched people around the lobby. She had short gray-blond hair and wore a sweater that was very snug on her.

It looked to me like it was real wool, too, and it made me itchy just seeing it.

"I need to buy a ski suit," I told her.

She stared at me. "We don't open until nine."

"But you are here, and you can charge it to my room. I really need this snowsuit. I have to get outside, and I can't go like this." I pointed at my tank top and shorts.

She frowned. "No, I guess you can't. You'd catch your death of cold."

"So can I buy a snowsuit from you? Please."

There must have been something in my voice, because she said, "All right. I haven't made nearly as many sales this weekend as I need to. You're very small. Let me see what we have."

She hummed as she went through the store looking at the clothes.

I clenched my jaw to keep myself from telling her to hurry up.

Finally, she picked out a purple ski coat and matching snow pants. I felt like a grape that was about to pop, but I wasn't going to be picky.

"What's your room number and name?" she asked.

I told her.

"It's nice to meet you, Darby. I'm Jayne Anne. If there is anything else you need from the ski shop during your stay, I will be happy to find it for you."

I put the pants and coat on over my tank top and shorts while she talked and shoved my phone in a pocket. As she rang me up, I ran out of the shop shouting my thanks.

When I got outside, the cold hit me like an icy wall. I gasped, and my breath was sucked out of me. The sky was bright blue and the ground was white with fresh snow. The glare off the snow blinded me for a moment.

I didn't have boots on, so it was just a matter of seconds before my running shoes and ankle-length socks got soaked through. I could feel my toes curling in from the cold. I walked the distance to the mountain where the skiers took off from. It was the length of a basketball court, but felt much farther in wet shoes and wet hair from my run. I pulled my hood up and pulled the ties tight, close to my head.

It was a beautiful, cold but crisp day. It looked just like the first day of the year should. Everything was bright and shiny, and fresh snow fringed the trees. Pristine and perfect, just like the brochure for the lodge claimed it to be.

I had to concentrate on not falling in the slick ice and snow. The side of the mountain was perfect for downhill skiing. What it wasn't good for was running shoes. I really should have bought a pair of boots when I was in the ski shop.

I slipped and fell on my back end and skidded down the mountain toward the fallen person. I tried to slow myself down with my hands and dig in my heels, but it was no use. I couldn't stop.

I ran into the man's ski pole and grabbed it. Digging the end into the snow, I finally stopped myself about ten feet below him. I lay on my back for a second to get my bearings. I really hoped that no one was looking out the window just then and saw my slide down the mountain. I took a survey of my body, and other than being a tad sore, I was fine.

Using the man's ski pole, I struggled to my feet.

I turned and climbed to him. "I'm sorry I grabbed your pole like that. Are you..."

I was going to ask him if he was okay, but the words died on my lips. He most certainly wasn't okay.

Dr. Garret Madd was dead, with an arrow sticking out of his back.

Chapter Seven

BEFORE LONG, A FEW MEMBERS of the hotel staff had joined me on the mountain where I stood, shivering, a few feet away from Dr. Garret's dead body. I'd called 911, and I'd tried and failed to reach Tate on the phone. Herschel, the manager, wrung his hands. "This is terrible. So terrible," he said over and over again.

We could all agree on that.

His Saint Bernard, Tiny, pressed his body up against his master's leg with a concerned look on his face.

"Darby!" a voice in the distance shouted.

I waved from where I stood. Moving was a challenge. My feet were all but frozen to the ground. What I wouldn't have given in that moment for a pair of warm fuzzy socks.

Carefully, a group of police and emergency workers came down the side of the mountain. Most were on foot, but two were on snowmobiles.

One of the snowmobiles stopped a few yards from me. My ex-boyfriend, Officer Austin Caster, climbed off the machine and strode to me. Much to my chagrin, he was looking as adorable as ever, with his bright blue eyes and blond hair that reflected white in the bright New Year's sunshine.

"When I got the call that there was a body found at Garden Peak Lodge, they didn't tell me you would be here."

"I guess they wanted to keep it a surprise."

Austin frowned at my attempt at humor.

Maybe right now wasn't the best time for jokes.

"Tell me what happened." He guided me away from the lodge staff. I shuffled after him.

He frowned. "What's wrong with your feet?"

"They're cold."

He looked at my feet. "Why aren't you wearing boots?"

"I will be as soon as we finish this conversation."

"All right," he said. "How did you find the body?"

I told him about being in the gym and seeing someone lying on the side of the mountain. "I really thought someone just fell down. Maybe broke an ankle at most. I never thought I would find Dr. Madd shot in the back with an arrow."

"Dr. Madd is the victim's name?"

I nodded. "Dr. Garret Madd."

"And why were you here?"

"I'm on a case," I said. There was no point in hiding my real motive for being at Garden Peak Lodge from Austin. He knew what I did for a living.

His eyes narrowed. "What's your case?"

"Dr. Madd and his wife were hosting a business event at the lodge this weekend. Over the last several months he had been receiving threatening notes. His wife, Cecily Madd, hired Tate and me to look into it."

"Sir," an officer walked over to us. "There is an arrow in his back, like the report said."

Like I would make up the arrow in his back, I mentally grumbled.

"But it appears by the arrow type that it was shot from a crossbow," the officer went on. "Could be a hunting accident. Dr. Madd was in the wrong place at the wrong time."

Austin thanked the officer, who nodded and went back to the scene.

I grimaced. Somehow a crossbow sounded like an even worse way to die. In any case, the mode of death was medieval. "Isn't hunting illegal this time of year? And isn't crossbow hunting always illegal?" I had never been nor wanted to go hunting myself, so I wasn't up on all the rules and when the seasons began and ended in the Finger Lakes.

"There is some crossbow hunting, but you're right. It's not this time of year. But that doesn't mean people aren't poaching. Winter is the easy time to hit a mark. There's little foliage to block the view, and the deer, or whatever the quarry is, stands out more against the snow."

"If it's such an easy time to hit the mark, then why did the hunter hit Dr. Madd? I don't think he was dressed like a deer."

Austin frowned.

"He was shot in the back. That seems to imply that the shooter was above him on the mountain when he fired. How could a hunter looking down a mountain mistake a man on skis for a deer?"

Austin didn't have an answer for that.

"I think you need to consider this a homicide. He

was getting threats. His wife is convinced the person sending the threats was here at the lodge this week-end."

"And what exactly was this business event?" he asked.

"The Madds threw a New Year's weekend for friends and for people who would like to work with them."

"Who would like to work with them? What does that mean?"

"Dr. Madd is a famous dermatologist and has a very expensive skincare line called MaddlyCare. From what I gather, he is using this weekend to have pro-spective partners pitch ideas at him."

"So they are competing against each other."

"Right," I said.

"And have you figured out who the person who sent the threats is?"

"Not yet," I said. "We've been on the case less than twenty-four hours. I wish I had figured it out before this morning. If I had, Dr. Madd might still be alive."

"You have suspects?" He studied me.

I nodded. "A few."

"You need to tell me who those people are."

I opened my mouth, but before I shared my short list of names, an EMT called out to Austin. "Caster, this is your chance to take one more look at the scene before we remove the body."

Austin turned, and I peered around him. There was a break in the human circle around the crime scene, and I caught another glimpse of Dr. Madd ly-ing dead on his stomach with an arrow sticking out of his back. How long had he been lying there before I arrived? Had it taken him long to die?

"I need to get back to the scene," Austin said. "I'll catch up with you later. I want to know everything."

I nodded. "I'd like to stay and wait until you're free to talk."

He looked down at my feet. "Not in those shoes, you're not. They're soaked through, and if you stay out here much longer, you're bound to get frostbite. Go inside and get warmed up, and I'll find you later."

I wanted to argue, but as he reminded me of my wet feet, the nerves in my toes reacted with a fresh shot of pain. "All right, but don't leave the lodge without talking to me."

He looked me directly in the eye. "I wouldn't even consider it."

"There's one more thing."

He waited.

"Benny B is here. He caught wind of all the celebrities who would be here for the weekend and infiltrated the lodge."

"Good to know," he said.

I turned to head back up the mountain. Luckily there was a rope railing I could grab to help me. I wished I'd noticed that before I did my dramatic slide into the crime scene.

The climb up the mountain in wet running shoes, even with the rope to assist me, wasn't nearly as unladylike as my slide down the mountain, but when I finally hit flat land, I bolted for the lodge. My stride was off because I could no longer feel my feet. I prayed that Austin was wrong about the whole frostbite thing.

When I reached the lodge, I tried to call Tate for a third time, and for the third time it went directly to voicemail. I lost track of how many text messages I had sent him. There was every indication that his phone was off. That wasn't something that sat well with me when we were on a case.

Before going up to my room to change, I went back into the gym to grab my water bottle and towel. As I shuffled through the door, I heard a woman crying.

I followed the sound into the pool area. There was a petite young woman perched on the side of one of the lounge chairs in tears.

I approached her gingerly. "Are you okay?"

She looked up at me. "No! Someone killed Dr. Madd!" Her curly red hair framed her face and bright hazel eyes. She didn't look a day over twenty.

"I know that Dr. Madd is dead," I said. "It's terrible news." I paused. "But why do you think someone killed him?"

"I think the arrow in his back is reason enough."

"How do you know Dr. Madd?" I asked, and sat on another lounge chair nearby.

"I'm his personal assistant. He was skiing early this morning and wanted me to meet him at the top of the ski lift when he finished at precisely seven forty-five, so we could go over his meeting agenda for the day. He had many meetings planned." She paled. "What do I do about all those meetings now?"

"I'm sure people will understand they need to cancel."

"Right." She removed her phone from her pocket, like she was going to start canceling the meetings right then and there.

"Don't do anything yet," I warned. "We need to take this one step at a time. What's your name?"

She looked me in the eye for the first time. "Mindy Carn."

"Okay, Mindy," I said. "How did you hear that Dr. Madd was dead?"

"I was running a little late for the meetings, so I ran outside just as the police got here. An officer told me not to go outside. I was upset because I knew Dr. Madd was already going to be angry because I was late. I asked a lodge staffer what was going on and he told me."

"Are you okay? Do you need help back to your room?"

Tears welled in her eyes. "I'm all right. I think I just want to sit here a moment. One minute I was organizing his schedule. The next minute, I learn he's dead. It's a lot to process."

Her mentioning meetings again reminded me of the two men I had heard fighting in the weight room just before I saw the body on the slope.

"I just don't know what will happen now." She sniffled. "What will become of MaddlyCare without Dr. Madd?"

It was a very good question, and one that just might lead me to the killer.

Chapter Eight

AFTER LEAVING MINDY, I JUMPED into the elevator, and when the elevator doors opened, I ran to Tate's room. I banged on the door. There was no answer. After being in active service with the Army, I supposed he could sleep through just about anything.

I knocked on the door harder. "Tate!" I shouted.

A second later, he threw the door open. "What is going on?" His eyes were wide. He stood in front of me in a T-shirt and sweat pants. His feet were bare. "Darby? What's gotten into you?"

"What's gotten into me? What's gotten into you? I called and texted you a hundred times."

He shuffled back into the sitting room of his suite rubbing his eyes. He picked up his phone from the kitchen counter. "It's dead. I forgot to charge it last night. We got in so late." He rubbed his eyes and then took a better look at me. "Why are you wet? Where on earth did you get the Purple People Eater snowsuit?" he asked, and then wrinkled his nose. "And you don't smell great, either."

"I went for a run in the gym and then bought a

snowsuit so I could go outside. I have a very good reason for waking you up. We have a problem."

He yawned. "A bigger problem than your outfit?"

"Everyone looks ridiculous in a ski suit."

"You have a point."

"And this is a very big problem. Garret Madd is dead."

He sat on a chair. "What? Are you sure?"

"I'm positive. I found the body, but if you don't believe me, take a look for yourself." I opened the shades that overlooked the side of the mountain. Police and hotel staff crawled all over the slope. By the looks of it, they were canvassing the area for clues. Perhaps Austin had taken me seriously that the dermatologist's death might not have been an accident, but murder.

I grabbed my camera with the long scope that I used for surveillance. Even with that, I couldn't see Garret's body. It was possible that it had already been removed from the scene. That's what the EMT had told Austin they were planning to do.

Tate headed to his bedroom. "Get cleaned up. I'll meet you on the slope."

"I'm coming with you now."

"You can't," he called from the bedroom. "Your hair is wet, and your running shoes will never be the same. You need to take a shower to warm up. When you're dry and bundled up, meet me on the slope." He came out of the bedroom in jeans, T-shirt, and socks and hastily pulled a sweater over his head. Grabbing his coat and boots, he was out the door before I could argue any further.

Even moving as fast as I could, it still took me

thirty minutes to shower and warm up. While I blew-dried my hair, I made coffee in the room coffee maker. It tasted terrible, but I needed the caffeine. The early morning adrenaline was wearing off, and I needed a boost. It promised to be a very long day.

I went down to the lobby wearing flannel-lined jeans, snow boots, a turtleneck sweater, and my new ski coat slung over my arm. I shoved my hat and gloves into the coat pockets. I wasn't going to be caught off guard this time if I had to go outside.

When I stepped out of the elevator, I looked to my left, to the bay of floor-to-ceiling windows that overlooked the slope. It was crawling with lodge personnel and police. I guessed it would be like that for several more hours. I scanned the crowd for Tate, but I couldn't pick him out.

He had to be somewhere on the mountainside.

"Darby!"

I recognized Austin's voice and turned.

He marched over to me with an odd expression on his face. "I just spoke to the reception desk to ask for your room number. We need to talk about what you mentioned earlier."

I frowned. "Why didn't you just text or call me? It's not like you don't have my number."

"You and Tate Porter are listed in adjoining rooms," he said, like it was some sort of accusation.

"And that's important because..."

"I just found it odd. I hope you know better than to get romantically involved with your business partner."

"I'm not an idiot, Austin. We are on a job."

"Right," he muttered.

If I didn't know better, I would have said Austin

Caster was jealous. But that couldn't be possible. He was the one who had dumped me, more than once. To be honest, it was three times he had broken my heart. The third time was the last straw, and I vowed that I would never go back, no matter how much I missed him. I would never admit that I missed him to anyone, especially not to Austin.

I wasn't missing him so much now, since he was making outlandish suggestions about my relationship with Tate, which was none of his business to begin with.

"Did you see Tate?" I asked.

Austin nodded. "Last I saw him, he was on the side of the mountain, looking down at the snow, trying to be Sherlock Holmes. The Herrington Police Department knows what it's doing when it comes to an investigation. We don't need any interference."

"We aren't interfering. We were hired for this job. We were here first. How were we to know that the main client would end up dead?"

"If you were better detectives, you might have figured it out," he remarked.

I winced. In that moment, I didn't miss Austin one bit.

He held up his hand as if he realized he had gone too far. "I take that back. That was a low blow."

"Very low," I agreed, and folded my arms around my bulky coat.

"That doesn't change the fact that if there were substantial threats, they should have been reported to the police. I have found no report files. I contacted the district where the Madds lived in New York City; there was no report filed there either."

I had said the same thing to Tate two days ago, but to Austin, I came to the Madds' defense. "They wanted to keep it discreet. They're a public couple with a huge company. They wouldn't want to do anything that brought negative attention to their business."

Thinking of money made me realize that I hadn't seen Cecily in all of this. "Have you spoken to Dr. Madd's wife yet?"

He glanced down at me. "No. We're having trouble finding her."

"What do you mean?"

"We haven't been able to locate her anywhere in the lodge. She's not in her suite, the spa, the restaurant, anywhere."

I nodded and considered this. Did Cecily know that her husband was dead? And who else could be next of kin?

"Does Dr. Madd have any children?" I asked.

He glanced at me. "No."

"He does have an ex-wife," I said. "And she's here."

Austin stared at me. "Dr. Madd's ex-wife is here this weekend? Why?"

I shook my head. "I don't know, but another guest told me she was here. I haven't seen her, not that I'd know what she looks like."

"I'll want to talk to her."

"I will, too," I said.

He frowned. "Tell me what you know."

I quickly filled him in with information about the job, and about Dr. Madd's speech the night before and the people he had upset. I wasn't the kind of private detective who kept information from the police. I felt it was important that we worked together.

There were benefits to working with the police, too. Since I was honest with them, they shared information with me when, in truth, they legally didn't have to. So even though Austin and I were no longer a couple, I had worked hard to keep him on my side since the split. I needed him when it came to my job, and he actually needed me for his, not that he would ever admit that.

"That about sums it up, Officer Caster," I finished.

"Detective," Austin said, meeting my eyes.

"Excuse me?" I blinked.

"It's Detective Austin Caster now. I was promoted." He stood just a little straighter as he said it.

"I didn't know that the Herrington Police Department had detectives."

"We didn't, until I was promoted. It was something the town council wanted to do after Samantha Porter's murder. Since I solved her murder, they chose me for the promotion," he said in a voice tinged with pride.

I bit my lower lip. I had actually been the one to solve Samantha's murder, and had almost died doing it. Well, Tate and I had, but Austin had helped...I guessed.

"Wow," I said with as much enthusiasm as I could muster. "Congratulations. That's a great step up."

He studied my face, as if checking to see if I was mocking him.

I wasn't. He was a good cop. I knew that it had been Austin's dream to be a detective someday. He had hoped to make it in a big city, but for some reason, he'd never got around to leaving Herrington. I had wondered many times what it was that kept him here. Considering his promotion, maybe it was good that he had stayed.

"I see you're more prepared for the weather this time. I was just about to head outside. One of the officers found the place from where the arrow was shot, or believes he did. Want to go with me to check it out?"

"You want me to come with you?" I asked in disbelief. As soon as I said the words, I wanted to reach out, pluck them from the air, and shove them back in my mouth. It wasn't a good idea to give Austin any reason not to invite me along.

"The coroner is leaning to this being a hunting accident, based on the method of death."

"There's no way this was an accident," I said.

He shook his head. "You have made your opinion abundantly clear. It's just good to remember that if the most logical explanation is hunting accident, then they will happily go with hunting accident instead of searching for other possibilities."

I frowned, not sure how that was any different from what I had just said, but I didn't want to argue with him. I very much wanted to see the location of the shooter.

I followed Austin outside, pulling on my ski coat, hat, and gloves as I went. It was in the twenties, I guessed. I zipped the coat all the way up under my chin and made a mental note to go back to the ski shop and buy a scarf. This case had cost me more money than I had made..but then, it hadn't made me a dime yet.

A dark bloodstain in the snow marked the spot where Dr. Madd had come to rest. Tate stepped away from the three crime scene techs there and strode to us up the mountain, not bothering with the rope. It seemed that he didn't need it. I wonder if he was part goat or had special mountain boots made just for him.

When he reached us, he and Austin stared at each other a little too long to be comfortable.

"Tate," Austin said.

"Austin," Tate replied.

I rolled my eyes. "Where did your officer say the location of the shooter was?" I looked to Tate. "Austin is going to show me the location."

"I'm coming too," Tate said, leaving no room for debate.

Austin didn't seem to feel it was worth debating because he started toward the very top of the mountain. There was a small building there that looked down on the slope. It had a small café inside: a place skiers could wait in style until it was their time to go downhill.

Dr. Madd had been shot in the back, so he was going in the direction that I expected. From this vantage point, I could see straight down the mountain and have a clear view of where he stopped. If Dr. Madd's death was even considered an accidental hunting incident, then the arrow would have had to originate in the woods. This wasn't the woods. Someone had stood at the top of the slope, taken aim, and shot Dr. Madd in the back, knowing all the time what he was doing.

There was a young officer standing to one side of the building. "Detective Caster, over here," he called.

"Detective Caster?" Tate whispered to me.

"He got promoted."

"Is it a good thing or a bad thing that the town of Herrington now thinks it needs a detective?"

"It's a sign of the times," I said.

Austin walked ahead of us. "What do you have, Officer LaMont?"

The officer pointed at the ground. There was an unmistakable impression in the snow."

"It looks like someone has been kneeling here," Tate said.

I took a closer look. The knee marks pointed down the ski slope.

In a wide circle, I walked around the impression and then stood ten feet behind it to line up with the imaginary person in front of me. Not wanting to make such a large mark in the snow, I squatted in place. My line of sight, if not exact, would be very close to the shooter's. I had a clear view of the bloodstain on the mountain and the crime scene techs searching for any scrap of evidence that might have fallen in the snow.

I stood up. "There is no way this was an accident. I was a good ten feet farther back than the shooter was, and from here, it's clear to me that those are people, not deer."

"But it was early in the morning," Austin argued.

"It was, but the sun was coming up, and there would have been lights on the slope. Otherwise, the lodge never would've let him go downhill."

Tate had taken my place behind the imaginary

shooter. "Darby is right. There is no way the shooter could've thought Dr. Madd was a deer. Furthermore, he was kneeling, which meant he was taking time with the shot. This isn't a wild shot that went wide; this was a shot to kill."

The young officer who had found the spot paled. I guessed he had never been involved with a homicide investigation before. He wasn't one of the officers I knew from Herrington.

"I wish I could argue with you on this," Austin said. "But I can't. Darby, I think you're right. Dr. Garret Madd was murdered."

"So what do we do now?" the younger officer asked.

Austin turned to him. "You're going to take a photo of every angle. Use a ruler to take measurements. This is a delicate crime scene, and the snow can melt or be disturbed at any time."

Office LaMont swallowed. "I'm on it, sir."

Austin turned to Tate and me. "As for the rest of us, I think we have a suspect list to question."

"It's just a start," I said. "I think those names I gave you from last night were just the tip of the iceberg when it comes to Dr. Madd's enemies."

"I think we start with the wife," Austin said. "We just need to find her."

"I'll talk to Cecily. I can find her," Tate said.

Austin frowned, but to my surprise, gave Tate the nod.

Chapter Nine

$\mathcal{W}$E WALKED BACK TO THE lodge, and my brain was reeling from what we had learned. I had suspected it before, but now, looking at the location of the shooter, it was proof enough, to me at least, that Dr. Madd had been murdered. And even though Cecily Madd was the reason Tate and I were at Garden Peak Lodge this New Year's weekend, it would be foolish to ignore that she was the number one suspect for the crime. She had motive. Her husband was throwing her over as the face of MaddlyCare for a young actress, and he'd publicly embarrassed her. She had opportunity. She was at the lodge. The question was, did she have the means? Did she know how to shoot a crossbow? Where would she get it?

I wanted to talk to Cecily, but Tate claimed to have that covered. At least for the moment, I had agreed to speak to other people of interest. One person I wanted to speak with in particular was Heather Madd, Dr. Madd's ex-wife—if I could find her. I still thought it was weird she was invited to this weekend. Cecily and Dr. Madd had been married for almost a decade. Why was Heather still in their lives? Anderson, the distributor, had hinted at the fact that she got to keep her job at MaddlyCare as part of her divorce. Why would she have done that?

When we reached the lodge, the three of us split up. I knew Tate would look for Cecily, but I didn't know what Austin planned to do. I mentally went over my list of people I could talk to. There was Kiera Bellworthy, the new spokesmodel for MaddlyCare. Frederick Hume, the cosmetic scientist who wanted to impress Dr. Madd. I didn't know how Dr. Madd's death would benefit Kiera or Frederick. It seemed to me that with him dead, their deals with MaddlyCare could be dead too. Unless there was some sort of binding document, I thought that was even truer for Kiera.

Of course, there was also Mindy, Dr. Madd's assistant who had been crying by the pool that morning. And Anderson Bray, the distributor who was being dropped by MaddlyCare.

Cecily's reaction to being replaced by the younger woman was not good. There was no way that Cecily would keep Kiera on as the new face of MaddlyCare if she didn't have to. My guess was, with the kind of attorneys Cecily could likely afford, she would be able to maneuver out of any contract, no matter how binding it might be.

Thinking of the people who might want Dr. Madd dead, my prime suspects, based just on last night, were his wife Cecily, Anderson Bray, and Dr. Madd's ex-wife, Heather, just because exes often carried grudges. Anderson was my next quarry.

I went to the reception desk and found Herschel and Tiny behind the desk. The pair of them usually appeared to be so composed, but at the moment, Herschel was not. He dabbed at his forehead with a white handkerchief with the letter 'H' embroidered on it. His usually pristine silver hair was mussed and his glasses sat crookedly on his nose.

"May I help you?" His voice wavered as he asked the question.

I studied his face. "Are you all right?"

He patted his forehead again. "I'll be fine. It's just been a day, a terrible day. I can't believe this has happened here, of all places. Garden Peak Lodge has always been a tranquil place."

Tiny walked around the desk and put his giant nose in my hand. It was cold and damp, but he seemed perfectly fine being so close to me, so I didn't step away from him.

"Oh, I'm so sorry. I spoke out of turn. I must blame that on the stress I'm under. I have never dealt with a murder before. It's next to impossible to keep all the guests happy when they are trapped in the lodge. I have been begging the police to reopen the mountain, so at the very least they can ski and be out of my hair for a moment." He blew out a breath. "How can I help you?"

"Well, it's in relation to what you were talking about just a moment ago. I'm Detective Darby Piper. I was wondering if you could tell me the room number for Anderson Bray."

He swallowed. "You're with the police?"

"I'm working with the Herrington Police Department, yes," I said. It was true…kinda.

"Okay." He patted his forehead again. "I want this to be over as much as the guests do. I'm happy to help." He shoved his handkerchief into his jacket pocket and began to type on his keyboard. He stopped typing, and his fingers hovered over his keys. "Are you asking about Mr. Bray because you think he might know something about what happened to Dr. Madd?" He lowered his voice to barely above a whisper. "I don't think I can stand it if I was that close to a killer."

I scratched Tiny's head. "We want to talk to everyone who knew Dr. Madd, so that we can figure out what happened this morning."

"Oh," he said, sounding somewhat disappointed. He nodded. "Room 202."

I thanked him and left the desk. Instead of taking the elevator, I went up the grand staircase to the second floor. It was hard to believe that less than twenty-four hours ago, Tate and I had been coming down that very staircase, knowing little of the investigation we were walking into. Now it was a homicide investigation. As of yet, we had not had a real sit-down conversation with Cecily Madd, the client. I was more than a little concerned that no one had been able to find her so far that day.

I knocked on the door of room 202. There was no answer. I knocked a second time, a little bit harder. A sound came from inside the room.

"Hold on!" A man's voice called.

The door was flung open, and Anderson Bray stood on the other side. He was wearing the same tuxedo that he'd worn the night before at the New Year's Eve party. Although the coat and tie were missing, and it looked a little rumpled, to say the least. He blinked at me. "You're not room service."

I shook my head. "Nope. Sorry."

He started to close the door.

I stuck my foot by the doorjamb. I was glad that I had worn sturdy snow boots in case he decided to slam the door. "I'm here to talk to you about Dr. Garret Madd."

"Why do you think I want to talk to anyone about that traitor?" He squinted at me. "Hey, aren't you the woman who beat me at poker last night? I almost didn't recognize you in that coat. It's very purple."

"So I've been told. When was the last time you saw Dr. Madd?"

"At the party last night, just like everyone else." He squinted at me. "Why are you asking me this? Listen, I'm not interested in whatever it is you're selling. I have work to do. I'm trying to salvage my business."

My foot was still blocking him from closing the door. "Did you have a long night?" I nodded at his wrinkled tuxedo.

"I wasn't up partying, if that's what you think. I was up working. I can't live a life of luxury like some people. I have to grind to make a go of it. And now I have to find a client to replace MaddlyCare. Do you have any idea how impossible it will be to find a client to replace him? The disloyalty."

"Did you know Dr. Madd's plans for the morning? What he was up to? His schedule?"

"If I answer your questions, will you go away?"

"Sure," I agreed.

He frowned. "Yes, everyone did. He sent us all an itinerary of his days at the lodge, so people knew when and when not to approach him with their pitches. He is that controlling. He even wants to control when people speak to him."

"Do you have a copy of the itinerary?" I asked.

"It's in here somewhere." He turned around, and I peeked at his room. A laptop sat in the middle of the made bed, surrounded by files and notebooks. There were two coffee mugs on the nightstand. It did appear that he'd been up working all night.

He rifled through the papers on the bed. "Here it is." He walked back over to me and handed me the piece of paper.

Sure enough, it read, *7:00-8:45am: Skiing. Do Not Approach.*

It was followed by a breakfast that never happened.

The day was detailed all the way down the page like that. On the other side of the page was the schedule for the next day too. "Nothing for Monday?" I asked.

"Apparently not. That's the day everyone was supposed to leave. Maybe Garret believes that everyone worth making a pitch to him will have done it by then."

I noticed that he spoke of Dr. Madd like he was still alive. If he was holed up in his room all morning, he might not know about the dermatologist's death—or he was a stellar liar.

"If that's all, I need to start packing. I'm leaving today. If I'm not working for MaddlyCare any longer, I don't have to be here." He started to close the door. "The Madds are the last people on earth I want to spend the first day of the year with."

I stuck my boot in the doorway again. "I think this is the point when I tell you that you can't leave."

He jerked his neck back. "I *can't* leave? I can do whatever I want."

"You can't leave because the police are going to want to talk to you. There has been an incident."

He paled. "What does that mean? An incident?"

"Dr. Garret Madd was found dead on the side of the mountain this morning. He died while skiing."

Anderson covered his mouth, and then his hand fell to his side. "You know, I'm not surprised at all that he died in a skiing accident. That just seems like the way a man like that would end. It's just such an uppity way to go. Only rich people die that way."

It wasn't a skiing accident, of course, but I thought I would let the police fill in that part.

He narrowed his eyes. "Why would the police want to speak to me? I wasn't there. I don't even know how to ski."

"Because there are some oddities about the accident."

He sucked in a breath. "Whoa! What oddities? What are you getting at?"

"The police just want to talk to you. Have that conversation with them and then leave. I know they'd appreciate it."

"Well, I don't want to talk to them."

He started to slam the door, and I pulled my foot back just in time. He closed it with such force I doubted that my snow boot would have been much protection at all.

Chapter Ten

I TEXTED AUSTIN TO TELL HIM he might want to send an officer up to room 202, because Anderson Bray was about to break out of the lodge. A text came right back and told me he was sending someone up right away.

I hesitated outside Anderson's door. Should I stay and keep guard until the officer arrived? Fortunately, I didn't have to wait long, as a police officer soon came up the stairs.

"Hey Piper, are you scaring suspects out of the lodge?" Officer Jack Parsons asked me.

Parsons had worked at the department for as long as I could remember. He was in his early fifties and in great shape, as he was a long-distance runner. Every weekend he was off from the department, he was in a race.

Because he and I went way back, he knew of my past relationship with Austin. Whenever I went into police headquarters, he liked to remind me about that and tease me.

If the teasing had come from anyone else in the department, I would have been mad about it. In his case, I just rolled my eyes and changed the subject to running, since it was something we both enjoyed.

Parsons knocked on Anderson's door.

There was no answer.

"Knock a little harder," I suggested. "I know he's in there."

Parsons did as I instructed him, but there was still no answer.

Behind us, we could hear pounding feet running down the hallway. I turned to see Anderson running for the hall, holding his briefcase.

"What in the world?" Parsons asked.

"I think he's making a run for it."

"From what?" the officer asked. "Me?"

I made it to the landing in time to see Anderson trip, fall, and roll down the grand staircase. He lay splayed on his back on the marble floor. His arms and legs were spread-eagled. He rolled his head back and forth on the floor and groaned.

Parsons ran down the stairs. "Are you okay?"

Anderson looked like he might cry. "I don't know what's going on, but I didn't do anything. I just want to go home. Let me go home."

People milling around the lobby stopped and stared. They whispered to each other. I heard someone whisper, "Fired distributor." After the party, it was well known that Dr. Madd planned to remove Anderson from his business.

"Mr. Bray, I only want to ask you a few questions about Dr. Madd," Parsons said.

Anderson squeezed his eyes shut, as though if he closed them hard enough, all his problems would go away. "Why does everyone want to talk to me about

Dr. Madd?" He sat up and, with as much dignity as he could muster, stood. Then he groaned. "I think I hurt my knee."

"We can call an EMT and have you checked out," Jack said.

Anderson waved his hands. "No, no, I don't want anyone touching me. Where's my laptop?" He looked around frantically.

I spotted a laptop case across the lobby. It had slid a long way. I hoped for Anderson's sake it wasn't damaged. I collected the case and held it, reluctant to give it back to him. Who knew what was in there, and what part of it might be related to Dr. Madd's murder?

"Give me the laptop!" Anderson said.

Parsons gave me a slight nod. He knew what I had been thinking and why I wanted to hold on to the computer. I handed it over. Bray held it to his chest.

"Can we talk, Mr. Bray?" Parsons asked.

Anderson looked around the lobby. Everyone stared at him. He nodded.

"Then follow me." Parsons started to lead him down the hallway.

I started after them too, but Parsons wasn't having it. He looked over his shoulder. "The conversation with Mr. Bray is confidential, Darby."

"Come on, Parsons. It won't hurt if I sit in."

He gave me a look.

"Fine, fine, do your cop thing." I folded my arms.

He shook his head, and he and Anderson went down the hallway. They disappeared into what I believed was a small conference room. Had the lodge given the police the space to work in throughout the investigation?

I wondered if Anderson had been one of the two men I heard in the weight room that morning. I tried to remember the exact tone of the man's voice, but I wasn't sure.

Had I been thinking at the time, I should have recorded the conversation with my phone. The only trouble with that was that I could get in a lot of trouble from recording a conversation without someone's permission, and the recording would be thrown out of court, assuming it ever came to that.

I turned back to the lobby and shot Tate a text that I had spoken to Anderson, and he was now with the police. I asked, "Did you find Cecily?"

The text back came almost immediately. "Yes, meet me in the conservatory with some rope."

"Are you trying to be funny?"

"No. I'm in the conservatory with Cecily, and we need rope."

"Why?" I asked.

There was no response. Again.

I hoped Tate was amused by the fact that he was sending me on a wild goose chase for rope in some twisted real-life game of Clue.

Where on earth was I going to find a rope? I stepped into the lobby and spotted my trusty ski shop again.

The same woman, Jayne Anne, who had sold me the ski suit that morning, was there.

"Oh!" she said. "Are you coming back for the matching boots? I have a pair in the same shade of purple."

There were boots that matched my grape outfit?

That was a lot of purple. Probably more than was legal.

"No, I was looking for some rope."

"We have rope. Not a lot, but some."

Jayne Anne walked me to the corner of the store for hiking, camping, and other sports. "I don't make many sales out of this corner of the shop in the winter," she said, "so there aren't many options. The ropes are really in camping gear, and that picks up in the spring. Not many people want to do winter camping in the Finger Lakes." She shivered. "I don't even like to go outside myself. I prefer summertime. I'm just counting the days until my husband retires, and we can move south to a warm climate."

She didn't appear close to retirement age to me. "Is your husband close to retirement?"

"It's about seventeen years away."

That was a lot of days to count.

Something hanging on the wall caught my eye, and I froze. A crossbow and arrows. There were various kinds of bows and arrows to purchase.

"You sell weapons?" I yelped.

"Weapons? Oh no. Whatever do you mean?"

I pointed at the crossbow.

"Oh." She relaxed. "That's not a weapon."

"I'm pretty sure it is."

She noisily cleared her throat. "Yes, I suppose it is, but in the summers at the lodge, archery is one of the main activities. They shoot at targets. Sometimes after taking the classes, people find a passion for it and want to buy some bows and arrows."

"Do you know how Dr. Madd died?" I asked in a

low voice. Another customer had just wandered into the store.

She looked confused. "He died skiing."

I glanced around. The other customer had wandered back out of the shop. Good. "He was skiing, but he died because he was shot in the back with a crossbow."

"No!" She covered her mouth, and her eyes glued themselves on the crossbow hanging on the wall.

"Did you sell a crossbow recently?" I asked.

Jayne Anne shook her head. "No. It's not the time of year for that, but there would be others on the grounds for the summer lessons. I don't know where they keep them. I just work in the shop, like I said."

I nodded. Now that I knew a crossbow would be readily available at the lodge, that multiplied the number of suspects. Assuming they, unlike the shopkeeper, knew where they were stored.

I chose a bright yellow nylon rope that was thirty feet long. Tate had not told me the length or strength of the rope he needed, nor had he told me why he needed it. My selection was a complete shot in the dark. "This should work," I said, not knowing if it was true.

I followed her back to the checkout counter.

She rang me up. "I'll charge it to your room again. I remember the number. It's been a slow day. Everyone who comes in here is all worked up about Dr. Madd's death. You would think it would make them want to spend money, but no such luck."

"Oh? What are they saying?" I asked, guessing that she wanted to talk about it.

I guessed right, because she handed me the rope

in a shopping bag and said, "All sorts of things, but the most common comment I heard was that he deserved it. From what I gathered, Dr. Madd wasn't very well-liked by the people coming to his party." Jayne Anne looked me over. "Maybe I shouldn't be talking to you about this. Aren't you part of his party?"

I shook my head. "I had never met the man before yesterday."

She nodded, as if I had eased her conscience somehow. "Yes, I didn't think you had the right look to be part of his group."

I wanted to ask her what the right look was, but thought better of it. "Did everyone have unkind things to say about him?"

"Pretty much. Except for that movie star. She was really in tears over his death."

"Kiera Bellworthy."

Jayne Anne nodded. "Have you ever seen a woman more beautiful in your life? She might blind you like the sun if you look directly at her. She stepped in here not long after you bought that coat slung over your arm."

"She was up early?" For some reason, this surprised me.

"Oh, yes. And it wasn't the first time I saw her this morning. She was outside when I came in to work at six."

My eyes went wide. "What was she doing outside?" I asked.

In my jeans pocket, my phone buzzed. I knew it was Tate asking where the rope and I were, but this conversation felt too important to leave just yet.

"She was crying. Crying her eyes out. I asked her

if there was anything I could do to help her, but she thanked me and said no. She was very polite—not at all what I would expect of someone so famous. When she came in the shop later, she apologized for the mess she was earlier. I was shocked that she even recognized me as the woman who offered her help, and then she bought seven hundred dollars' worth of gear. I don't even think she really looked at anything she bought. She just told me to charge it to her room and have it all sent there. After that she left. She never did tell me why she was crying so early in the morning."

I gripped my shopping bag with the rope inside it. If Kiera Bellworthy was outside when Dr. Madd was shot, that meant she had opportunity. I thought back to the prints we had seen in the snow. We'd all assumed they were a man's, but maybe they could've been made by a very tall actress.

Chapter Eleven

THE CONSERVATORY WAS ON THE top floor of the lodge, in the back of the building facing the ski slope.

I took the elevator up to the fifth floor. The doors opened, and I found myself in a hallway with few doors. I was on the penthouse level. Cecily and Dr. Madd's room was on this floor. The penthouse itself was down the hall to the left, but directly in front of me there was a set of French doors. "Conservatory" was etched on a silver sign to the right of the doors. So apparently meeting Tate in the conservatory wasn't a joke. I still wondered what the rope was for.

I stepped through the doors and felt like I was stepping into a jungle. The air was humid, and tropical plants and vibrantly colored flowers surrounded me. To my shock, a brightly feathered bird flew by.

The yellow bird landed on a branch just inches from me, opened its beak, and sang the most brilliant song. I felt like I had stepped into Oz or some other faraway, magical place. If a Munchkin popped out of the foliage, I wouldn't have been surprised. I wondered how many of the guests even knew this place was here.

A heady smell hung in the air from the plants and humidity. It wasn't long until my fascination was replaced by dread—namely from the heat. My legs began to sweat in my flannel-lined jeans, and I was dying to take my thick winter boots off. I removed my coat and fanned myself. Another bird flew over my head.

I ducked. "Tate? Are you in here?" I didn't call his name very loud. This didn't seem to be a place where you should shout.

There was no answer as I stepped farther into the room. I followed a short winding flagstone path. It moved through the conservatory like some sort of tropical snake.

The path ended with another set of French doors that went into a second room. This room was very similar to what my mother would have called a sun-room. It had a few plants—nothing like the jungle room—and lots of rattan-backed chairs. Cecily was sitting in one of them, looking like she might just be overcome with the vapors.

The windows in the room faced the ski slope and had a spectacular view of the snow-capped mountains, and Tate Porter was leaning so far out of one of the windows that his feet weren't touching the floor.

I hurried into the room. "Tate, what are you doing?"

I startled him, and he tipped farther out the window. I ran forward, grabbed him by the back of his shirt and yanked. He had to outweigh me by sixty pounds at least, but I had fear on my side. I yanked hard, and his boots hit the tiled floor with a thud.

Tate grabbed at his shirt collar. "You're. Choking..."

"Oh!" I let go of his shirt. "I'm sorry. It looked like you were going to fall out the window."

"I wouldn't have almost fallen out the window if you hadn't scared me. I had everything under control." He pulled on his collar as if he could still feel the fabric digging into this neck.

"Looks like it," I muttered.

"Someone has to get my bag!" Cecily cried.

"Your bag?" I asked. "Out there?" I pointed to the open window.

"Yes," she snapped. "Didn't you want to see the notes? Now they're my proof that I didn't kill my husband. Why would I have killed him if I was protecting him from the person sending these notes? Why would I spend all this money to hire the two of you if I planned to murder him? I don't just throw away money. It's ludicrous."

They were both good questions, but I couldn't get the look on Cecily's face out of my head when her husband announced he would make Kiera the new face of MaddlyCare.

Before I got too far in promoting Cecily to my suspect list, there was the mode of death to consider. Had he been stabbed or shot in their suite, Cecily would be in police custody by now, but he had been shot with a crossbow as he was skiing down the side of a mountain. Assuming it wasn't some freak hunting accident like the police had first thought, that mode of murder seemed to take more premeditation than a crime of passion. Even more than that, it took skill. What were the odds that someone could hit a target so perfectly while said target flew down the mountainside? The chances were slim at best. Whoever shot that crossbow knew what they were doing and knew how to hit a mark. A moving one, at that.

"Can I see the rope?" Tate asked.

"What are you going to do with it?" I held the shopping bag away from him. I'd give it to him when I got some answers.

"I'm going to go out the window and grab the purse so we have that evidence. We not only need it to prove Cecily's innocence, but to find out the identity of the person who wrote the notes. That person could have killed Garret Madd. I'd even go as far to say they're the most likely candidate."

I held on to the shopping bag and peeked out the window, and saw the small purse hanging from the edge of the brick face. "How did it get out there?"

"My husband threw it out the window early this morning," Cecily said. "It was when we came back to our room after the party. We had a terrible fight. I told him that I hired you to look into the threatening notes. I wanted to show him what a good wife I was to him and why he should have been more sensitive to my feelings about his big announcement about Kiera," she added bitterly. "I got out the purse to show him the threatening notes. He wouldn't look at them. He never wanted to look at them. It was almost as if he never saw them, they didn't exist.

"He said I was making up the threatening notes." She took an unsteady breath. "I wasn't making them up. I have them with me all the time in that purse. When I went to show him, he grabbed the purse from me and threw it out the window. Can you believe that?"

My radar was up. Cecily seemed to be angrier and

put out by her husband's behavior than sad that he was dead.

"You can't reach the purse from your penthouse veranda?" I asked.

She shook her head. "No, it's closer to the conservatory. He threw it like a disc. It's a miracle it didn't disappear down the side of the mountain."

"That's why I needed the rope," Tate said.

I held up the shopping bag. "This was the best I could do on short notice. I'm guessing there must be more rope around the lodge for repairs and accidents. I can ask if this doesn't work. I have certainly spoken to reception enough times that they're used to my asking questions." I looked over my shoulder. "Are you sure we should be opening the window?" I asked. "What if the birds get out? They would never survive the cold."

"The birds are just in the first part of the conservatory. When you came through that second door, you left them behind," Tate said.

I wasn't so sure about that. I didn't know what kept the birds from sneaking through the second door. But as I looked around this much smaller room, which wasn't nearly as humid, I didn't see any wayward feathered friends.

I leaned out the window. The purse was pretty far out on an outcropping of brick. It wouldn't be an easy grab by any means. "Why not just call Austin?" I asked. "The police or the fire department, if need be, will be able to retrieve it using a ladder or even a fire truck."

"I don't want the police to have it. If I did, I would have called them already," Cecily said sharply. "The notes are none of their business."

I internally winced. She wasn't going to be happy when she found out I had already told Austin about them. Considering how upset she was at the moment, I would keep that little detail to myself for now.

Tate wiggled his fingers at me. "The rope. The sooner I get out there and grab it, the better."

"No," I said. "I should go. I'm smaller, and I have more recent experience climbing, since I rescue Mrs. Berger's cat from her tree at least once a week. Also, I'm not sure the rope I have will support your weight. You're strong enough to pull me in if needed. I wouldn't be able to do the same for you."

Tate looked like he wanted to argue with me, but then he sighed. "You're right, but it's too dangerous." He turned to Cecily. "Darby's right; we should talk to the police."

"No!" Cecily snapped. "If you want to get paid for this weekend, you will get that purse now without involving the cops."

I frowned. "You signed a contract."

She looked down her nose at me. "I can get out of it if I need to."

I was certain she was right on that point, but I wasn't going to outwardly agree with her.

"I'll get it," Tate said.

He started toward the window.

I clenched my teeth. If I didn't climb out that window right now, I knew Tate would.

"No, I'll go," I insisted.

"Someone has to go out there," Cecily said in a sharp voice. "It might as well be her."

Tate's brows knit together as if he was questioning his old friend for the very first time.

Chapter Twelve

ATE TIED ONE END OF the rope around my waist. As he did, I had the sensation that this was one of the dumbest ideas I'd ever had. Tate and I should walk away from this job right now. We could go back to our boring background checks and saving cats from trees. The background checks were really boring, but there was no chance of falling five stories to your death doing them. As for saving cats from trees, it wasn't as scary as this.

I sighed. I could be as stubborn as Tate, maybe even worse—not that I would tell him that.

I slung my right leg out the window and carefully straddled the frame. Gingerly, I swung my other leg over and slid down to the ledge. The rope cinched around my waist. I was going to have bruises and a nasty case of rope burn, for sure.

The wind was blustery and cold outside the building, but I had opted not to wear the bulky winter coat out of fear it would hinder my movement.

Cecily's purse was a whole body length below me. I looked up and saw Tate's anxious face sticking out the window. "If anything happens to you, your parents will hunt me down."

"Don't forget Maelynn and my little sister DeeDee," I called. "They'll also be out to get you. You don't stand a chance."

"How could I forget them? Now I'm even more afraid."

I looked down. "Lower me a bit more to the next ledge. From there, I should be able to reach the bag."

"Got it." He stared into my eyes. "I've got you, Piper. I will never let you fall."

My breath caught. Maybe I was reading too much into this, but to me it felt like he was talking about a lot more than my falling off the side of the building.

Slowly, he lowered me some more. I passed a window. As I slid by, I spotted a man sitting on his bed reading a book. It must have been a really good book, because he didn't notice the woman hanging outside his window.

Finally, I was at the same level as the purse. I reached for it, but just barely grazed it with my fingertips.

A cold wind came off the mountain and rocked me back against the building. I bumped into it with a thud.

"Piper! Are you okay?" Tate cried.

I clung to the rope and the brick wall. "Yes, but I'm going to need a massage in that fancy spa after this."

"Deal. Just don't die," he called back.

"I wasn't planning on it." I inched a little farther along the bit of ledge until I reached the end. One centimeter to the right and I would be in the open air.

The only thing that would keep me from plummeting to my death was Tate's brute strength.

But I could grab the purse now. I carefully removed it from the outcropping and slung the delicate strap over my shoulder. I let out a sigh of relief. "I got it!" I looked up.

Tate hung halfway out the window. "I see that. Hold on tight to the rope, and I will pull you up."

"You're going to pull me straight up?" I yelped.

"Sure. You're not that heavy."

"Thanks," I said uncertainly.

"One! Two! Three!"

My whole body jerked as I lifted from the ledge. The rope around my waist tightened painfully. My hands held onto the rope for all I was worth, trying to relieve whatever pressure on my waist that I could. Bit by bit, I was lifted upward. My legs dangled. I held my feet off the wall to keep the rest of my body from banging into the side of the lodge.

Finally, my head came over the windowsill. When my shoulders cleared the sill, Tate said, "Let go of the rope and grab the window frame."

He seemed to know what he was doing when scaling a building, so I did as instructed.

Tate grabbed me by the shoulders and pulled me into the room. We fell into a heap on the floor just as the French doors of the conservatory opened. Austin and two other police officers stormed into the room.

Cecily scowled at us. "Did you call the police?"

"No," I said, out of breath, and scrambled to my feet. I grunted as a sharp pain pierced my waist just where the rope was. I was definitely going to have a bruise—more than one.

"The hotel was getting calls that a woman was hanging out a fifth-floor window," Austin said. "I hoped it wasn't you, Darby." His voice was heavy with disappointment.

"I wish it wasn't me, either. It wasn't a great experience." I rubbed my middle.

Austin turned on Tate. "How could you put Darby in such a dangerous situation? Do you care about her at all?"

"Austin, I was the one who volunteered to go out there," I said.

He glared at me. "I'm not talking to you."

I put my hands on my hips and winced. "You should be talking to me if it involves me."

"I would talk to you if I thought you had one iota of common sense."

I clenched my jaw. "I know what I have to do to solve a case. What I do is worth the risk."

Austin snorted, and I wanted to smack him. I crossed my arms instead.

After a moment of glaring at each other, Austin asked, "Why did you go out there, anyway?"

"I went to retrieve a purse that had fallen out the window."

"A purse? You nearly died for a purse?" he asked, and then his eyes narrowed. "What's in it? There are better ways to get it than hanging off the side of the building with a bit of rope. There must be something in it that is worth the risk."

Cecily jumped to her feet and walked up to me. She held out her hand. "That's mine, and I will be leaving now. Thank you for getting it for me." She took the purse and marched toward the conservatory like Mrs. Peacock fleeing a crime scene.

The two police officers who had come in with Austin blocked the way out of the room.

She stopped. "Excuse me."

Neither one of them moved.

"Mrs. Madd," Austin said. "I need to speak to you about your husband, his death, and the threatening notes he has been receiving."

Cecily spun around and glared at me. "You told the police about that?"

"If those threatening notes are in that purse, I need to see them too. My guess is they are something Darby would risk life and limb for."

She clutched the purse to her chest. "You need a warrant to do that, don't you?"

"I can get one, because the notes might be related to your husband's murder." His voice was even. "It would be much easier if you just handed the purse over, though."

"I'll hold onto them for now." She pressed her lips into a fine line.

Austin frowned. "Don't you want to find out who killed your husband?"

Her shoulders slumped, as if reality was just starting to sink in. "I think I have to sit down."

Austin nodded. "I imagine this is a shock. Officers Parsons and LaMont will get your information. I'm just going to walk Tate and Darby out of the conservatory."

Cecily returned to her rattan chair, looking much smaller than she had a moment ago. Parsons and

LaMont sat on identical chairs in front of her and began asking her hushed questions.

I wanted to sit in and hear every word of it.

"Darby," Austin called.

I turned and saw him by the double doors leading into the conservatory. Tate was already inside the indoor garden.

The colorful birds were disturbed by all the comings and goings through their home, because they fluttered and chattered above our heads. If one of them tried to dive bomb us, I wouldn't be the least bit surprised. It would be fitting for how my day had been going.

Austin continued through the garden with a purposeful walk. There would be no stopping to admire the flowers and birds. I raised my eyebrows at Tate, and he shrugged his shoulders. He appeared to be as clueless as I was about what Austin was thinking.

When we were out in the hallway, I let out a sigh of relief. The garden was too warm to be comfortable in flannel jeans and carrying a heavy winter coat. I wished I had left the coat downstairs before coming up to the fifth floor.

"Let us be there for your conversation with Cecily," Tate said. "I know her. I'll know if she's telling the truth."

Austin glared at him. "You should leave this to the police now. It's time for you to go home. The two of you poking your noses in this case complicates my investigation. Cecily didn't appear to be pleased with either of you."

Tate shook his head. "People lash out when they're grieving."

Austin arched one eyebrow, a skill I'd always found annoying when we were dating, when he used it on me. "And you think she is grieving?"

I pressed my lips together, not saying a word. It was something that I wondered myself about Cecily. She didn't seem to be heartbroken over her husband's death. True, everyone mourned differently, but she seemed much more concerned with saving her purse than the loss of her husband.

"It's not my place to judge how another person deals with tragedy," Tate said diplomatically.

"It would be a whole lot easier for me if you both went back to town." Austin folded his arms.

"But we've already helped you with the investigation in countless ways," I said. "You wouldn't know about the threatening notes or have a head start on a list of suspects without us."

He glanced at me. "That's true, but the police can take it from here. You'll just muddy the waters."

Before either Tate or I could take issue with that, Austin said, "Right now, I have work to do. If the two of you knew what was good for you, you'd just leave this mountain now." He went back into the conservatory.

I ran into the garden after him. "Austin!"

The birds cried in the trees. They really didn't like his activity in their space.

He spun around. "What?"

I stared at him. In all the time I had known him, I had never seen him this uptight. I wondered if the pressure of proving himself after his promotion had gone to his head. "I just wanted to tell you that you will want to speak to Kiera Bellworthy, too. She was seen outside close to the time of the murder, and she was crying."

"Thank you," he murmured, mollified. "I'll do that."

I nodded and was about to turn and leave when he said, "How could you be so stupid? You could have been killed! Do you have any idea what that would have done to me?"

I blinked at him. "Done to you?"

"Yes, to me." His eyes bore into mine. "Just because we aren't together doesn't mean I stopped caring about you. I don't want you getting hurt. You could have been killed, Darby."

I stared at him. So this was why he was acting so strangely. It wasn't the pressure of the promotion. It was *me*. I'd never thought Austin still cared about me. He was the one who'd said he wasn't ready for marriage. Now he was angry at me because he cared too much?

His expression dissolved back into an irritated mask. "Go collect your boyfriend and leave the lodge now. That's the only way I'm going to know for sure that you're safe." He stomped down the path and disappeared into the foliage.

Alone, I stared dumbfounded into the garden, as the colorful birds circled overhead in the steamy air.

Chapter Thirteen

*T*ATE WAITED FOR ME IN the hallway and held up his hands as if in surrender. "Okay, that didn't exactly go as planned."

I cocked my head. "You think?"

"I do. I also think we need to take some time to regroup. I will catch up with Cecily later. I'm sure she'll want to keep us on the case, especially since Austin said in no uncertain terms that she is the primary suspect. It's getting to be afternoon. Have you eaten anything today?"

"I don't remember. Maybe? No?"

"Okay, I take that as a definite no. Let's get something to eat and make a plan. We need to take a more methodical approach to this case. We have been running in too many directions."

I certainly agreed with him on that point. There were so many people I wanted to talk to about the case, but I couldn't keep grinding if I didn't have fuel and a plan. "Okay."

"Perfect. Meet me in the hotel restaurant in thirty minutes."

"In thirty minutes? Why don't we go right now?" I asked.

He pointed at me. "I'll let you know at lunch. Just give me thirty minutes." With that, he bolted to the exit door that led to the hotel stairwell.

Part of me wanted to run after him, but a larger part of me was just plain tired. I had gotten very little sleep the night before and had been running since five that morning. I sighed and walked to the elevator bay, planning to drop the purple coat I had been carrying all over the hotel in my room.

When I reached the third floor, I noticed that my door was ajar. My body tensed. A lot had happened that day so far. It seemed my body was just expecting more bad news.

I pushed open the door with my toe. "Hello?" I held my coat in the air like I was about to throw it at someone. It wasn't much in the way of a weapon, but I hoped at least that it would catch an assailant off guard.

A woman in a maid's uniform stepped out of the bathroom, holding a spray bottle. I noticed the bed was neatly made, and the blankets on the couch were folded and tucked and hanging over the arm.

The woman stared at my raised arm, holding the coat.

"I'm sorry." I dropped my arm. "I didn't expect anyone to be in here."

"It's all right," the maid said with a smile. "Everyone has been so jumpy today with that poor man's death."

It was interesting that she would say "poor man's

death." I didn't think anyone else referred to Dr. Madd in that way.

"I have just finished up your bathroom, and I'll get out of your hair." She gathered up her cleaning products from the bathroom.

"What's your name?" I asked.

"Priscilla," she said without hesitating. "If that's all you need, I'll be on my way." As she went out the door, she added, "Have a good day."

The door closed behind her with a click.

I sat on the edge of my bed. The urge to lie back and rest my eyes for a few minutes before I had to meet Tate in the restaurant was overpowering. I rubbed the sore spots around my waist where Tate had tied the rope. It had been a very long day, and it wasn't over yet. I kept wondering where Tate was off to. What was he doing right now that he couldn't tell me about? I wished he was more open about his plans.

Since we'd started working together, he'd told me repeatedly to trust him, but that wasn't easy to do when he ran off all the time with no explanation.

There was a knock on the door. "Housekeeping!"

I frowned. Did the maid forget something? I went to the door and opened it. There was another maid on the other side of the door, and she had a large cart that held new towels, spray bottles, a vacuum cleaner.

She smiled. "Would you like your room cleaned?"

"A maid was just here and cleaned the room. She left no more than five minutes ago."

"That's not possible. I'm the only one working on this floor today, and I haven't been in your room yet."

My stomach tightened, and it had nothing to do

with the rope. "There was a maid named Priscilla who was here a little while ago."

"There is no one working at the lodge with that name." She sniffed and pushed her glasses up the bridge of her nose. "If there were, I would know. I've been here for twelve years."

"Maybe I misheard her," I said, knowing that I hadn't. My stomach sank. "I don't need the room cleaned. I'm fine."

She nodded and handed me a stack of extra towels. "If there's anything else you need, just call house-keeping." She pushed her large cart to the next room.

When I had walked in on the first maid, she didn't have a cart. It seemed all she had with her was a spray bottle and a uniform. It had been an excellent cover story, one that even I might have used if I had to get into a person's room on a job. There was only one reason someone would want to come into our room, and it had to do with Dr. Garret Madd. Did the other guests know that Tate and I were hired private detectives now? It was entirely possible. The Herrington police officers on the grounds knew, and I had told Herschel, the lodge manager, and Anderson, the distribution guy, myself. Others would soon know, if they didn't already.

I picked up the landline and called the reception desk.

"Yes, Ms. Piper," Herschel's pleasant voice said on the other end of the line.

I sucked in a breath and then remembered that, of course, reception would know who was in what room. It was a logical guess that if a woman was calling him from our room it was me. "Can you tell me the name of the maid who works on my floor?"

"Is anything wrong?" he asked in a worried voice. He sounded like he was just one more emergency away from losing it. A murder at the lodge had certainly frazzled the staff.

"No, everything is fine. I just didn't catch her name. I wanted to leave her a thank-you note."

"Oh," Herschel sighed with relief. "Her name is Laney. She's a great employee and has been with us for a long time."

"She said twelve years," I said.

"Yes, that sounds right. Was there anything else you needed?"

"Just one more question. Is there a maid who works for the lodge named Priscilla?" I asked.

"Priscilla?" He was clearly confused. "No, we don't have anyone here by that name," he said with as much certainty as Laney had a few minutes ago. "Do you need me to find someone with that name?"

"Oh, no. I must have heard the name wrong— maybe it was referring to someone else. Thank you so much for your time."

"My pleasure. Please let us know if there is anything else you need."

I thanked him and ended the call.

Why would someone pretend to be a maid to get into my suite? To search it, probably...or to plant incriminating evidence. I shivered, but I took comfort in knowing that there wasn't anything in the room to find. Tate and I worked from our phones when we were out of the office. We never carried client files or computers with us. That was intentional. Even with password protection and encryption, computers and electronic files could be compromised. Since our phones were always with us, they were the best way to keep any information safe. A smartphone could still be compromised, but it was just a bit more challenging.

I searched my room to see if anything had been planted or had gone missing. I found nothing new, and all my possessions seemed to be in the same places I'd left them that morning. Other than my clothes and other essentials, I had very little with me.

That's when I noticed that the door between my and Tate's suites was slightly ajar. I went over to it and opened the door on my side. The door on Tate's side was wide open. It hadn't been like that when I left in the morning. At least, I knew the door on my side had been closed and locked.

I stepped into his suite and looked around. I had searched through my things to see if anything was off. Should I search through Tate's things, too?

Before I could change my mind, I went into his bedroom. Tate's old Army knapsack sat in one corner. My fingers hovered over the bag's drawstrings. It would be a major violation of privacy to open it, but I reminded myself that Tate agreed with my method of not bringing any personal effects with him on a case.

I untied the drawstrings and looked inside.

I removed shirts, jeans, and socks. There was nothing out of ordinary, and if something had been planted or taken, I wasn't sure how I would know. I opened the front pocket of the bag and took out a novel. When I tossed it aside, a photo fell out.

I picked it up and peered at it. It was of Tate,

maybe fifteen years ago. He was laughing. There were fewer lines on his face, and he wasn't alone. He held the hand of a much younger and much more natural-looking Cecily.

Why would he bring this with him? To show Cecily and talk about the old days? It just seemed so odd to me that this would be in his things unless it was important to him. He had kept it for a very long time.

Something wasn't right here. Who was the fake maid working for? Or was she working for herself?

I left Tate's room and went back into mine, but not before making sure both doors between our rooms were closed and locked. Tate and I were going to meet up at the restaurant soon, but I had to check out something first.

I took the elevator to the lobby, and as always, I found Herschel behind the main desk.

He smiled at me. "Ms. Piper, how can I help you?"

Tiny lay to one side of the counter, gently snoring. It had been a busy and tense morning for everyone at the lodge.

"I just called about the maid named Priscilla."

He swallowed and fixed his glasses. "Yes, and as I told you on the phone, we have no one who works at the lodge by that name."

"If that's the case, someone broke into my room pretending to be a maid, and I want to know who that person is."

"Ms. Piper, I assure you that our lodge is very secure."

I squinted at him. How he could say that with a straight face when Dr. Madd had just been killed on the slope?

"I'd like the keys changed on both Tate Porter's and my rooms."

"Certainly," he said.

"And I'd like to know where you keep the maids' uniforms."

"Excuse me?" He adjusted his glasses.

"The maids' uniforms. Would it be hard for someone to take one?"

"It wouldn't be difficult," he admitted. "They're in the staff area, and we have a large staff. There are people coming and going from there all the time."

I frowned. "Where is it?"

"Ms. Piper," he said. "I really don't think we need to continue this conversation. If something was taken from your room, I'm happy to replace it to the best of my ability. But I can't do much more than that and changing your room keys."

I nodded. "I have to meet Tate for lunch. I'll stop by afterward and pick up the keys."

Our conversation might have been over, but I wasn't done with the mystery maid just yet.

Chapter Fourteen

I KNEW I WAS RISKING BEING late for my lunch meeting with Tate, but that couldn't be helped. I had to find out more about the woman who broke into my room.

After I left Tiny and Herschel, I walked around the lobby and the main floor of the hotel looking for a service door. I found a door labeled *Employees Only* just outside the spa. I tried it, but it was locked. There was a key card reader on the door just like on the guests' doors.

I stood outside the spa and wondered what to do. I knew Herschel wasn't going to let me into the employees-only area. He just wanted to make my fake maid Priscilla problem go away.

A woman in a white uniform came out of the spa. She smiled at me as she walked to the employees-only door. I pretended I was interested in reading a brochure about the lodge someone had left on the side table as she unlocked the staff door with her key and went through.

Just as the door was about to close, I grabbed its handle and held it just enough that the latch didn't click. I then counted to ten, which I guessed would give the woman enough time to go wherever she was headed.

I slipped through the door and found myself at the top of a set of stairs. It seemed that the staff area in the lodge was in the basement. A dank smell hung in the air. The lodge was an older building, and even with the white walls and tiled flooring, nothing could hide the fact that it was an old basement that had been dug into the mountain. When I reached the bottom of the stairs, I touched the stone wall, and it was ice-cold.

There was laughter coming my way. A maid's cart was tucked to one side of the hallway. I ducked behind it just as two young waiters walked by, presumably on their way to the lodge restaurant.

I could hear my heartbeat in my ears. I needed to find where the maids' uniforms were kept and get out of there.

At the end of the hallway I found a large room full of lockers. This was the place I was looking for. I went to the first locker and opened the door. A purse and winter coat hung inside.

I was surprised that not a single locker had a lock on it. Either it was lodge policy that didn't allow locks, or every single person who worked for the lodge was very trusting of their coworkers. I knew that wouldn't have worked for me, but I was a private investigator, so I stopped trusting most people long ago.

The third locker I opened held a maid's uniform. *Jackpot.* I had my answer as to how a person could have stolen a uniform. But I wasn't any closer to finding out who that person was.

I turned to leave. Even though I was a private investigator, I wasn't there to invade the staff's privacy, unless one of them showed themselves to be a viable suspect.

A crumpled piece of paper caught my eye and I bent to pick it up. It was a computer printout about the lodge and its amenities. There wasn't anything odd about that. I was certain everyone on the staff, from Herschel the manager to a hostess at the restaurant, had to be well-versed in all the lodge had to offer, so it made sense that something like this might be in the locker room.

What stood out was that it was from a real estate website for luxury hotels and resorts that were for sale.

I was reminded of my conversation with Jeremy Stone, the winery owner, at the New Year's Eve party. He wanted to buy this place. He'd made no secret of that, and apparently, it was really up for sale.

I folded the piece of paper and stuck it in my jeans pocket.

The hotel restaurant was busy even at three in the afternoon. The bar was particularly packed. At the police's request, the partygoers couldn't leave the lodge, and the ski slope was closed. There wasn't much to do other than eat, drink, and gossip about the murder.

As I stepped into the room, I sensed tensions were high. I didn't know how much longer the Madds' wealthy guests would be willing to be cooped up in the ski lodge.

I scanned the room for Tate, but didn't see him. I went to the bar, not because I wanted a drink, but because it was the best place for gossip. I needed to know more about Dr. Madd and his wife, and why these people had decided to spend their holiday weekend in the Finger Lakes with the two of them. I knew some of them hoped to work for MaddlyCare, but was that true for everyone?

"How long do you think the police are going to keep us captive?" a man with a grizzled beard asked.

"They can't after the weekend. I have a nonrefundable return flight to the city," the woman sitting on the barstool next to him said. "If the police make me change my flight, they're going to have to pay for it." She sighed. "It's a shame that all those deals we planned to make with him are now dead in the water. I wouldn't go into business with his wife."

"Anyone who goes into business with Cecily Madd is in for a whole heap of trouble. They'd better watch their back," the man replied. "As for how long we'll have to stay here, it can't possibly go on for that long. Anyone can see his wife did it. Did you see her face when he said he was replacing her? I'm surprised she didn't spontaneously combust. It made me a bit relieved that they passed on my campaign to revamp the branding for MaddlyCare. The emotional price of working for them would not have been worth it. My mental health is worth more than what they can pay."

The woman nodded. "Another job will always come around. That's why I'm in marketing. Something goes off badly, there's always another campaign I can jump on."

"Maybe I should change careers and do straight

marketing. Branding can get tedious. Clients always want tweaks."

"Miss?" a voice asked me, in a tone that told me it was not the first time he had tried to get my attention.

I turned, and a bartender with a precise goatee was looking at me expectantly. "What can I get you?"

"Umm, a glass of white wine. Thank you," I said, turning my back to the woman and man I had been eavesdropping on. I didn't want them to see my face.

"What kind?" He rattled off a list of white wines.

"Whatever you recommend. I'm not picky." I was mostly not picky because I wasn't well-versed enough in wine to know the difference. He nodded and moved down the bar to get the next patron's order.

There were no barstools open, so I hovered near the two people I was eavesdropping on.

"It kind of blew my mind to see Tate Porter here," the woman said. "I haven't seen him since he was in New York. That must have been ten years ago."

I froze and turned slightly to take a better look at the younger man she was talking to. I didn't recognize him.

"Yeah, that's when I met him for the first time," he said. "He and Cecily go way back."

Had Tate visited Cecily in New York? I had been under the impression that he hadn't seen her since high school.

"Miss?" The bartender held a wine glass out to me. I accepted it and set several bills on the counter. He nodded his thanks and took the money to his till.

"He and Cecily were close back then—"

"Donaldson," a hostess called out.

"That's us." They picked up their drinks and went into the dining room.

My head was spinning. I wished I had interrupted them and asked them how they knew Tate. It was also interesting to me that at least some of the guests had known Cecily outside the confines of business.

I took one of the stools the couple had vacated and waved at the bartender.

"Would you like something else?" the bartender asked. He studied my face. "Hey, I know you. I see you at Floured Grounds a lot chatting with Maelynn."

The bartender was about forty and had thick black hair and tanned skin, even though it was the beginning of January. He did look familiar. "Maelynn is my best friend."

"Right. You're Darby. She talks about you all the time. I think she said you and I would make a cute couple."

Inwardly, I sighed. Ever since I had broken up with Austin, Maelynn had gotten it into her head to play matchmaker.

"I'm John Paul," the tan bartender said.

"It's nice to officially meet you, then. I'm sorry. I told Maelynn I'm not interested in dating anyone right now." Not that Maelynn really cared.

He laughed. "Don't worry about it."

"I was wondering if I could ask you anything about the couple that was just sitting at the bar. Do you know anything about them?" I asked.

He started cleaning a glass. "Not really. They had been nursing drinks at the bar since eleven. To be honest, I'm glad to have the stools freed up."

"Mind telling me what they were talking about?" I asked, and slid a twenty-dollar bill across the bar.

John Paul looked at it, palmed the bill, and tucked it into the pocket of his black jeans. "Mostly, they spoke about the murder like everyone else in the lodge. It's crazy what happened. I mean, who gets shot in the back with a crossbow? It's like something out of a movie."

I had to agree with him on that. I had never heard of anyone killed in that manner before. I wrote my cell number on a napkin. "This might be a stretch, but can you call or text me if you hear anything interesting when it comes to the murder?"

He tucked the napkin in his pocket where the twenty-dollar bill had disappeared. "Maelynn said you were a detective. Are you working?"

I looked up and down the bar. "I'm a private investigator, which is quite a bit different from a police detective, but I am working with the police on the case. It would be a great help if you told me if you heard anything interesting about the murder."

He frowned and looked as if he would say something when a woman at the other end of the bar waved at him. Before he left to take her order, John Paul said in a low voice, "I can't make any promises."

I nodded, still grateful he took my number. What I had learned in this private detective business was, you never knew where the next lead would come from, and it was best to be open to all sources of information, even if it was a guy your best friend wanted you to date.

Chapter Fifteen

SOMEONE TAPPED ME ON THE shoulder. I turned and found Tate smiling at me.

"What's with the long face?" he asked.

"I'm fine," I said.

He cocked his head. "In my experience, when a woman says she's fine, she's not. Not even close." He squeezed my shoulder. "Let's get some lunch and talk."

I stood up from the barstool and followed him into the dining room. Like the rest of the lodge, the restaurant was decked out in what I was starting to think of as Northwoods Chic. There was a large, stone, two-way fireplace—of course—in the middle of the room, and dark beams decorated the ceiling.

"You already have a table?"

"I made reservations." He glanced over his shoulder. "Just after we left Cecily and Austin."

"Oh." Tate usually wasn't one to plan ahead like that.

A hostess showed us to a small table that over-looked the ski slope. All the emergency workers and police were gone. There were metal rods in the snow with yellow crime scene tape to mark where Dr. Madd had fallen near the top of the mountain.

"I bet we didn't get this table by accident," I said, looking out the window.

"I put in a special request. The hostess likes me," he said, with the confidence of a man who is aware of his good looks.

A waiter appeared at our table and took our drink orders. I still had most of my wine, so I asked for water. Tate ordered a Coke. We also ordered our food at the same time. Tate ordered a specialty burger, and I went for comfort and asked for a grilled cheese and fries. It really had been a long day.

When the waiter left, I folded my hands on the table. "Where did you go when we left Cecily in the conservatory? And why didn't you tell me where you were going? And what's the deal with you and Cecily? What's your relationship, or past relationship? Why do guests of the Madds know who you are?"

He held up his hands as if in surrender. "Whoa! Whoa! Where are all these questions coming from?"

The waiter appeared with our drinks before I could answer. He set them on the table and disappeared again. It gave me time to think about my answer.

"I need to know what's going on with you. If we're going to be partners, I need to trust you one hundred percent, but if you're withholding information from me, it makes me question if I can do that." I picked up my wine glass and took a long drink.

"Okay," Tate said. "I haven't been as forthcoming with you as I should. I thought I was helping by letting you focus on your part of the investigation while I focused on mine."

"That's not how it works." I set the wine glass down, which was now empty. "It is our investigation, which means we're doing this together as a team."

He swallowed, as if, for the first time, he realized how upset I was.

"And it's not just this case," I continued. "You keep information to yourself all the time. How are we supposed to make Piper and Porter Detective Agency work that way? You tell me to trust you, but in truth, you don't trust *me*."

He sighed. "I'm sorry. You're right."

"I'm right?" I had geared myself for an argument, and I deflated into my chair.

"As much as I have told you to trust me, I haven't always trusted you. I spent too much time wandering around the world. I've learned to be careful. Maybe too careful. My aunt trusted you, and that should've been enough for me." He leaned back in his chair. "So ask me what you want to know. I'll tell the truth."

I eyed him and wished I had ordered a second glass of wine. I felt like I might need some liquid courage. "Okay, I'll start with Cecily. I need the backstory between you two."

"We were close friends in high school. We dated on and off. It was nothing serious, just a high school romance. I knew then that I wanted to go into the Army, so we knew it wouldn't last when I entered the service."

Thinking back to the conversation I overheard, I asked, "Did you ever visit her in New York?"

He frowned. "Once or twice not long after high school when I was on leave, but after she got married, I hadn't spoken to her until this week."

"But you've never been to this lodge before, even though it was owned by her father?"

"No, she didn't have a good relationship with her dad. I never met him. I don't even remember him coming to her high school graduation or anything like that. All I know is he was some sort of big hotel chain executive, and he left corporate life to run the lodge on a smaller scale sometime after Cecily's parents divorced. I think she was still small when they broke up. Maybe even a baby."

"He lived so close to his daughter and he didn't try to forge a relationship?"

"As far as I know, he didn't. He remarried shortly after his first divorce and concentrated on his new family."

"New family?"

"He had a son with his second wife."

"Son? Cecily has a brother?"

"Half-brother, yeah."

"What happened to the second wife?" I asked.

"They divorced. From what Cecily says, she's living in California."

"And the son?"

"Oh, you saw him already," Tate said.

I blinked. "I *saw* him? I haven't met anyone claiming to be Cecily's brother."

"I don't know if he would tell anyone that. Cecily made it very clear that she thinks her brother is a screwup. The two of them have barely spoken since Cecily arrived, by her accounts."

"Who is he?"

"He's the ski instructor on staff here."

"Was he the one wearing jeans at the party?"

"Bingo," Tate said, as if I'd won some sort of prize.

I thought back to that eventful night of the New Year's Eve party. I noticed the man right away because when everyone else was in black tie, his casual attire stood out. As did his attitude. As the other members of the party had put on pleasant faces, he'd scowled as if he'd rather be any other place on earth.

I tried to remember seeing my fake maid Priscilla in that group of people, but I couldn't. Then again, she was a fake maid, so she wouldn't have been there, would she?

"I tried to talk to him at the party, but he blew me off."

"I'm not surprised to hear that. By the way Cecily tells it, he blows everyone off."

"What's the brother's name?"

"Ridge Tragger."

"That sounds like a ski instructor's name."

"I thought so too," he said.

"What does this all mean for the case?"

Tate shrugged. "I don't know. Just that Cecily's ties to this place are much deeper than we first thought."

"That seems significant."

He nodded. "It does."

"How long have you known her brother works here?" I asked, thinking that was an important bit of information that he should have shared with me.

"I just found out. When I left you, that's when I learned it."

I frowned. I would come back to that comment in a moment. There was something more pressing that I wanted to ask him. "Before you came to the bar, there was a man named Donaldson there who seemed to know a lot about you and Cecily. How many people here this weekend do you know?"

"Donaldson?" he said as if testing out the name. "Oh, do you mean Peter Donaldson? Yeah, he went to school in a neighboring town. I know him from sports camps and football from middle and high school. You probably don't know him because he is three or four years older than Cecily and I. I wouldn't call him a friend. I haven't said much more than 'Hi' to him all weekend."

"Where did you go after we left Cecily?"

He stared at his water glass for a moment as he considered his answer. "I met with Benny B."

I flattened my hands on the table. "*What*?" I would have shouted it if I hadn't been afraid the whole restaurant would overhear me.

"That reaction is why I didn't tell you." He sipped his Coke.

"What could you have to speak to Benny B about?" I asked.

"I wanted to know what he knows. He's a smart guy and has been at this lodge a lot longer than we have. He knows the place, and he was preparing for this weekend for a long time. He had time to do the research that we didn't have the luxury of time to do. He, not Cecily, was the one who told me her half-brother is the ski instructor here."

"It's worrying to me that Cecily didn't see that as essential information to share."

"I think Cecily only shares the information that *she* wants to be seen as essential."

"So he just told you everything he knew?" My voice dripped with doubt.

"Not for free."

The waiter showed up then, but my appetite was all but gone. "What was the price for the information?" I asked, not touching my food.

Tate didn't have the same qualms about eating, because he wiped at his chin with a napkin after his first big bite of burger. It was so large, it looked like it might fall apart in his hands, but somehow he kept it together and didn't drop anything on himself. If it had been me eating such a messy meal, I would have looked like I'd purposely rolled in it after one bite. "I told him we would give him information for the article that he wants to sell about this weekend."

I stared as him as if he'd put the burger on top of his head and worn it like a hat. "Tate, we can't do that. If it gets out that we spill the details of our cases to reporters after they close, it could hurt our reputation, and then we'll have an even more difficult time trying to find clients."

"I told him he can't reveal us as the source," Tate said, as if that took care of it.

I knew it hadn't taken care of anything. He was playing with fire, striking a deal with Benny B.

"And you trust him to do that?" I still couldn't believe what he had done. "Depending on the information you give him, Cecily will be able to surmise that we were the ones who leaked to the press."

Tate set his half-eaten burger back on the table, as if it had hit him what he'd done.

"This is why you have to clock so many hours

before you can get a private detective license in the state. There are ethics involved in being a P.I."

Tate looked down at his plate, and I regretted my words. "Look, you made a mistake. Everyone makes mistakes. When it's time to give Benny B information about the case, we'll be careful about what we tell him."

Tate lifted his head. "I should have checked with you first. I was just so gung-ho about the idea that I didn't ask. I knew what you would say. To be fair, what you've said isn't wrong."

I nodded. "Was it worth it? What did he tell you?"

"It was worth it. I already told you the part about Cecily's half-brother working here, and the other stuff he had to say was very interesting."

"Go on."

"The Madds were here a full day before the guests arrived, and most of that time, the couple spent apart. I'm not sure what Dr. Madd was doing, but Cecily was in a number of meetings with the lodge staff, especially Herschel. It appears that after her father passed, he left it to her. Up until this point, she has let the lodge run itself, but it seems she wants to be more involved."

I raised my brow. "What about Ridge? Didn't he get part of the lodge?"

"I don't know the arrangements of the inheritance," he said. "Benny B didn't know either, but he suspects Ridge got a raw deal in their father's will, since Cecily is listed as the sole owner of the property with the county, and Ridge is an employee."

"Benny B looked up the property records?"

"You bet he did. You know the guy is thorough."

That was true. It was why Benny B was so good at his job. "Then what do we do next?"

"We need to speak to Ridge. That's number one. I think we should do that together. He's a little hard to track down."

"Why's that?" I asked.

"Benny B didn't even know where to find him. With the ski slope closed, he seems to have evaporated into thin air. Benny said when the slope was open it was easy to find Ridge. He was always there hours before the slope opened and hours after. He took his job seriously."

"He was *always* there?" I asked. Tate nodded as if he didn't know what I was getting at. I spelled it out for him. "If Ridge is always there, then wouldn't he also have been there when Dr. Madd was shot?"

"Exactly, and that's why we need to talk to him together. I'd rather you not try to speak to him alone."

"I'm sure Austin will also be looking for him," I said. "And we have to find Dr. Madd's ex-wife, Heather. She's a guest this weekend too."

"I will leave that part to you, since you already have an in with Herschel. He seems to be willing to work with you."

"I don't know if I would call it an *in*, but I have certainly made a nuisance of myself. Maybe he's willing to answer my questions because he wants me to go away."

"It might be the way you get most of your information." He picked up his burger then and took another bite.

I narrowed my eyes.

After a sip of his Coke, he waved his hands. "I'm kidding."

"You'd better be," I grumbled.

He grinned.

I picked up a French fry. For whatever reason, bickering with Tate always made me hungry.

"We don't have much time to solve this case before everyone leaves," Tate mused. "I'm certain as soon as the police say people can leave the lodge, there will be a mass exodus."

I nodded, having come to the same conclusion. "What's the point of doing all of this, though? In Cecily's mind, she's probably already fired us."

"I'm going to talk to Cecily."

"But will she listen?"

"She will to me," he said with confidence.

I didn't question him why he was so confident about that. If he was going to trust me, I was going to have to trust him too.

Chapter Sixteen

ATE AND I FINISHED LUNCH, and I felt a whole lot better about our partnership. There were still some kinks and details to work out, but I was confident that at the very least, we would be able to get through this case and address the remaining issues when the weekend was over—which wasn't that far away. It was already late Saturday afternoon, and conceivably, everyone who was at Garden Peak Lodge that weekend would be gone by Monday afternoon. It sure didn't give us a lot of time to find a killer. The odds of finding the culprit after everyone left the lodge were slim to none.

"Darby!" a voice called as Tate and I went our separate ways in the lobby. I knew he'd gone in search of Cecily, while I was off in the other direction to find Heather, the ex-wife.

Edwin waved at me from a table just outside the lodge spa. He was sitting at the table with his fiancé, Pierce. I walked over to join them. "Hi! How's business?" I asked.

"Sales are good!" Pierce said. "Guests don't have

much to do right now other than eat and shop. The shopping here is limited to the ski shop and us."

Edwin nodded. "I feel bad, because all the guests here really want to leave. Every last one has told us this. But keeping everyone in the lodge has been a real boon to our business."

"Edwin," Pierce said. "You can't say things like that. It makes us seem unfeeling."

"I'm not unfeeling. I feel terrible that a man died. I'm just happy to be starting the New Year in the black. I can be both things." Edwin turned to me. "Did you hear the news? They're opening the mountain back up for skiing tomorrow morning, so at least people will be able to get outside and ski. We really must all go for a few runs before we leave here."

I started to tell him that that wasn't going to happen, but then I remembered that Ridge Tragger was the ski instructor for the lodge. If I was a novice skier, I would have to work with him. It might be worth it to take a lesson. "I'm in," I said.

"Really?" Edwin asked. "I thought you wouldn't ski because there was too high a risk of injury."

"There is, but I think it's something I should try at least once, right?" I hoped my voice stayed steady as I said it.

"Right!" Edwin said. "And you're a former ballerina. You should be great at it. It's all about balance. You'll have no problem at all."

I wasn't so sure that being able to stand in pointe shoes more than ten years ago translated into the ability to stand right up on skis today.

"I'll set up the lesson," Edwin said quickly, as if

he was afraid I might back out. "You can do it at the reception desk."

"Be sure to include Tate," I said. "He'll want to ski too."

More than wanting to ski, he would want to talk to Ridge.

"You got it," Edwin said. "It'll be like a double date."

I scowled. "It's *not* a double date."

Edwin grinned. Out of the corner of my eye, a woman hurried by us. She was no longer in the maid's uniform I had seen her wearing in my suite, but I recognized her. I didn't even say goodbye to Edwin and Pierce before I took off after her. She went out the lodge's back door onto the wide patio that overlooked the ski slope. When she hit the patio, she kept going in the direction of the ski house, a place where no one from the lodge was supposed to be today, per the police.

I decided to hang back and follow her to see what she was up to. She went around the back of the ski house, and I followed. I was in my turtleneck sweater, flannel-lined jeans, and snow boots, but I wished I had brought that giant purple coat with me. The cold breeze froze my ears and cut through my sweater.

As I peered around the ski house, I saw her go inside. I inched closer to the door. There was a large window just before the door, and I peeked over the windowsill. From my vantage point, I saw the woman who called herself Priscilla standing in the middle of the ski house with none other than Benny B. That guy was always popping up to make my life more difficult.

I was no longer worried about hiding. I stood up and marched into the ski house. Throwing open the door, I asked, "What's going on in here?"

Benny B yelped and hit the floor like a bomb had gone off. Priscilla looked down at him in annoyance.

He opened one eye and looked at me. "Darby Piper, you just about scared me to death."

I glanced at the woman. "It's nice to see you again, Priscilla. I see you're no longer wearing your maid's uniform. Get off work early?"

She scowled at me.

"Or did you put it back into the locker you stole it from, since there is no maid, no employee actually, who works at the lodge by the name of Priscilla?" I accused her.

"Who's Priscilla?" Benny B asked, clearly confused.

I pointed at his companion. "Her. Or at least that was the name she gave me when she broke into my room posing as a maid."

Benny B nodded. "Nice. I don't think I would have gone with Priscilla. It's too unique, but it was great to give an alias."

She lifted her chin. "It's my cat's name."

"What's your real name?"

She looked at me for a long moment, and I thought she wasn't going to answer. Finally, she said, "Heather Madd."

"You're Dr. Madd's ex-wife."

"Wow," she said sarcastically. "You really are a crack detective."

"How do you know I'm a detective?" I asked.

Heather pointed at Benny B. "How do you think?"

I clenched my jaw. I knew Benny B would end up telling someone why Tate and I were really at the lodge that weekend. "Why were you in my room?" I asked in a sharp voice.

"I heard that someone sent threats to Garret. I assumed Cecily gave you the notes, and I wanted to see them for myself."

"You didn't find them," I stated.

She pressed her lips together. "No, I didn't."

"How did you get into my room?"

"That was easy. I took the maid's uniform and the master key from a locker in the service area. The locker was unlocked. I knew I could put it back before anyone noticed it was gone, and I did, too, even though you interrupted my search."

It's what I had expected after seeing the unsecured staff locker room myself.

I didn't tell her why she hadn't found the notes because I hadn't even seen them yet, even after being on this case for two days.

"What are the two of you doing here together?" I asked, looking from Heather to Benny B and back again.

"None of your business," Heather snapped.

I folded my arms. "Benny, Tate told me about your arrangement. You won't be getting any information from us if you don't tell me what's going on with the two of you."

Benny B's face reddened. "Heather told me about this weekend, and I thought it might make a good article. I never thought Garret would up and die and make it a *huge* story."

I looked to Heather. "Why did you tell Benny B about the weekend?"

"His mother is an old friend of mine, and I know she worries about him."

"So it had nothing to do with your ex-husband?" I asked dubiously.

She didn't say anything.

"Why are you here this weekend? It's pretty unusual to invite an ex-wife to an event with your current wife. I have to say, it's even stranger that you work for your ex-husband."

She frowned. "I still work for MaddlyCare. It was part of the divorce settlement. I either took Garret for half of everything he had at the time, or he gave me a permanent job and ten percent ownership in the company. I'm a smart cookie. I knew the company was in its infancy and would just get more popular and make more money as time went on. It was the wiser move to stay on and have a share of the company and a steady salary."

"What do you do for the company?"

"I'm in sales. That's where I started. I manage the account for a large department store. Actually, my account is one of the brands I brought to MaddlyCare. That's how Garret and I met."

I nodded. It seemed that Garret Madd had made it a pattern to meet his significant others through his work. It made sense. His work had been his pride and joy, and the place where he spent all his time.

It seemed I had solved one small mystery from this weekend, which was how Benny B had learned about the event. It made me feel a bit better.

"What in particular did you want Benny B to learn about Garret's company?"

"That he was going to sell it to the highest bidder. That he was going to get out, and his wife was opposed to the idea. That the only way he saw to diminish her say in the sale was to diminish her position in the company."

I stared at her. This wasn't good news for Cecily. It was giving her even more motive to kill her husband.

"Who knew about Garret's plans for the company?"

She snorted. "Who didn't? Garret was the least private person you ever met. He was so confident about his place in the world. He would say anything and tell you anything about himself. He never thought anyone could hurt him or touch him. It was the benefit of being raised in privilege and staying there as an adult."

"If so many people knew his plans, why did so many other distributors and pitch people come here this weekend? It seems like it would be a waste of their time, if he was preparing to sell the whole thing."

"It's a free all-expenses-paid vacation," she said with narrowed eyes. "Why wouldn't they want to come?"

"That might be true for a good number of the attendees, but I'm sure someone like Kicra Dellworthy could afford a fancy getaway. She doesn't need this weekend, and she doesn't need to take the risk of signing on with a company that is up for sale."

"Sure, if she ever had any chance of being in the movies again."

"Why wouldn't she?" I asked. "I thought she was the It Girl in Hollywood right now."

Heather clicked her tongue. "Do you live in a bubble? She was in the middle of a huge social media scandal. I don't remember what she did exactly, but Hollywood has blacklisted her. She can't even get a bit part in a sitcom. This endorsement with Maddly-Care was her way back in."

I winced. I obviously needed to spend more time reading about pop culture if I was going to interact with it. I changed the subject back to the notes. "Why were you trying to find the threatening notes?"

"Because they're proof that Cecily killed her husband," Heather said. "Because I would bet my stake in MaddlyCare that she wrote them herself." She looked me square in the eye. "How does it feel to be working for a killer?"

"How do you know I was working for her? And I don't agree that she's necessarily the killer."

She smiled at Benny B. "Benny clued me in. Your little charade of being a couple with your business partner is a waste of time. Anyone who's around you can see that the two of you have no chemistry, no interest in each other."

I wasn't sure how I felt about her statement—relieved or worried. How many people at the ski lodge knew that Tate and I were P.I.s and not a couple? It could become a problem. Witnesses might be less interested in speaking to us.

Benny B crossed his arms "Heather, if you found the notes, were you going to share them with me?"

She waved away his concern. "Yes, yes. Don't worry so much, Benny. You're always afraid that someone else will scoop you."

"I'm afraid of it because it's happened on more

than one occasion. I won't be double-crossed," he said bitterly.

I grimaced. That didn't bode well for the information-sharing deal that Tate had struck with Benny B.

Heather chuckled. "Don't use that tone with me. You wouldn't even be here without me."

I watched the two bicker with interest. I could use their distrust of each other to my advantage. I just didn't know how yet.

"Where were the two of you early on New Year's Day morning?"

Benny B's eyes went wide. "I had no reason to kill Dr. Madd, if that's what you're getting at. I mean, his death is a great story for me, but I had a good story already, without killing someone. There was plenty of material to work with before he died. I mean, Kiera Bellworthy is here. Just her presence will get me noticed in the tabloids."

"Just so we cover all the bases, where were you?" I pressed.

"I was asleep in my room. It was a late night," he said, but the way he wouldn't meet my eyes told me he was lying.

"And you?" I asked Heather.

"The same. I was in bed. I'm not one for a late night, and I had trouble waking up. Also, I have never even seen a crossbow before. If you think I shot my ex-husband in the back with one, you're crazy." She folded her arms. "Don't you think if I wanted to kill him, I would have done it by now? I sure wouldn't wait until he was at a big party with friends and clients. There are much quieter ways to remove a person you want out of the picture."

That wasn't as comforting as she seemed to believe it to be.

"Why are the two of you out here now?" I asked.

Heather scowled at me. "I wanted to know if Benny learned anything more about my ex-husband's death."

"I've been trying to," Benny B said in a whiny voice. "But no one here will give me the time of day since I'm in a lodge uniform, and they view me as a servant, not a person. This weekend is really going to change how I treat people in service positions in the future."

"What's the staff saying about the murder?" I asked.

He glanced at me, and at first, I didn't think he was going to answer. But then he said, "I think they're relieved. They think if Cecily Madd gets arrested, she can't sell the lodge."

"The staff knows she wants to sell?" I asked.

"That's the rumor. There was a lot of fear when staff started to talk about Cecily taking over. Many thought she would sell the place or just use it for her fancy friends. She promised a lot of changes, but she was never specific as to what they would be. It was almost worse than her coming right out and saying what her plans were. People have some wild imaginations."

"Why do they think Cecily is the murderer?" I asked

"Isn't the significant other always a suspect?" he asked.

I shrugged. That wasn't much to go on.

"And her brother Ridge? What does he think about all this?"

Benny B nodded. "Hard to say. He keeps to himself. My guess is he's not happy about it, though. From what I have gathered over a month of working here, Ridge was left out of his father's will, except he was promised housing at the lodge as long as he worked here. I think it's a cushy setup for him. He skis and gets free room and board. Some of the other staff complained about it. They believe he gets special treatment because he was the late owner's son."

"Have you spoken to him since you've worked here?"

"I've tried. It hasn't gone well." He wrinkled his nose. "And I don't think he likes me."

"He doesn't like anyone," Heather muttered.

Benny B nodded at her, and then looked back at me. "You can ask him yourself. He lives in the ski cabin at the edge of the woods."

Chapter Seventeen

I WAS PRETTY SURE TATE WOULD not want me knocking on Ridge Tragger's door that evening. I could've waited to speak to him at the ski lesson, but my patience with this case was running thin. It was close to five now and almost completely dark. This close to the winter solstice, the sun began to set around four-thirty. After I left the ski house, I called Tate, but he didn't answer.

I stood ten yards from his cabin and dithered over what I should do. Smoke rose out of the cabin chimney. Ridge was home. I rationalized as I walked toward the cabin that I would just check the place out. I would wait to knock on the door until Tate was with me.

Who was I kidding? I wanted to speak to Ridge now.

The log cabin was much taller than it appeared from the ski house, which made me believe there was some type of second floor loft on the inside. All the blinds and curtains were closed over the windows. That was good, because no one inside the cabin could see me. But it was also bad, because I couldn't see what was going on in there, either.

I stood to the side of the cabin, going back and forth in my head about whether I should knock.

"Hey! What are you doing?" A man in a heavy winter coat came around the side of the cabin carrying a large stack of dry firewood. "Guests aren't supposed to be out here," he said in a gravelly voice. "This is private property. Make your way back to the lodge." He unceremoniously dropped the wood to the left of the cabin's front door.

I shuffled a few feet back from him. "Sorry if I bothered you."

"You can prove that by leaving." He turned to open the door to his cabin. His hand was on the doorknob.

"You're Ridge Tragger, right? The ski instructor?"

He glowered at me. "I know you rich folks think you're more important, that you can ask me anything day or night, but that's not true. The ski house is closed right now, which means I don't have to answer your questions. If you have a question for me, bring it back when you can ski. Otherwise, get lost."

I was definitely not one of the rich folks he was talking about. Any of my credit card companies could set him straight on that.

"I'm not here about a ski question. I wanted to talk to you about Garret Madd of MaddlyCare."

He turned slowly around and gave me the once-over. "And why do you think I would know anything at all about that?"

"Because your sister is his wife."

He glared at me. "Who are you?"

"A detective. I'm working with the police on the case involving your brother-in-law's death."

"I've already spoken to the police. I have nothing else to tell them or you."

If it wasn't for the porch light, I wouldn't have been able to see him at all at this point. The sun had completely disappeared over the mountain. "Did you see anything the morning Dr. Madd died? You would've been the closest person to the ski house."

"Did you not hear what I just said? I've spoken to the police. Talk to that Detective Caster. He can tell you what I saw. I'm not going to repeat a story."

I wasn't sure Austin would share that information with me.

"It must have been stressful for you to have your sister here this weekend."

"What do you mean?"

"Were you afraid your sister was going to sell the lodge?" I asked.

He narrowed his eyes at me. "She would never do that. The promise was that I would always have a place here."

"But didn't your father say that you had a place here as long as the lodge was operational? If she shut it down and turned it into something else, you might have to move."

Even in the dark, I could see his fists balled up at his sides. Perhaps I had pushed him a tad too far, but I was stubborn, and I kept going. "Why did your father leave the lodge to Cecily, whom he didn't raise, but not you?"

"He cut me out because I made some bad choices growing up. I fell in with the wrong crowd and didn't live up to his standards. The truth is, no one could live up this his standards, not even Cecily, and she's basically a robot in human skin."

I cringed at the description of Cecily.

"Now get off my part of the mountain." He went into the house and slammed the cabin door closed in my face. A second later, the porch light went out.

Well, I had gotten myself into a situation. I turned and started back to the lodge. Luckily, it was gigantic and lit up like a Christmas tree, so it was easy just to follow the lights.

Along the treeline, I heard movement in the woods. A twig snapped, and there was muffled movement in the snow. All I could think about was Dr. Madd being shot in the back.

A bear ran out of the woods, and my heart stopped for a second when it came right for me. When the bear barked, I started breathing again.

"Tiny," I rasped.

The big dog jumped in front of me.

"What are you doing here? Shouldn't you be with Herschel?" I looked around, but it was impossible to see in the dark whether the lodge manager was nearby.

"Let's go back to the lodge. I'm freezing. I don't have the great big fur coat that you do." I turned to go.

Tiny gave a sharp bark and hopped in the direction of the woods.

"Tiny, let's go in." I wrapped my arms around myself.

He barked again.

Weren't Saint Bernards rescue dogs? They were

sent out into the mountains to save people. Was that what Tiny was doing right now? What if he was trying to take me to a person who needed help?

"Is Herschel in trouble?"

Bark! Bark! Bark!

The dog galloped into the woods.

I glanced back at the warm and brightly lit lodge. This was such a bad idea.

When I stepped into the dark woods, I realized how ill-prepared I was to follow Tiny. It was freezing, and the snow collected in drifts so high between the trees that they went over my boots. Icy snow fell into my boots and soaked my wool socks. Was there anything more miserable than wet feet?

Surely Tiny's feet had to be soaked too, but the big dog didn't seem to mind.

My foot ran into something hard in the snow. I assumed it was a branch that had fallen from the trees and been buried. But when I pointed the weak light of my phone toward it, I saw it was black plastic.

I bent down to pull the piece of plastic out of the snow. It was halfway out of the ditch when I realized it was a crossbow.

I let go of it like it had burnt my hand and quickly backed up. In doing so, I tripped over an actual branch hidden in the snow and landed hard on my backside.

I scrambled to my feet. "Tiny! Come!"

This time the big dog didn't disobey me, and he followed me as I ran all the way back to the lodge.

As soon as I hit the brightly lit patio, I took a breath. Tiny was at my side, panting along with me. Saint Bernards were great endurance dogs for climbing mountains and saving stranded adventurers. But they weren't sprinters, and Tiny and I had just done a five-hundred-yard dash.

I needed to gather myself before I went back inside the building. Though it seemed I wouldn't have a chance to do that, because Austin Caster stepped into the patio lights. "I hope you weren't up to another dumb stunt."

I wrapped my arms around myself because I was freezing. My whole body began to shiver.

His face morphed from annoyance to concern. "How long have you been out here without a coat?" He walked over to me. "We need to get you inside." He wrapped his arm around my shoulder and shuffled me into the building. The lobby was nearly empty, but I could hear loud voices floating to us from the bar and restaurant. It was getting close to dinnertime now.

My teeth were chattering. Tiny followed right behind us as if he wanted to keep a close eye on me.

Having had such a late lunch, I wasn't hungry. In fact, the thought of food made my stomach lurch. I chalked that up to exhaustion.

Austin sat me down on the hearth right in front of the roaring fire. He then removed his heavy winter coat and wrapped me in it like he was swaddling a child. "There. You should warm up fast."

"Thanks," I managed through chattering teeth. "Were you looking for me outside?"

He nodded. "The bartender mentioned that he saw you go outside."

Great. Now the hotel staff was spying on me. Not

that I could blame them. I had been asking a lot of questions.

"Listen, I know that I was hard on you about scaling the side of the building. I'm sorry if I came off harsh," Austin said.

I took off his coat. I was still cold, but to be honest, his coat smelled too much like him. I didn't want it on me. "I know you were just upset that I put myself at risk, but in both our lines of work, it's something that we have to do. Right now, we need to go back outside."

"No way—you're freezing."

Tiny rested against my leg.

I leaned toward Austin, and his eyes went wide. What did he think I was going to do? Kiss him? That was never going to happen. "I found the weapon," I said in a hushed voice.

He jerked back. "The murder weapon?"

"It was definitely a crossbow that someone buried in the snow. In the dark, I couldn't see any footprints around it, but it snowed last night. They could be covered over."

He stood and put on his coat. "I'll go check it out."

I stood too, even if a little more slowly.

"You can't come outside again. You're too cold. Stay here and warm up. Tiny can show me where the crossbow is. Right, Tiny?"

The dog barked in agreement.

I wanted to argue, but I was very cold. So cold, in fact, that my hands were curled into claws. I fell back into my seat.

"Stay here," Austin said. "We won't be long."

The police detective strode out of the lodge with a galloping dog/bear behind him.

I sat on my hands to warm them up and debated going to the closest restroom to run them under hot water to warm them up more quickly.

"Darby, have you seen Tiny?" Herschel asked, looking frantically around the empty lobby. "I let him out an hour ago to do his business before bed, and he never came back in. I called and called him until I was hoarse. He's never done this before. I'm really worried."

"I saw him outside, and now he's with Detective Caster."

Herschel's mouth made a little O shape. "Why would he be with the detective?"

"Tiny found something in the woods, and Austin went to check it out."

Herschel adjusted his glasses. "What did he find? Can't it wait until morning? It's freezing and dark out there. I don't like Tiny being outside so late."

Austin stepped into the lodge carrying the crossbow and followed by Tiny. The Saint Bernard had a spring in his step. He had done well, and he knew it.

"What's that?" Herschel asked.

"A crossbow," Austin said.

Herschel opened and closed his mouth. "The one that killed Dr. Madd?"

Tiny walked over to his master's side and stood on his foot. Herschel had no reaction to the dog on his foot. Maybe he was used to it.

"It's hard to know for sure, but it's most likely. The doctor was shot about four feet from where I found it in the woods. My guess, it the killer threw it in the woods, hoping correctly that the snow would hide it until he got away."

"Does this mean you're close to solving the case?" Herschel asked.

"The case is ongoing. I need to take this to the station."

Herschel looked like he wanted to say more, but someone rang the bell at the reception desk. He and Tiny left us by the fireplace.

Austin looked down at the crossbow. "Let's hope this is a break in the case."

"I'm surprised you removed it from the scene."

He pressed his lips together. "I didn't have much choice. I took what pictures I could of its position, but I couldn't leave it there. The killer could have come back and taken it to hide elsewhere, and it's supposed to snow again tonight. I couldn't risk it getting buried again."

I nodded. "One more question before you go. Did Cecily give you the notes?"

"Yes," he said. "From the way she was talking about it, I thought there was a lot more to it. There were only three threatening notes. Why didn't she show them to you and Tate?"

"She never really gave us a good reason, which I find suspicious." I looked him in the eye. "What did the notes say?"

"I knew you were going to ask that." He opened the side pocket of his coat and brought out a piece of paper. On it, there were three small photocopies of typewritten notes. "The originals are at the police station."

I nodded. I wouldn't have expected anything else. I took the paper from his hand and read them.

The first note was the one Tate and I had seen. *It will come to the point where you will have nowhere else to hide. You know what you did. If I have to spend the rest of my life hunting you, I will. This is your fate for ignoring my warnings.*

The second note read, Life is more important than money, with the exception of yours. Watch your step.

Finally, the third note said, *MaddlyCare will be ruined if you sell. You caused this crisis. The only way out is to remove you.*

I shivered. "So whoever wrote these knew he was thinking of selling the skincare line." Before Austin could stop me, I removed my very cold phone from my pocket and took a picture of the paper. "So I can show Tate," I said, by way of explanation.

Austin sighed and took the sheet of paper from my hand. "I should have expected that."

"You should have," I agreed. "How did the rest of the interview with Cecily go?"

"As well as I expected. Her attorney is flying in, and we are planning to interview her again in his presence."

My eyes went wide. "What did she tell you?"

"No much. I got more from the assistant."

"Mindy Carn?" I asked, surprised that I had all but forgotten the young woman. She was the one who'd told me Dr. Madd was dead. I made a mental note to speak with her again. "What did she have to say?"

"From what I gathered from Mindy and others, the Madds had hit a sour patch in their marriage. At the same time, both of them were looking to sell their businesses. Dr. Madd wanted to sell MaddlyCare, and Cecily wanted to sell this lodge. I can't say if those decisions were related to the talk of divorce of not."

"Do you think either or both of those things are the motive for murder?"

"Definitely, if the spouse in either case had a say in the sales."

Why had Cecily hired Tate and me to find the person writing these notes, when she wanted to leave her husband? It was a question that only Cecily could answer.

Chapter Eighteen

As LUCK WOULD HAVE IT, when I hit the treadmill Sunday morning, I wasn't the only one working out. Kicra Bellworthy came into the gym when I was in the middle of my run. I had a mile left to clock, but I slowed down when she took the treadmill next to mine, so I could speak without gasping. "Hi!" I smiled brightly at her.

She nodded at me and put in a pair of earbuds. *Oh-kay*, now wasn't a good time to talk. I thought over what I would say to her when she finished running. I guessed she wouldn't want to talk about her social media scandal.

I passed the three-mile mark, but she was still jogging away on her treadmill. I kept running. It didn't hurt me to put in a little more time. I felt better that morning than I had the day before. I'd gotten more sleep, and no one was running through the gym crying over having seen a dead body. That thought reminded me that I wanted to track down Mindy Carn, Dr. Madd's assistant.

I ran a little faster as my anxiety about the case amped up. Tate and I were running out of time. It was the last full day at the lodge, and tomorrow all the suspects, assuming the police would let them leave Monday as scheduled, would leave and return to their respective homes.

Kiera got off the treadmill. "You've been running a long time. Do you run marathons or something?"

I slowed to a walk to cool myself down. I looked down at my screen. I had run five miles. It'd been a while since I'd tracked that many. Maybe treadmills weren't as horrible as I thought. "No, I just try to run every day. I've done a few races, but it's not really my thing."

She walked over to the fridge in the corner of the room and grabbed a bottle of cold water supplied by the lodge. That's how fancy Garden Peak was. They didn't expect you to bring your own water to the gym.

She said, "I have found there are two types of runners. Those who run for themselves and those who run for the medals."

I nodded and drank from my water bottle.

"I used to run for the medals. I'm a goal-setter, but then it became too hard. I only do virtual races now."

"Too hard because of scheduling?"

She looked at me over her bottle of water. "Too hard because people follow me. It gets old after a while. It's been nice this weekend that there's no press around. I thought when..." She shook her head like she was trying to erase a memory. "I thought when everything happened that the press would show up, but so far I haven't seen a single reporter. It's refreshing and so different from LA. Out there, if a celebrity stubs their toe, paparazzi show up to get the shot," she said in disgust.

"Herrington doesn't have much of a news source. We have a regional paper, and that's it. I think the police have been able to keep Dr. Madd's death quiet, but I don't think they'll have much luck keeping it from the press much longer."

"Oh, Dr. Madd." Tears came to her eyes. I assumed that she was tearing up over a man's life lost in such a tragic way. She quickly disproved this by saying, "His death ruins everything for me."

"For you?" I stepped off the treadmill.

She patted her forehead with a clean white towel. Even though she had been running, her skin was flawless. It just had a slight hint of a dewy glow. I, on the other hand, could feel sweat trickling down my neck. I grabbed a towel from the rack as well.

"I was informed last evening that my services with MaddlyCare would no longer be needed."

"Cecily told you that?"

"Yes." She sniffled.

"Did you sign a contract yet? If you did, it might still be binding no matter what Cecily Madd said."

"No. We were supposed to do that early yesterday morning at seven sharp. I was to meet him at the ski house."

That would explain why the ski shop owner saw her outside so early on Saturday morning. Had she seen Dr. Madd's dead body before I had?

Her face clouded over. "You seem to know a lot about MaddlyCare, and I have never met you."

"I worked for the Madds for a time, and they invited me to this party." It wasn't a complete lie. I had worked for Cecily Madd for a day, and she did invite me to the party.

She frowned. "You seem kind of too normal to work for them."

"I'll take that as a compliment."

"Do you know Cecily well?" she asked.

"Well enough."

She bit her lower lip. "Do you think you can put in a good word for me with her? I'm hoping she'll change her mind. I need this contract. It could turn my life around."

"Maybe if you tell me your story, I can help?" I tried to keep the eagerness out of my voice.

She studied my face, and then her shoulders sagged. "I don't have anything else to lose. I already lost everything."

Kiera and I found a quiet booth in the restaurant. When the server came around, Kiera said, "Get whatever you want. It's on me." She then proceeded to order a carrot juice and an egg white.

I guessed that my plans for chocolate chip pancakes were out. The main reason I ran was because I loved to eat.

"Umm, I'll just have a coffee and a fruit cup, please."

The server gave me a look, as if to say, *That wasn't what you were going to order, was it?*

Once he was out of earshot, I said, "Tell me why you need to be the face of MaddlyCare so badly. You're a famous actress. I would think you have a lot of opportunities for endorsement deals."

"I was a famous actress. Now I'm just a notorious one."

The server brought our food with our drinks. It

hadn't taken long at all. It wasn't like there was a lot to carry.

When he left, Kiera said, "You don't know anything about me, do you?"

I wrinkled my nose. "Not much."

She sipped her carrot juice. "It's kind of refreshing that there are people out there who don't know my story. It gives me a little hope that I can rewrite it. I'm praying it's true that the general public has a short memory."

"What did you do?" I asked, as dozens of scenarios flew around in my head, none of them good.

She swirled her juice like it was a fine wine. "I was working on a movie and unhappy with the script. In hindsight, I should have never taken the job, but it was going to be a major blockbuster and it was for a lot of money. I'll admit, as an actor I sometimes picked jobs based on the money, but I'm not the only one who does that, not by a long shot." She looked down. "I spoke to the executive producer about the script. There were some changes I thought would give my character more credibility. He blew me off." Her face flushed with anger. "I then spoke to the screenwriter and the director. They treated me the same. They acted like I didn't know what I was talking about. I just wanted my character to be a little more real, but they were happy to make her one-dimensional arm candy. When I got home that night, I was so angry."

I pressed my lips together and waited.

"I posted on social media about the role I was playing and how I deserve respect. Then, I attacked the people behind this big movie. I said some very unkind things and took it too far. It snowballed and got out of control. I did it at night after a long day of shooting a movie I didn't believe in. I was burnt out. I wanted to tell the world what I truly thought, and it was a huge mistake."

Reckless tweeting. It always seemed to trip up the famous.

But I couldn't help but wonder what she wrote. "Did you post true things?" I paused. "Did someone harm you and you posted about that?"

She stared into her juice glass. "I know what you're getting at, and it was nothing like that. I was never hurt. I mean, sure, some of the people I put on blast were rude, bossy, and plain unkind, but they never hurt anyone physically, as far as I know. I mostly just shared my personal opinions about their personalities, lack of talent, and even their looks. The more shares I got on social media for my opinions, the worse my opinions became. It was like a game, until it all came crashing down on my head."

It seemed to me that it was a stupid game to play, considering her reach as a celebrity. How could she think that those she gossiped about wouldn't find out? Maybe she knew then, and just didn't care, but I knew she cared now. I could understand that she might've gotten caught up in the likes, shares, and initial positive attention. And I couldn't help but think of some actors who had done worse things and had still been able to find work. That hardly seemed fair.

I grimaced. "What happened after that?"

"By the time I woke up the next morning, it was all over the internet and even the national news. They put me on par with other young women actors who snapped from the stress and constant scrutiny. I immediately deleted my accounts. People had hundreds of screenshots of everything I said, though. Nothing on the internet really goes away. Remember that."

I already knew that to be true. As a P.I., I did a lot of my background checks online and was continually amazed by the things people posted. Something you post at eighteen can haunt you when you're looking for a job at thirty. It was just the reality of the inter-connected world we lived in.

"What happened after that?" I speared a piece of fruit.

"The movie dropped me. My agent and manager did too. I lost all the upcoming roles I had lined up. No production wanted to take the risk I would put them on blast if I didn't like something. Where I was in my career, it was a lot. I had filming scheduled out for over two years. In a second, it was all gone." She took a deep breath. "So I went underground. I thought if I disappeared for a little while, it would be better for everyone. The truth is, I have enough money from past work to support myself for a long time to come, but I want to go back. I miss acting. It was a year ago that this all happened. I've been punished enough. I made a mistake. How many times do I have to say I'm sorry?"

"You thought MaddlyCare was your way out?" I sipped my coffee.

She finished her carrot juice. "Yes. When Dr. Madd called me, I thought it was a joke, and I still don't know how he got hold of my private number. No one has it. I changed my phone number after everything that happened. The press hounded me. When he told me what he had in mind, I couldn't believe it. He mentioned inviting me to this weekend, and I couldn't say no. It wasn't like I had other plans for New Year's Eve."

"So you knew he was going to make that announcement at the party?"

"Not exactly." She shook her head. "He said he was going to tell everyone sometime this weekend. I assumed after we signed the contracts. But when he made the announcement, I wasn't upset by it. I was thrilled. I thought after telling all those people, he couldn't possibly go back on his word. He told me we'd do the paperwork in the morning after his scheduled skiing time. He promised me there would be no interruptions then." She sighed and stared down at her plate. "How was I to know he was going to get killed before I could sign the contract? I don't think I have cried over someone's death so hard in my life. He was my way back."

I tried to keep my face neutral, but I could see how Kiera might have said the wrong things online in the past. She wasn't the most tactful person I had ever met. "When you were outside the lodge waiting to meet him, did you notice anything unusual? Did you see anything?"

"No. I was pacing." She paused. "And smoking. I know it's a terrible habit, and I would be hung from my toes in California if anyone knew I was doing it. I only smoke when I'm terribly stressed. I need it. I've gotten very good at hiding the habit. You have to be sneaky if you smoke in L.A."

"The merchant at the ski shop said she saw you pacing outside."

"Did she see me smoke?" Kiera gasped.

I shook my head. "She didn't mention it."

Her shoulders sagged with relief. "That's comforting to hear. I don't want it to get out in the media about my habit. It would be just another thing to keep me from regaining my career."

"Did you see anyone else when you were outside?" I asked.

She frowned as if she thought this over. "I saw the shop owner. Oh, and Cecily Madd."

"You saw Dr. Madd's wife the morning of his murder?"

She nodded.

That didn't fit with Cecily's account of what had happened that morning. She said she was alone in bed when her husband died. That implied she didn't get up until later that morning, at which time she learned about her husband's murder.

"What happened when you saw her outside?" I asked.

"Nothing."

"Nothing?"

"Yes, nothing. I said hello, and she wouldn't even look at me. The way she kept looking around, I thought she must have been waiting for another person. I left her be. I wasn't going to get any more on her bad side. Dr. Madd was the only one who hired me—or almost hired me. I knew I would have to work with Cecily eventually, and it would serve me well if I made friends with her." She looked down. "But I don't think she wants to be my friend."

That was an understatement. Cecily wanted nothing to do with Kiera. She just wanted her to go away.

I had to admit that this was looking worse by the

second for Cecily. Tate and I would have to talk to her if she wanted any help avoiding going to prison.

"What are you going to do now?" I finished my coffee.

"What I have been doing all this time—wandering around and waiting for the time I can finally leave. This whole experience has been a disaster." She poked at her plate.

She hadn't taken a single bit of her egg white, but my bowl of fruit had been empty for a long while. If she was a runner and ate like this, it was no wonder she was so thin.

I pulled a business card out of my purse. It only had my name and cell phone number on it. I had a set of business cards with the name of the agency, my title, and even more information. But this card was simpler. It was the one I gave potential witnesses to a crime, and to people to whom I wasn't ready to divulge what I did for a living. "One last question: Did you ever have a movie role where you had to shoot a crossbow?"

"Sure."

"So you know how."

"Of course I do, but to be honest, I learned for the part from a video online. You can learn just about anything on the internet. It's not like shooting a bow and arrow. It's more like pulling a trigger on a gun, and anyone can do that."

I frowned. That didn't help me narrow down the suspects at all, then.

Kiera thanked me. "I needed this," she said. "It helps to talk about it. I've turned into such an outcast in Hollywood, and no one wanted to listen to my story. It's nice to speak to someone who I think is actually listening."

I was listening. I was listening with every part of my being.

Chapter Nineteen

AFTER MY CONVERSATION WITH KIERA, I wanted to head up to my suite and change out of my running clothes. I stepped into the elevator and leaned against the wall. It was unbelievable to me that less than twenty-four hours since we took this case, Dr. Madd, the client's husband, who was receiving the threatening notes, was dead, and not just dead, but murdered.

The elevator doors were about to close when someone shoved a hand between the closing doors and forced it to open. Benny B waltzed into the elevator. "You don't mind if I ride up with you, Darby, do you?"

I shook my head.

"You know, Darby, we could be partners. Like I told you before, our jobs aren't that different."

"There are differences." I straightened up. I had to be on my guard if I was being questioned by Benny B.

"What I want to know is what your conversation with Kiera Bellworthy was all about. I have to say, I was quite intrigued when I saw the two of you eating breakfast together, fresh from the gym. Were you bonding over working out?"

I scowled at him and said nothing. How long was this elevator ride, anyway?

"You wouldn't be talking to the actress if you didn't think it would help you solve the case."

I didn't say anything.

"Did Kiera tell you how she self-imploded on social media?" He clicked his tongue. "It seems to be the Achilles heel of the celebrity who doesn't have enough of a filter. But she didn't do anything she can't come back from. There's nothing Hollywood loves more than a comeback story."

The elevator pinged and the doors opened on my floor. I stepped out without saying a word.

Benny B didn't follow me, and I saw the elevator was headed back down to the main floor. "You're not getting out?" I asked.

"Nope. I just wanted to ride up with you." He waggled his fingers at me as the elevator closed between us.

I ground my teeth. I shouldn't let Benny B get on my nerves like that, but the guy really rubbed me the wrong way. I knew, deep down, part of it had to do with the fact that he wasn't wrong. In truth, our occupations weren't that different from each other's, and I hated that.

I walked down the hallway to my room and found a note taped to my door. It read, "Meet me at the ski house at nine a.m. Wear the Purple People Eater suit," and there was a sketch of a skier going downhill.

Great. I knew that I'd told Pierce and Edwin I was up for a skiing lesson, but now that time had arrived.

At ten before nine, I made my way down to the lobby in my purple snowsuit. I was well aware of the looks I received in the elevator and from the restaurant. The cut of the snowsuit wasn't horrible. It was a snowsuit, after all, so its purpose wasn't to be flattering. It was serviceable. The problem was the shade of purple.

I liked purple as well as the next girl. Purple flowers, purple ribbons, and even purple nail polish. It's all fine with me. But a head-to-toe purple suit was a little much. I was a walking grape. Who wanted to be that?

Edwin and Pierce were making their way to the ski house, and I called after them. The couple turned around, and they both gasped.

"Darby, what on earth are you wearing?" Edwin asked, looking a tad green. It was as if my outfit made him physically ill.

I jogged to catch up with them. "It's a ski suit. I had to buy it at the last minute. I didn't come prepare to do any skiing this weekend."

"You look like you did a log roll in a kiddie pool full of Welch's grape juice."

"You do know this is a ski lodge, right? That you might have been asked to ski, right?" Pierce asked, as if he didn't believe my story.

"I know that," I said. "But we came last-minute. I didn't have time to go shopping before we left."

"Not to mention," Edwin said. "Darby hates to shop. You should have texted me. I would have found something for you, and at a discount, too. I shiver to think of how much you spent on that...that...whatever it is."

"I spent more than I wanted to," I admitted. "This was all the ski shop had in my size. It's not that bad, is it? Everyone looks ridiculous bundled up in winter clothes, right?" My voice went up an octave when I asked that.

"You look like a jar of grape jelly threw up on you," Pierce said.

I grimaced. That was worse than Edwin's grape juice description.

"Pierce," Edwin admonished. "You can't say something like that."

"Don't tell me you weren't thinking it," Pierce replied.

I held up my hand. "Okay, okay, can we please stop talking about what I'm wearing? Tate left me a note that we're going skiing. I guess you got us the time, Edwin?"

He smiled as if this was his greatest achievement. "I did, and something even better."

I waited, knowing Edwin would tell the story of how he got us the slope time at the pace he chose, no matter how much I might want to rush him.

"I got us a private lesson with the lodge's ski instructor, Ridge Tragger. Pierce and I need to brush up on our skills, and you said you've never skied before. I thought it was the perfect choice." He sighed. "I'm convinced that Tate is a talented skier and won't need the lesson. Is there anything that man can't do?"

As luck would have it, Edwin was right about Tate's skiing skills. Just as we approached the ski shop, Tate took off down the hill on a set of skis. He expertly wove back and forth down the mountain. He never came close to running off-course or hitting another skier. At the bottom of the mountain, a cloud of snow kicked up in the air as he brought himself to a complete stop. When the snow settled, he waved up at us.

Pierce clicked his tongue. "I think it would be boring to be good at everything. Where's the uniqueness in that?"

Edwin smiled. "You're right, hon. There's a bunch of stuff we're bad at. That's what makes us perfect for each other. Even better, we're bad at completely different things, which mean we complement each other."

"Are you the Yule party?" a man asked.

When I turned around, I found myself looking into the face of Ridge Tragger. He scowled when he saw me standing with Pierce and Edwin.

He pointed his clipboard at me. "You! What are you doing here?"

Edwin looked from the ski instructor to me. "You two know each other?"

"Not exactly," I said with a red face.

"She was at my cabin last night accusing me of murder!" Ridge said.

"Darby, you have to stop going around and doing that," Pierce said. "It's going to be impossible for you to meet someone if murder is all you talk about. You have to think about your future."

"I don't just talk about murder," I muttered.

Edwin and Pierce shared a look, as if they weren't so sure about that.

"I'm not giving her a ski lesson," Ridge said, and started to leave.

"Wait!" Edwin said. "We paid for this lesson. You're obligated to give it to us."

I waved my hand. "Edwin and Pierce, you two take the lesson. I'm happy to sit this one out."

Edwin frowned.

Ridge folded his arms. "I'll give the two of you a lesson. Just not her."

Pierce and Edwin looked at each other.

I made a shooing gesture. "Go. I don't mind. Really." It was true. Not having to ski was a relief, and I didn't think I would have much luck questioning Ridge after the stunt I'd pulled last night at his cabin.

"All right," Pierce said. "You'll meet us back at the restaurant for lunch?"

I smiled. "Sure, and you can tell me all about skiing." I waved to them and started back to the lodge to prove to Ridge I was leaving.

The three of them made their way to the ski house. When they disappeared inside, I gave a great sigh of relief. I didn't want to ski. There weren't many things I was afraid of, but hurling myself down the face of a mountain on a couple of slick boards was one of them. Any bravado I'd been feeling when I first said yes to the idea had dissipated.

I realized something as I made my way back to the lodge. Pierce and Edwin's lesson was forty-five minutes long. Ridge would be busy for that time. Which would give me a perfect opportunity to check out his cabin again, this time unnoticed.

Before I could change my mind, I walked to the path that led to the ski instructor's cabin.

Halfway down the path, I looked behind me to see if anyone was following me. No one was. Though I saw an immediate problem. The snow. I was leaving boot prints on the path. Unfortunately, it was something that couldn't be helped. I would just have to be quick and mask the prints as best I could when I left the cabin.

Ridge's home came into view, and it was far less intimidating in the daytime than it had been the evening before. I approached.

I stopped a few yards from the small building. I hesitated, then walked up to the front door. With the boot prints I was leaving all over the place, Ridge would know that someone had walked around his home.

I was just about to move forward when I heard a great *woof* and a man shouting. I was hit on the right side by a truck.

Okay, it wasn't a truck, but it sure felt that way as I rolled onto my back in the snow. Tiny, wearing his giant Saint Bernard grin, dripped a glob of dog slobber on the front of my coat. Ick.

"Tiny!" I struggled to sit up, but the dog wouldn't have it, and pushed me down by the shoulder with one of his mighty paws. He then proceeded to lick me up one side of my face and down the other.

I waved my hands. "Okay. Okay! I give!"

With another *woof*, he hopped off me.

I sat up slowly. I wasn't hurt, just slobbered. As cute as Tiny was, my ick factor was at an eleven plus.

Herschel ran over to me. "Darby, I'm so very sorry. Tiny still thinks that he's a puppy. Even when he was a puppy, he was too big to jump on people."

I got to my feet and brushed snow off myself. "It's all right. He didn't do any harm."

"I'm glad." He looked around. "If you don't mind

my asking, what are you doing this far from the lodge?" He glanced at Ridge's cabin nervously.

"I was just out for a walk."

He relaxed. "It's a lovely day for it." He sighed. "Tiny and I were out doing the same. It's been such a stressful weekend. I'm hoping that the lodge will survive it."

"You think Dr. Madd's murder will have a lasting impact on the lodge?"

A black cloud floated across his face. "I'm hoping that's not the case, but Cecily will have to decide what she wants to do. The last I heard, she was putting any changes to the lodge on hold for now because she would have to take over MaddlyCare, which is far more work than management of Garden Peak Lodge. I promised her that we had everything here under control. To be honest, she has never had much interest in Garden Peak until recently."

"Why do you think she developed a sudden interest in the lodge?"

Herschel looked around as if to see if anyone was watching us. We were alone. There was a faint sound of music floating to us from the ski house, but we couldn't even see the building from where we stood.

"I don't know exactly. I think she and Dr. Madd were having marital problems. The lodge is something that she owned without her husband. Maybe she saw it as a backup plan."

It reminded me of what I had heard about the prenup between Cecily and her husband too. If she stood to get nothing in the divorce, then the ski lodge might be her best hope of financial security. It would still be a step down from her penthouse life in New York, though.

"If they were having issues, why did Dr. Madd agree to hold the party here?" I asked.

"I don't know." He sighed. "It's just a mess, and I hate to sound selfish, but I don't know what this will all mean for the lodge. Cecily's father was a good man, a great boss. I wish his children had followed in his footsteps, but it wasn't to be. They were too spoiled. While their father had to work for everything he had, they got handed everything."

"Isn't Ridge a good ski instructor?"

"He is. When he's sober. Did you know he was bound for the Olympics? Everyone was convinced he would go, especially his father. And then, he went to the trials when he was twenty and completely froze up. He couldn't make himself kick off. They gave him chance after chance, and he wouldn't budge. His father was devastated. He had put so much into Ridge's success. He had sent him to the best ski schools and trainers all over the world. But when the moment came to show the world what he could do, he couldn't do it."

"I imagine his father was disappointed."

Herschel nodded. "He was a mess afterward. He felt like he'd wasted money that could have been poured into the lodge. Instead, he'd wasted it on his son. Ridge couldn't deal with the guilt of it. He drowned his disappointment with himself into alcohol. He fell in with the wrong crowd. He even went to jail a few times."

I made a mental note to ask Austin about Ridge's

past arrest history. "Was that why his father cut him out of the will?"

He nodded. "I suppose he reduced Ridge's inheritance. Cecily got everything, but Ridge got a permanent job and place to live here as long as the lodge stayed in the family."

"As long as the lodge stayed in the family? What if she decided to sell? It could go for a handsome price."

He shrugged. "Then Ridge would have to go."

Ridge had just gone up three notches on my suspect list.

Chapter Twenty

As much as I wanted to snoop around Ridge's cabin, it wasn't something I could do with Herschel and Tiny looking on. The only good thing to come of it was Tiny, who galloped around the cabin like a newborn colt, completely destroying any evidence of my footprints. I decided to walk back to the ski house and catch a glimpse of Pierce and Edwin skiing.

I wasn't too worried about Pierce. He was an athletic guy, and I often saw him cycling on the roads around town when I was out for a run. Edwin, however, was about as athletic as Mrs. Berger's cat, which meant he was willing to give just about anything a try, but more often than not, got stuck and needed to be rescued.

Just as I reached the ski house, Tate jumped off of the ski lift. "Hey, where did you go? I thought you were taking a ski lesson this morning. And what's on your coat?"

I looked down at the drooly stain on the front of my coat. It was a fashion statement. "I ran into Tiny."

"Oh." That was explanation enough.

"As for skiing, Ridge refused to teach me because of the investigation."

Tate took off his skis. "I guess I can't blame the guy."

"It's fine. I didn't want to do it anyway."

"What's the deal with you and skiing? I have never seen you so determined to avoid something before."

I gave him a look. "I just have a fear of breaking my leg. I spent over half my life training to be a ballerina. A skiing injury wasn't worth the risk of losing that dream."

"But you're not a ballerina now, and you haven't been for over a decade."

"Thank you for the reminder, but that still doesn't mean I want to break my leg."

"I don't think anyone wants a broken leg. I can teach you. Just go down the run once, and I won't ever ask you to do it again."

I shook my head. "No. We have a case to solve." I paused. "Or do we? Have you spoken to Cecily?"

He frowned. "I'm working on it."

"It looks to me like you're skiing."

"I am, and so is Cecily. I asked her to come out with us this morning to relax and blow off some steam. I'm positive she'll put us back on the case. Anytime it comes up, it's clear she is terrified of going to jail. I remind her time and again that hiring us back on is the best way to avoid doing that."

"Tate, we're running out of time."

"I know," he said. "Listen, Cecily just started her first run, so I can get you started on going downhill. I think it will benefit your investigation to see what Dr. Madd saw just before he died."

That was a stretch, even for Tate.

"Will you give it a try?" he asked.

"Will you stop asking me if I'm willing to try?"

He clapped his hands together. "You bet."

Together, we walked the rest of the way to the ski house, where the Madds' guests were chattering and talking outside.

"That's one of the steepest inclines I've even been on," one of the guests said.

I shot Tate a look.

"I'll send you down the less steep part," Tate claimed.

This was such a bad idea.

Inside the ski house, there was a line of skis of various sizes, and men's and women's ski boots. Tate went over the line of skis, grabbed a pair, and picked out boots in my size too. "These will work."

Resigning myself to my fate, I put on the ski boots. They were a perfect fit.

Tate and I went back outside, and he walked me through a quick lesson. "Point your skis straight to go faster. Turn them ninety degrees to slow down. The lower you are on the skis, the faster you will go, because there is less wind resistance. Be sure that you're in control. You don't want your legs pulled out from under you. That's how you get hurt."

Terrific.

"Also, lean over your skis for better balance. You may be inclined to lean back, but that will backfire on you. Any questions?" He beamed.

Tate was a little too excited over the idea of me skiing for my liking.

"Yes. Why am I here?" I lowered my voice. "How is this going to help us find out who killed Dr. Madd?"

"Get in line, and you'll see."

I was about to protest until I saw that Cecily stood at the end of the line of skiers waiting to make their way down the mountain.

I shot Tate a glance and joined the end of the line. I'd stand in line and play the part, but there was no way I was going down that mountain.

Cecily looked over her shoulder at me. She sniffed. "Shouldn't you be trying to find out who killed my husband?"

"That's what we are doing. This is the scene of the crime, you know."

She sniffed.

I changed the subject. "I spoke with your brother a little while ago."

She looked over her shoulder. "He's my half-brother, and barely worth that title."

I raised my eyebrows. "It's nice of your father to let him stay and work at the lodge."

"It's ridiculous. Ridge never worked a day in his life, and he gets free room and board and a cushy job? As long as I have this place, I'm stuck with him."

I nodded. "I heard that as long this lodge was in the family, that was true."

"That's why I have a mind to sell it. I came back here for that very reason. I wanted to see how everything was going and what I wanted to do. I realized that managing a lodge wasn't for me. It would serve me much better to sell it and pocket the money. I've been putting out feelers to see if there is interest."

I removed the flyer I had kept from the staff locker from my pocket. "Like this? Posting it's up for sale on websites?"

She ripped the paper from my hand. "Where did you get this?"

"That doesn't matter."

"It matters to me."

"It would also seem to matter to the lodge staff. It seems Herschel and the rest of the staff have done an impeccable job."

She nodded. "I'll give them that. It might help me, too, because I think I can sell it all for a high price. There are many new entrepreneurs out there who have so much money they don't know what to do with it. Several have expressed interest in the lodge. They might as well give their money to me. I can reinvest it into MaddlyCare. Now that my husband is dead, I own eighty percent of the company. Garret's ex-wife owns ten percent." She made a face. "And the other ten is owned by a small number of employee share-holders. I have a clear and strong majority, which means that I can make all the decisions pertaining to the company moving forward."

I didn't know if Cecily realized, or maybe she did and thought she was untouchable, but she had just given me a very good reason as to why she might have killed her husband.

"But will you have time to go through the sale if you are in charge of MaddlyCare? I imagine the company will take up a lot of your time."

She looked at me. "I'm capable of both, and it

doesn't mean I have to be here to hold anyone's hand. As you said, Herschel has done a great job caring for the property. I don't doubt for a second that he will do the same through the process of selling. I'm not concerned with finding a buyer."

The skier in front of us went down the mountain. I was running out of time.

"I might hold off on trying to sell it," I said.

"Why?"

"You don't know yet how the investigation into your husband's death is going to go. If MaddlyCare's assets are frozen, or—"

"That is not going to happen," she snapped.

"We don't want it to happen, but the longer this murder investigation drags on, the more likely it will cause some trouble for your husband's company and, in turn, you."

"What can I do about it?" she asked.

"Cooperate to find your husband's killer."

"Fine." She turned all the way around and pointed a polished fingernail at me. "But you'd better find out who did this to my husband quick, or I'm suing you both."

I didn't bother to tell her that wasn't how it worked.

"You're next," said the young woman who was directing the skiers downhill.

From behind, I felt someone give me a little shove, and my skis tipped down. The next thing I knew, I was heading down the mountain.

I tried to remember everything Tate had told me in what seemed a very short lesson. He said to keep my feet pointed straight ahead. When I did that, I went faster, so fast that I was hurtling toward a group of skiers going at a much more leisurely pace. What had he told me to do to slow down? I had no idea. My mind was a complete blank.

"Move! Move!" I shouted to everyone in my path. I couldn't control the skis. I had no idea how I was staying upright. I wanted to fall to my side and bail out, but I was scared. My boots were so tight in the ski bindings that I didn't see how I could flop to the side without snapping an ankle. I was going too fast to bail out safely.

A skier appeared at my side, matching my pace. When I dared glance in his direction, I saw that it was Tate.

"What are you doing?" I shouted at him.

"I'm trying to help you. Turn your skis ninety degrees."

"I don't know if I can do that." I flailed my ski poles, but then regained my balance.

"Just turn your feet toward me."

"Are you crazy?"

"Stop arguing with me and do it," he snapped.

I turned my toes toward him. I felt my descent slow just a little. I was still going way too fast for comfort.

"Fall!" he shouted.

"What?" I screeched.

"Fall! Let yourself fall!"

"What if I break my ankle?"

"Piper, look at me."

I couldn't break my gaze away from the steep slope in front of me.

"Darby," Tate said in a gentler voice.

I looked at him then. He never called me by my first name.

"Darby. Fall."

I glanced down the slope and then back at his eyes.

"Just fall." He said it so quietly that I didn't even know if I heard him say it, or if I read his lips.

So I fell as if I were a bird shot out of the sky.

Unfortunately, since I was me, I fell the wrong way. I came to a dead stop right in Tate's path. He fell on top of me in a heap.

"Can you please get off me?" I asked, while cataloging in my brain what on my body hurt. I was a bit sore from the fall, but I didn't feel any intense pain.

"One second," he muttered. "I have to get out of my skis." He used his ski pole to release the clasps on one ski, then the other. He crawled off me and used his ski pole on my skis too, freeing my feet.

He grinned. "So, what do you think? Is skiing your sport?"

I was lying splayed flat on my back on the side of a frozen mountain. I gave him a look, and he laughed.

"That will be the first and last time I go skiing," I said, and heard him snicker. "You'd better stop laughing at me."

"Darby Piper. I would never laugh at you." Then he chuckled. "I'm sorry. You look like a smashed grape."

What a compliment.

"Honestly, I'm a little surprised you went down the slope," Tate said. "I thought you would turn back after you spoke to Cecily."

"I was planning too, but someone pushed me."

"What?"

I struggled to my feet and was about to pick up my skis, but Tate was faster and collected them for me.

"You were pushed? You're sure?"

"It's the only thing I'm sure of this weekend."

An odd look crossed his face.

Chapter Twenty One

AFTER TATE AND I RODE the ski lift back up to the top of the mountain, Edwin and Pierce shuffled me into the lodge.

"You poor thing," Edwin said. "You need rest. You need to take a seat. I have an idea. You can sit at Pierce's and my table while we finish up with our ski lesson."

I frowned at them. Sitting at a table and trying to sell health goods to the Madds' guests wasn't my idea of rest or a good time. Although before I told Edwin and Pierce what I thought of the idea, I realized that the health food store's table was the best place to be. It was right in the middle of the lobby. From where I sat, I could see Herschel at the reception desk, peek into the restaurant, and see everyone coming and going from the ski house.

"All right." I sat at the table.

Pierce wrinkled his nose. "You agreed a little too quickly to this. What's up?"

I smiled up at them and started tidying the items on the table for sale. They were hitting the natural beauty products hard, as those took up half the table's length. Was that in direct competition with MaddlyCare? "I just want to help out," I said in my most cheerful voice. "And if sitting here means I don't have to go out there and try to ski again, sign me up."

Edwin laughed. "Don't worry, Darby. No one will ever ask you to ski again. That was terrifying!"

Still laughing, he and Pierce went back outside.

I let out a breath and struggled out of my coat. It was nice to have it off. I could move my arms much more naturally without it.

When Edwin and Pierce had offered to bring me back to the lodge, Tate stayed behind at the ski house. He planned to ask around if anyone saw who pushed me.

I really didn't think there was much question as to who it had been. Cecily had been directly behind me when I went down the mountain. I guessed Tate wasn't ready to believe his *friend* would do such a thing.

At the health food store table, I was loosening my snow boots when someone walked up to the table.

"Do you have anything for anxiety? After this weekend, my nerves are shot," a young woman's voice asked.

I looked up from my laces to find none other than Mindy Carn, Dr. Madd's assistant, standing right in front of me. Her eyes were large and round, and she nervously tugged on her ponytail like it was some sort of lifeline for her.

I sat up straighter. "We have several things that might help you. What we have here is only trial size, but if you like it, we are happy to order it and ship it to your door. Everything is all natural."

She smiled. "Good. That works for me. I can try a few things and see what helps me." She leaned over the table. "What do you have?"

I quickly scanned the table and was relieved to see the items organized by ailment. I guessed that was Pierce; he was the more organized of the two of them.

"We have supplements with everything from lavender to lemon balm."

"Are there any that you recommend?" She twisted her hair. If she kept pulling at her hair like that, she might pluck herself bald.

I wasn't a health guru like Pierce and Edwin, so I was a little leery of making such a recommendation. I stuck with one I knew. "I've heard great things about the lavender aromatherapy, and you just put it under your nose and sniff it."

She nodded. "I'll try that."

I rang her up on the tablet and put the aromatherapy in a small gift bag. As I handed her the bag, she asked, "Do I know you from somewhere?"

"We met briefly. I was in the gym..."

She smacked her cheek. "Oh! You're the woman by the swimming pool. I'm so embarrassed I acted so crazy."

"There's nothing to be sorry for. You had a giant shock," I said soothingly.

She held her bag to her chest. "It was a huge shock, and I have no idea what will happen now."

"What do you mean?"

"Will I still have a job? I was Dr. Madd's personal assistant. The only thing I did for the company was cater to his every need. With him de—gone, what is my role now?"

"Have you spoken to Cecily about it?" I asked.

She shook her head and then looked over her shoulder as if Cecily would jump out of the fireplace and scare her. "Not yet."

"Why not?"

"First of all, it didn't seem right to barge in on her about me when she just lost her husband, and second of all, she scares me." She lowered her voice. "You should have heard the loud fights that went on between her and Dr. Madd. Many times she would come to the office, and the two of them would start arguing. It wasn't good. The last time they fought, Dr. Madd said he wanted a divorce."

"What did they fight about?"

"What *didn't* they fight about? She complained that he worked too much. She also complained that he didn't work hard enough. She said he was trying to diminish her role in the company and she wouldn't stand for it." Mindy lowered her voice. "Honestly, I think he was, because she was always so angry with him. I'm not giving Dr. Madd a pass, by any means. He could be very difficult to deal with—I should know—but she was always on his case. Because of that, it wasn't any surprise to me that he wanted to make changes to the company so she wasn't around as much."

I bit the inside of my lip. Tate had confirmed with Cecily that we were still working the case for her, and I was becoming more and more concerned that we just might be working for a killer. The logical thing to do was pack our bags and quit, but quitting wasn't something I was particularly good at.

"I shouldn't say any more." She looked this way and that, as if she believed the walls had ears. "I said too much as it is. You were just so kind to me the other day. I just might have fallen in that swimming pool if you hadn't been there."

"It was no trouble at all. Did you like working for Dr. Madd?" I asked.

She glanced at me. "It was all right. He paid extremely well. In my first two years of working for him, I paid off my college loans. Who can say that right out of college? The money was a good reason to stick around. I knew I wouldn't be in the job forever, but it was all right for now. I was having a little fun here and there, but most of all, I was putting my money in the bank. I'm glad I did, because now I have a little nest egg until I find the right job."

My eyes went wide. I wished I had been as good with money when I was her age. "How long have you worked for Dr. Madd?"

"Five years. Between you and me, I have been the only person to hold down this job for so long. I think it was because I always had my eye on my endgame to make money and leave. Also, I didn't take his outbursts personally. I know he can be horrible to everyone, so it wasn't about me."

"Outbursts?" I asked.

She nodded. "Oh yeah! Dr. Madd was notorious for throwing fits. He was upset about something or other every day, but he would blow his top once a week. The problem was you had no idea what would set him off. Something huge like losing a big account might do it, but other times he just let big things roll off his back, and he lost his mind over the sink in the staff kitchen not being bone dry."

"Wow. It must have been hard to work for him." It sounded to me like Dr. Madd and Cecily were a match, if an unhappy one.

"It was, but like I said, the money was worth it for a while. I don't think I could do it more than two more years. It had always been my plan to leave after seven years. If I stayed on longer than that, I was afraid I would become as short-tempered as Dr. Madd. They do say you become the people you spend the most time with."

"They do say that," I agreed.

"Well, I was going to have to leave, because I didn't want to be like Dr. Madd or his wife."

"His wife?" I asked. "Why wouldn't you want to be like her?"

"I would love to look like her, especially at her age. She looks like she's twenty-two."

I let the *her age* comment go, even though Cecily was no more than thirty-five and just a few years older than myself.

"But I wouldn't want to be her. She's just not a very happy person. Have you ever met someone who has it all and is still always in a foul mood? That's Cecily. Dr. Madd was hard to deal with because of his tantrums, but in between the tantrums, he was okay. Cecily, though..." She shivered. "She was chronically in a bad mood. That's so much worse."

I nodded. I had noticed that too about Cecily, but I thought it might be the stress of the weekend's festivities and then her husband's death.

"Maybe it will be for the best if she doesn't keep me on," Mindy murmured, more to herself than to me.

"Did Dr. Madd ever give you the impression that he was afraid or might be in any form of danger?"

She stared at me. "What are you talking about? Dr. Madd was the most certain person you could meet. He wasn't afraid of anything. I think he's jumped out of a plane at least three times, and he swam with great white sharks. He wasn't afraid of anyone."

"Okay," I said. "Was anyone you know of afraid of him?"

She snorted. "Who *wasn't* afraid of him? The man was powerful in the industry. One comment to a supplier or manufacturer, he could ruin someone's career. And I've already told you what he was like at the office. Lots of people feared him. Honestly, I think that's why so many people are here and accepted his invitation. They were afraid if they didn't come, Dr. Madd would ruin them."

The question was, which one of them had decided to ruin Dr. Madd first?

Chapter Twenty Two

I WAS STILL WONDERING ABOUT WHO might have killed Dr. Madd when Pierce came up to the table. He smiled. "You're free to go."

"Where's Edwin?" I asked.

He chuckled. "Up in our room. It takes him a lot longer to change than it does me. You know how seriously he takes his look."

I stood up. "Edwin has wanted to give me a makeover for years."

He waved away my comment. "You don't need it—but it probably would be fun. I would love to see Edwin's vision for you. He's usually spot-on about what looks good for a person."

"If he and Maelynn ever join forces, I'm doomed." I gave a fake shiver.

He laughed and stepped behind the table.

"I made a few sales." I pointed to the iPad on the table.

He looked it over. "Wow. Thanks! If you ever get tired of being a private detective, you can work for us."

"In truth, the pay would be a whole lot better and it would be a whole lot less stress, but I'm doing what I love. Even if the job drives me batty."

"And even if your partner drives you batty, too?" he asked with a smile.

I wasn't going to comment on that. I already was well aware that Edwin thought Tate and I should be a real couple. I wasn't going to encourage Pierce to join him on the campaign. I said goodbye and headed back to my suite.

I hoped to be there only long enough to change and get back on the case.

As I stepped off the elevator, I was surprised to see Frederick Hume standing outside my door.

"Can I help you?" I asked.

Frederick jumped. "Can we go in and talk?" His eyes were round and worried. "I need to speak to you in private."

I wasn't comfortable inviting Frederick into my room. He was nervous and unpredictable. "What do you want to talk about?" I asked. "There's no one in the hallway. Tell me here."

"It's about the murder." He looked up and down the hallway. "I know something."

With just a few hours left to solve this case before the suspects dispersed to places unknown, I thought I didn't have much choice but to hear him out.

"All right." I waved my keycard at the door, and we went inside. Letting a strange man into my room was against my better judgement, but I did want to hear what he had to say.

I shut the bedroom door and sat on the desk chair

in the living room. Frederick perched on the end of the couch.

"I—I heard that you were a private investigator."

I wasn't surprised that he knew that. Since Dr. Madd died, the secret was out. There were just too many people at the lodge who knew Tate's and my occupation. They were going to figure it out. Even so, I asked, "Where did you hear that?"

"I think his name is Edward. The guy from the health food store. I was talking to him about selling my eye cream. It's all natural. He said he would be interested when I had a manufacturer."

"Edwin," I said. I should have known that Edwin would let it slip.

"Right," Frederick said with a decisive nod as if I had just solved a major riddle. He studied my face. "Have you used my eye cream?"

I shook my head.

He nodded. "I didn't think so. You still have lines around your eyes. They would be gone by now if you used Miracle Smooth." He held the bag to his chest.

"Did you give that sample to Cecily?" he asked.

"I haven't," I admitted. "It sort of flew out of my head when Dr. Madd was killed."

He frowned. "His death ruined so much."

I studied his face. "Frederick, why are you here? You said it was about the murder?"

He licked his lips. "Yes, yes it is. I—I will tell you if you can deliver these Miracle Smooth samples to Cecily Madd and put in a good word for me. I realized that one sample wasn't enough. She would need several if she wanted to try them on different skin types. No matter the skin type, the cream will work. I can promise her that. It would be an amazing addition to MaddlyCare's quiver." He set the bag on the couch cushion closest to me and gave it a little push in my direction with the back of his hand.

"Did you say quiver?" I asked.

"Yes, like arrows. Maybe I meant arsenal. Sometimes I get my idioms twisted up."

I frowned. I didn't think he got his idioms twisted up at all. He had said "quiver" for a reason. I could not have forgotten so soon that Dr. Madd was killed with an arrow.

"Are you going to give these to her? If you do, I'll tell you whatever it is you want to know. You can keep the original tube I gave you. I think you need it."

I stood up. "Are you trying to bribe me and insult me? You think that will make me help you sell your product to Cecily Madd and MaddlyCare?"

He frantically waved his arm. "No! No! No!"

"Then what are you doing?"

"I'm just asking for a favor in exchange for information."

"I'm pretty sure that is the definition of a bribe. If there is something you can tell me about the case, I'll listen. Or if you prefer, you can talk to a member of the Herrington Police Department."

He hung his head. "I don't want to talk to the police."

"Why not?"

"You have to understand, I'm just trying to sell a product that can really help people. I can't distribute it to the masses, but MaddlyCare can. People need what I created."

I studied him for a long moment. "If you really believe that, have the bravery to speak to Cecily Madd yourself."

He dropped his gaze. "I—I can't do that. She wouldn't listen to me. I become too nervous and tongue-tied. She would have no patience with me. I've been to cosmetic chemist conventions before and have seen the Madds there." He swallowed hard. "Part of the convention is pitching your ideas to companies like MaddlyCare. I watched as others tried to sell their products to the Madds. Both Dr. Madd and Cecily chewed them up and spit them out. They had no patience for anyone who didn't speak clearly or have a clear vision for their product."

"So you're afraid to talk to her about it."

He folded his hand his lap. "I'm not proud of it."

"How are you able to speak to me about it, then?"

He looked up. "Because your opinion doesn't matter."

I cocked my head. "Is that supposed to be a compliment?"

He sighed.

I sat back down. "Why are you so desperate for MaddlyCare to buy your eye cream? There must be other companies you can talk to, and people who are more receptive to hear you out."

He swallowed and adjusted his glasses. "They are the best, and I truly believe that Miracle Smooth should be with the best."

"Doesn't Dr. Madd's death change that?" I asked.

"I—I don't know. It could. I don't know what the future holds for the company." He pressed his hands together so tightly that his knuckled turned a milky white.

"So maybe it's better to wait and see what they have planned before turning your eye cream over to them," I said softly. I couldn't help it—I was starting to feel for the guy. It was clear that he dealt with anxiety. I guessed that it had taken everything he had just to show up here this weekend, and when he made it, the person he most wanted to work up the nerve to speak to was killed. Talk about bad luck.

He picked up the bag and put it on his lap. "Maybe you're right. I was just so set on selling it to MaddlyCare. It's why I came up here. I spent everything I had on this trip."

"I thought MaddlyCare covered the cost of the weekend?"

He shook his head. "It might have for employees and friends, but if you were going to pitch to Dr. Madd, it was on your dime."

"Did you try to pitch to him at the New Year's Eve Party?"

He shook his head. "I didn't have the nerve to go up and talk to him at the party. He was always surrounded by people pitching their ideas. I knew my little eye cream would get lost in the shuffle."

"Did you speak to him another time?" I asked, stopping just short of saying *before he died?*

"I tried to. I really thought I could do it. I had myself all hyped up to speak to him."

I leaned back in my chair and waited. Since it was a desk chair, it bounced slightly when I changed position. "What happened?"

"New Year's morning, I knew he was skiing, and I made a point to wake up early so that I could speak to him on the slope."

"Wait, I thought Dr. Madd had an itinerary that said he wasn't to be interrupted when he was skiing."

He swallowed again. "It did, but I was desperate. I knew when he got back to the lodge and was open for meetings, he would be inundated by other sellers who were much better pitch people than me. I know I have a great product, but I would be competing against professional salesmen. I had to get out ahead of them."

I nodded. How many of the suspects were awake and outside of the lodge on New Year's Day morning? It seemed like it had been a rather high number.

"I knew what time Dr. Madd planned to be on the slope, and I arrived thirty minutes before him."

I took a breath. Frederick was about to tell me he saw the murder. "What did you see?"

"That dog was on the mountain," he said, barely above a whisper.

"Dog? Do you mean Tiny?"

He nodded. "He scared me away from the ski house. I was bitten by a dog when I was a small boy and have had a terrible fear of them since. Before Dr. Madd even arrived, Tiny chased me off."

"How did he do that?" It was hard for me to believe that the gentle giant of a dog would hurt him.

"He galloped toward me, and I ran back to the lodge. I was convinced he was going to attack me." He wrapped his arms around himself, as if he needed protection from the memory.

I was sure Tiny had just wanted to say hello to him. "Given your history with dogs, I can understand why you were scared. Was he trying to attack you, or did he want to play?"

"Is there a difference?" Frederick asked.

"Yes," I replied.

"Well, there isn't one as far as I'm concerned. I'm afraid of all dogs, no matter the size, and Tiny is the size of a bear."

"Did you see anyone else?" I asked. It was hard for me to believe Tiny was out there all alone.

"When I ran back into the lodge, I almost knocked over Kiera Bellworthy." His face turned bright red at the memory. "She was on her way outside."

I nodded. I already knew that Kiera had been outside when Dr. Madd died. She was on her way to her planned meeting with him...or so she'd told me. She was an actress. Could she have been lying?

"Anyone else?" I asked.

He shook his head. "When I came back inside, the lobby was empty. There wasn't even anyone at the reception desk."

I thought that was telling, because as soon as he'd told me that Tiny was loose on the mountain, I wondered if general manager Herschel was somewhere close by. If he wasn't at his post at the reception desk, he was more likely somewhere closer to his dog.

Frederick put his head in his hands. "I don't know what I'm going to do. I'm ruined. I can't even go to any conventions to pitch my product to other companies. I can't afford the admission prices. I really thought putting all my hopes in MaddlyCare was the best plan. How could I be so stupid?"

"I think what you need is to find a partner to do the selling for you," I said. "You need to work with someone you trust and who believes in your product. If the cream is as great as you say it is, then stick to what you know: the science. Let someone else do the legwork of selling it."

"I can't afford a person like that," he moaned.

"Think more creatively. There might be someone out there who doesn't care about the money upfront, but will want a share of the profit if the cream is sold. There is always another way to reach your goal. Don't be closed off to other scenarios."

He stood up. "Thank you. You have given me a lot to think about."

And he'd given me a lot to think about, too.

Chapter Twenty Three

AFTER FREDERICK LEFT, TAKING HIS eye creams, I changed into jeans and a sweater, which was my uniform November through April. I texted Tate to tell him what I had learned from Frederick and went in search of Herschel and Tiny.

To my surprise, Herschel wasn't at the front desk. A young woman was in his place.

"Can you tell me where Herschel is?"

She blinked Disney princess eyes at me. "Is something wrong? Maybe I can help you."

"Nothing is wrong. I just wanted to chat with him."

She looked concerned when I said *chat*.

"Is something wrong with Herschel?" I asked.

She chewed on her lower lip. If anything, the mannerism made her more adorable. "No."

Her no wasn't that convincing.

"Can you tell me where he is?" I raised my eyebrows.

"In the conservatory, I think," she said.

"You think?"

"It's where he said he was going when he called

me out of the restaurant to watch the desk," she said, sounding less than convinced herself. "I've never worked at this post before. I'm a hostess, not a receptionist."

I nodded and wondered what had called Herschel away from the desk. "Thanks for your help."

She relaxed. "If you need seating at the restaurant, let me know. I'm very good at seating people."

"I'll remember that," I promised.

I went up to the fifth floor, where the conservatory was. When I stepped off the elevator, the hallway was empty. I walked into the conservatory, and as soon as I did, I regretted my sweater. It was a balmy eighty degrees in the humid room. I wondered how much it cost the lodge to keep it going, especially since it didn't appear to be a major draw to guests. I was alone in the rainforest-like room with only the bright flowers and birds as company.

The hostess had said Herschel was up here, but I couldn't imagine the birds would be this docile and calm if a giant Saint Bernard was among them.

A green parakeet landed on the branch closest to my head.

"Aren't you a cutie?"

It started to clean its wings as if to ensure it was the prettiest bird in the room.

Unless they were hiding in the foliage, Herschel and Tiny weren't in the bird room, as I was beginning to think of it. I walked along the path until I came to the first of two sets of doors. I went through both sets and found Herschel and Tiny staring out the window at the ski house and slope. Herschel turned and looked at me with tears in his eyes.

Tiny jumped to his feet and galloped over to me. His giant tongue hung out of his mouth liked a flag.

I stepped back before he could jump on me and held out my hand. "Steady there, boy." I spoke to him like he was a horse. Since he was the size of a horse, I was okay with that.

"Tiny, stay!" Herschel said.

The dog came to an immediate stop and lay down on the floor.

"Wow, he's well trained."

"I can't take the credit for it. It was his previous owner who trained him so well." Herschel walked over to one of the rattan chairs and sat down.

"And who was that?" I asked.

"Michael Tragger, Cecily and Ridge's father. Tiny was just one year old when Michael died, no more than a puppy. Even as a pup, he had giant feet. There was never any doubt that he was going to be a sizable dog."

I looked at Tiny with renewed interest. "He was Cecily's father's dog?"

"Yes. When Mr. Tragger died, he left the dog to the lodge and asked that Tiny be cared for here until the end of his life. He became my dog, since I'm in charge of the lodge. He's a great dog. I don't think Cecily or Ridge have any interest in him. That's fine by me. We've become great friends, haven't we, Tiny? I wouldn't have it any other way."

When Tiny heard that compliment, he stood up, padded over to Herschel, and placed his mighty head on Herschel's knee.

"I can tell that he wouldn't have it any other way either."

Herschel scratched Tiny's jowls. The big dog closed his eyes in pure bliss.

"How long ago did Mr. Tragger die?" I asked. "Tiny doesn't look that old."

"He's getting up there in age. If you look at him close enough, you can see that he has some graying around the muzzle. He's eleven. That's close to ancient for a purebred his size."

I sat in a rattan chair across from Herschel.

"I give him supplements every day for arthritis. It's no fun getting old." He looked the dog in the eye. "Is it, Tiny?"

The dog gave a woof in agreement.

"Are you all right?" I asked. "I went to the reception desk to look for you, and the staff person said you pulled her away from the restaurant. And when I came in here, it looked like you'd been crying."

He nodded, still looking at the dog and not me. "I need some time to clear my head. I had just gotten some bad news, and I had to process it in private."

"What was the bad news, if you don't mind my asking?"

He seemed to consider this for a moment. "Cecily is selling the lodge. It's exactly what I feared would happen and tried so hard to stop. My goal for this weekend was to put on the best show for her and Dr. Madd. I wanted to show them that this place needed to stay in the family, and that the history of Garden Peak Lodge was important. Everything was going so well until Dr. Madd died. After that, my hopes for the lodge crumbled right in front of me."

"When did you learn she was interested in selling? Did she tell you?" I leaned forward in my chair.

He scratched Tiny's large head. "She didn't have to. I knew it was a possibility. For the last four months, realtors and potential buyers have come sniffing around the lodge. Finally, when pressed, one of the possible buyers told me he had heard from his realtor that he had seen the listing online. I looked for myself and found it. This was in November when I got the confirmation of what I already knew. I called Cecily right away."

"And how did that go?" I asked.

"You're working for Cecily; I'm sure you can guess. I'm lucky she took my call. She did confirm that she planned to put the lodge up for sale after the New Year. I told her she really needed to come back to Herrington and see the place before she made such a huge decision. While I was talking to her, I got the idea to host her friends here for a New Year's Eve party. I thought if she saw all the lodge had to offer, she would never sell it. What a fool I was," he said bitterly.

"The New Year's Eve weekend was your idea?" I asked. I didn't know why that surprised me, but it did. From the start, even knowing that Cecily owned the lodge, I thought Garden Peak Lodge was an odd choice for a big party with all the Madds' fancy friends and clients.

He nodded. "She said no at first. I asked her to think about it, and told her at the very least she would have one last fun weekend at the lodge before she sold it. She still said no." His face drooped. "But then she called me about two weeks ago and asked me to plan the party and said she wanted it to be the whole weekend." He shook his head at the memory. "Boy, did I have to scramble to get everything in place that quickly. I knew that Cecily would want the best of the best, and if I wanted her to keep the lodge, I had to deliver."

I considered this. "Did she say what changed her mind?"

He shook his head. "I wasn't going to question her about it. I was just glad for the opportunity."

Interesting.

"Did her brother know she was selling?" I asked.

"Ridge?" he asked with a raised brow. "I suppose he knows now, but I don't think he was aware of it before this weekend."

"What do you think finally made her want to sell? Dr. Madd's death?"

"No." The bitterness was back in his voice. "What I realized the night of the New Year's Eve party was that she never planned to keep the lodge. Some of those buyers and realtors who had come sniffing about over the last few months were on the guest list. She was using my party as an ad to secure the best price for the lodge. I have never felt so used in my life. And now she tells me that the sale is a done deal." He dug his fingers into Tiny's fur. "I came up here when I heard that. I just needed a little bit of time to absorb it alone."

"She was able to find a buyer?" I asked.

He nodded. "Jeremy Stone. He's a local vineyard owner, who is still here. It's no secret he wanted to buy this place," he said in a low voice. "He's been stopping in for months asking about it."

I remembered my conversation with the vineyard owner at the New Year's Eve party. I hadn't realized he stayed for the whole weekend. He had been charming. I racked my brain to remember if I had seen him since that night.

"Why are you so against selling?" I asked. "Just because she sells, that doesn't mean you'll lose your job. The new owner will still need someone to run the place. If that new owner is Jeremy Stone, he has enough to manage with his wineries in the region."

Tiny lifted his head from Herschel's lap.

Herschel placed a comforting hand on the top of the dog's head. "I just want everything at the lodge to remain the same as it's always been since Mr. Tragger opened the lodge. This place was important to him. I know he would feel the same."

"But he's been gone for ten years," I said softly. "Things can't stay the same forever."

He stared me in the eye. "Why not? Why can't things just be left alone when they're working? It's just like Cecily Madd to think that there's a better way, but what if there isn't? What if you're doing it the best possible way right now?"

I raised my eyebrows.

He removed a handkerchief from his pocket and patted his forehead. "I'm sorry. My predicament is not your fault. Garden Peak Lodge is more than a job for me. It's my whole life. I live and work here."

"Do you have a cabin like Ridge?" I asked in surprise.

"No, but I have a little apartment off the reception area. It's nothing fancy, but it's all I need. I added it not long after Mr. Tragger died. I have found that guests like access to the general manager at all times. Before I moved to the lodge, I was going up and down the mountain as many as three times a night. It was exhausting and a waste of energy. Worse yet, my living in town caused the guests to wait. Our guests do not like waiting. Since I moved here, we've done much better. Our reviews are impeccable because I'm here for the guests' every concern and wish."

"You're afraid you'll get kicked out if Cecily sells?" I asked, realizing that we were finally getting to the heart of why he was upset about the sale. It actually wasn't that different from Ridge's reasons for being upset.

He nodded. "And I'm afraid of what will happen to this place. I—we've worked too hard to throw it all away now. And for what? Money?" He said "money" like it was a curse.

I wanted to tell him that whether he liked it or not, Cecily was the owner, and whether he agreed with it or not, she had the right to sell the lodge.

But I held my tongue, because for the first time, I was looking at the anxious general manager as a suspect. I should have seen him as such before, but I'd judged that he was harmless. Why? Because he was jittery and nervous. Those were terrible reasons to write someone off as a suspect, though. I could write the cosmetic chemist Frederick Hume off for the same reason, but I had to consider him a suspect as well.

Herschel placed a protective hand on Tiny's shoulder. "And what will happen to Tiny?"

"I imagine Cecily will let you keep him," I said. "She doesn't strike me as an animal person."

"What good will that do? Tiny and I would be homeless together."

It didn't matter what I said. Herschel had a counterpoint to everything. "My advice would be to not panic and speak to Cecily about it. If she does sell to Stone or someone else, talk to that person about keeping your job and home."

He let out a breath. "You're right. I always jump to the worst-case scenario. It's what gets me in trouble time and time again."

Now that Herschel was moderately calm, I felt like I could ask him what I came to the conservatory to ask in the first place. "Why were you on the mountain the morning of Dr. Madd's murder?"

"I—I wasn't..."

He was lying, and we both knew it.

"I have an eyewitness who saw you on the mountain." That wasn't true. Frederick had seen Tiny, not Herschel, but Herschel didn't need to know that.

"That's not possible. I wasn't on the mountain."

I leaned forward. "Why should I believe you?"

"Because I wasn't there," he said.

"Tiny was. The big dog is hard to miss."

Tiny looked up from where he lay next to Herschel's chair.

Herschel visibly relaxed. "I let him out that morning. Whoever saw him just saw him outside, not near the slope. Tiny knows to stay away from the ski house. He wouldn't go up there without me."

"Did you go up there to talk to Dr. Madd about your worries about the lodge?" I asked.

"I told you, I didn't go there. Are you not listening to me?"

The conservatory door flew open, and Austin walked into the bright room.

"Herschel," Austin said. "I need to talk to you."

Herschel glared at me. "Did you tell them something about me?"

I held up my hands. "I haven't said anything to the police about you."

"Ms. Piper isn't involved in this. I just had some more questions about the last few days here at the lodge. We are trying to piece things together about Dr. Madd's movements. From what I hear from the staff, nothing happens at this lodge that you don't know about."

Oh, I was *Ms. Piper* now. *Great.* This didn't bode well for getting any more information from the police.

Herschel hung his head. "That may have been true before, but I don't know who killed Dr. Madd. I've told you this before."

"Still, I'd like to chat again." Austin gestured to one of the rattan chairs by the windows. "May I sit?"

Herschel sighed and nodded.

Austin turned to me. "Darby, can you give us a few minutes?"

"Is that what Herschel wants?"

The older man smiled at me. "I appreciate you listening to me, Darby. Not many people have that much patience to listen for so long. Tiny probably needs to go out. We've been up here a long while. Can you take him?"

I had been relegated from investigator to dog sitter.

Tiny whined.

"Sure," I said with a sigh. I did have a soft spot when it came to animals. "Let's go, Tiny."

The giant dog galloped to the door that separated the sunroom from the hot and humid bird room. Before I went through the door, I looked over my shoulder. Austin and Herschel spoke in hushed tones, and a feeling of unease fell over me.

Chapter Twenty Four

I LED THE DOG OUT OF the sitting room and through the rainforest room. He didn't so much as look at the birds. Herschel had him very well trained.

When we reached the ground floor, I spotted Tate near the reception desk, where two bellhops were trying to accommodate a long line of guests who all wanted to check out right then.

Tate spun around. "Where have you been?"

I wrinkled my brow. "I could ask you the same question."

He shook his head. "Sorry. I just sort of panicked when I couldn't find you."

I felt my cheeks flush. Tate had been worried about me.

"There is supposed to be a massive snowstorm tonight," he went on to say. "So the lodge said people can leave before the weather hits if they want to get off the mountain. I guess Austin and the police okayed it too. Anyone who stays might be stuck up here for another day or two."

I placed a hand on Tiny's head. "Should we leave?" I asked.

"Not as long as Cecily is here, I don't think. We'll be all right through the storm. The lodge has been here for over a hundred years and weathered much worse. They have backup generators and plenty of provisions. That being said, a lot of people are getting out. I think it's a combination of the weather, and that they're no longer under orders to stay here by the police."

"If the guests leave, the killer might leave too," I said. "What do you think that means for Austin's investigation?"

He shrugged. "That he doesn't think he can close the case before everyone leaves tomorrow. I'm sure the powers that be in Herrington don't want a bunch of wealthy people from New York City trapped on the mountain during a blizzard. That would be worse press for the town than the murder."

At my side, Tiny whined.

"Let's talk about this outside. I promised Herschel I'd take Tiny out." I walked toward the back doors and Tate followed me.

When we got outside, Tiny ran for the bushes.

"Why are in you charge of Herschel's dog?" Tate asked.

"I was talking to him in the conservatory when Austin came in and wanted to speak to Herschel in private. Tiny had to go out, so I got the job." I shrugged and wrapped my arms around myself. I really needed to learn when I needed my coat at the lodge and when I didn't. I was awful at guessing.

Tate was wearing his coat and noticed my shivers.

He took it off and put it over my shoulders. It was so big it was like a blanket on me. "No," I protested. "You need it."

"I have a sweater. I'm fine. I'm a lot more warm-blooded than you."

I narrowed my eyes. "So you're saying I'm cold-blooded."

He looked me in the eye. "I would never say that about you, Piper. You care too much."

Something caught in my throat, and I had to turn away when he said that. "I wonder how long Tiny's potty breaks last."

Tate barked a laugh. "Way to change the subject."

It was time to change the direction of the conversation. "Why is Cecily staying? I would think she would want to get off the mountain before the storm too."

"She has a buyer for the lodge and they have paperwork to go over."

"Jeremy Stone," I said.

Tate raised his eyebrows. "You know him?"

"I met him briefly at the New Year's Eve party, but I didn't know he was still here or that he wanted to buy the lodge so quickly until my conversation with Herschel just now," I said. "What does this mean for Herschel and the rest of the staff?"

"Stone claimed that he wouldn't make any changes to the staffing or how the lodge runs. But doesn't every buyer say that when they take on a new business? I guess in twelve to eighteen months a lot here will be different."

That sounded about right, and that was just what Herschel had been so afraid of.

"Cecily is determined to get this deal done and head back to New York with Stone's check in her pocket. She's willing to stay on the mountain for however long it takes. The storm can't stop her."

"I doubt much at all can," I said.

Tate cocked his head. "You don't like Cecily much, do you?"

I made a face. "Why do you have a picture of the two of you in your bag?" I blurted out. And then I clapped the giant sleeve of his coat over my mouth. It smelled just like Tate, like clove and lemon. I dropped the sleeve.

Tate stared at me. "You went through my bag." There was no accusation in his voice, just disbelief.

My cheeks felt red hot. "Not on purpose." I shook my head. "No, I went through it on purpose, but not to pry. I just wanted to see if anything had been disturbed. This was right after the fake maid, Dr. Madd's ex-wife, searched our rooms for the threatening notes against Dr. Madd."

He relaxed a little. "Okay."

"Okay? That's all you're going to say? You're not mad?"

"I trust you," he said simply. "If you searched my bag, you had to have a reason, which you explained to me."

I stared at him. "Wow."

"Wow, what?" he asked confused.

"I guess I didn't know you had that much faith in me."

He looked into my eyes. "Piper, you're my partner in all this. I have to have all the faith in you."

I looked away again.

After a beat, he said, "As for your question, I brought that picture because I found it in Aunt Samantha's house after she died. I thought it would be a hoot for Cecily to see it. Maybe we could talk about old times. I never did show it to her, though."

"Why not?" I asked barely above a whisper.

"She's different now. I just don't think she wants to reminisce about when we were kids. She seems more focused on her future, and now that her husband is dead, the future of her company, MaddlyCare."

I had to admit I thought he was right, but I couldn't miss the sadness that I heard in his voice, and it broke my heart. No matter what I might have thought of Cecily, she was a person who had been important to Tate once upon a time.

Tiny popped out of the bushes and barked at us.

It was a welcome interruption. I waved him toward me. "All done? Let's go in."

Instead of doing as I asked, he ran farther away from us and then stopped to look back. He barked again.

"He wants us to follow him," I said.

"Sheesh, did this dog go to Lassie school or something?" Tate wanted to know.

"Could he have found another murder weapon?" I asked.

"There's only one way to find out," Tate said, and jogged after the dog.

I sighed and brought up the rear.

I had expected Tiny to run toward the ski house or Ridge's cabin just beyond it, but he ran in the opposite direction. We followed him through the trees. There was a clear path here in the summer because of the break in the forest canopy overhead, but at the moment it was buried in several feet of snow.

Above our heads, the sky was turning a milky gray purple color, and the clouds looked like they were being stirred into billows of smoke.

"Tate!"

He turned and pointed up.

He tilted his head back. "Yeah, we need to go back. Whatever Tiny has to show us can wait." He stopped in the middle of the path, clapped, whistled, and called the Saint Bernard.

Although Tiny stopped, the dog didn't come back to us.

Tate put his fingers in his mouth and let out a shrill whistle. Tiny just cocked his massive head as if to ask if that was the best he had. He then turned and continued to walk down the path at a slower pace.

"Let's follow him," I said. "He won't go back to the lodge until he's shown us whatever he thinks we need to see."

"All right," Tate said, and started to run after the dog. Tiny began to run too.

I followed close behind both of them.

After a short while we came to a field with a shed. Across the field there were lumps covered with snow. Tate waded through the snow over to them. With his gloved hand he brushed the snow away, and I could just make out half a bullseye when I made my way across the field. It took me a little longer because of my much shorter legs and the high snow drifts.

"This is where they hold archery lessons in the summer," Tate said.

Tiny barked happily as if to tell Tate he was a good student.

Tate looked at the shed.

As if he and I were thinking the same thing, we hurried over to the shed. Again, he beat me there because of the snow.

I saw him open the shed door. There was no light inside. He turned on the flashlight on his cell phone.

In the shed there were quivers of arrows, more arrows, bows, bow strings, and crossbows. There was a riding lawn mower too, but that wasn't really what we were focusing on.

"It wasn't locked?" I asked.

"It was." He held up a padlock that had been sliced with bolt cutters.

"You think someone broke in here and stole the crossbow and arrow that killed Dr. Madd?"

"That's exactly what I think," Tate said. He pocketed the cut padlock. "We'll give this to Austin. Maybe he can look for prints. It's not doing any good keeping this place secure."

A big gust of wind slammed the shed door shut behind us. I looked through the small window and saw it had begun to snow.

I took some quick pictures with my cell phone. "If there's a whiteout from the storm, we could get lost. We have to get back to the lodge now."

Chapter Twenty Five

TATE, TINY, AND I MADE it back to the lodge just as the wind was really starting to pick up. The lobby teemed with people trying to get off the mountain before the worst of the storm.

Herschel and another desk clerk were in a mad dash to check people out and settle their accounts. As soon as Tiny saw how stressed his master was, he ran over to him. Herschel patted the dog's head and continued to help guests. Yet he seemed more relaxed to have Tiny at his side.

I handed Tate his coat. "It's chaos in here."

"Rats escaping a sinking ship."

"You think they're all rats?" I asked.

He smiled. "It's just an expression."

Mindy Carn, Dr. Madd's personal assistant—or I suppose *former* personal assistant was a more accurate title—waited in line to leave.

"I'll be right back," I said to Tate, and went over to speak to her.

I stopped her after she checked out and was

heading to the shuttle that would take her down the mountain. "You're not staying with Cecily?"

She shook her head. "I gave it a lot of thought after I spoke to you, and I turned in my resignation. It was one thing to put up with Dr. Madd as a boss, but there is no way I would have stood working for Cecily for more than a week. It was better to end it here."

The shuttle honked its horn.

"I have to go. I can't wait to get out of here." The window blew her long hair around her face.

I can't say I blamed her. I wished I was leaving Garden Peak Lodge, too.

Through the shuttle window, I saw Kiera Bellworthy. She glanced at me and nodded. She was leaving the lodge like she wished. I wondered what would happen to her career now without MaddlyCare to save it.

As the last shuttle scuttled down the mountain, it began to snow in earnest. It went from a few large flakes to a cloud of white in a matter of seconds. Looking out the back window of the lobby, I could no longer see the ski house, the ski lift, or the mountain itself.

The windows shook from the wind. I bit my lip and prayed that everyone who went down the mountain made it safely. There was no leaving the lodge now.

Cecily had told most of the staff they could go home before the storm hit. All that remained were the chef; one other member of the kitchen staff; John Paul, the bartender; and Herschel, of course. I hoped they would be paid extra for staying. Ridge counted as an employee who stayed behind, too, but I hadn't seen him in the lodge all day. I guessed that he was holed up in his own cabin for the duration of the storm.

The front lobby doors opened, and clouds of snow and freezing wind came into the building.

"Herschel! What were you doing outside?"

The lodge manager brushed snow from the sleeves of his coat and removed his hat. "I had to check that all the outdoor furniture hadn't flown away."

"The furniture isn't going to matter if you get blown away in a snowstorm."

He puffed out his chest. "I've been the manager of this lodge for a very long time, and I've always taken my responsibilities in that role very seriously."

"Trust me, Herschel. No one would think for a moment you weren't serious about your job."

Tiny galloped over to him.

Herschel scratched his ears. "It's so good to see you, my friend. We may need to move soon." His mouth turned down.

The big dog barked and stared at his owner's face with a pure expression of love. I doubted that Gumshoe had ever looked at me like that. Annoyance was the typical expression on my cat's face.

"Move?" I asked. "I already told you, you don't know if the new owner will want to make changes to the staff. I would wait it out and see what happens. It seems she's selling the lodge to Jeremy Stone. Wait until all the documents are signed and have a conversation with him about your future here."

"I won't be here to have that conversation."

"Why not?" I asked.

"I made a costly mistake. After Detective Caster questioned me again in the conservatory, I was just so upset at the idea of having to leave this place. People just don't understand that Garden Peak Lodge is my world. So I went to Cecily one final time to make a plea for her not to sell the lodge. I promised her I would make the lodge even better. I promised her I would attract A-list guests. I promised her that I would make her a fortune."

I rubbed my arms. "What did she say?"

He buried his face in his hands. "Everything I've worked for has fallen to pieces." His voice was muffled, and I had to listen hard to make out the words. "I thought I could keep everything just how it's always been. She said what she did with her lodge was her decision and no one else's, and she was tired of my questioning her. She fired me and ordered me to get off the mountain."

"She *fired* you?"

"Just now." Tears gathered in the corners of his eyes. "She said I had to get out now."

I glanced out the window. "You can't leave now. This storm is going to last through the night."

He frowned. "Cecily said I had to."

"She obviously didn't look out the window or at the forecast."

"I don't think she cares if I get caught in the storm."

"That may be true, but you're still not going. It's not safe. I'll talk to her. You can leave in the morning," I said.

He nodded. "Maybe you'll have more luck speaking to her than I have."

I wasn't sure I would, but Tate had a good chance.

Fortunately, I spotted him looking out the back window of the lodge at the cloud of white.

He turned to me. "It kind of looks like we're inside a bag of sugar."

"That's one way of putting it." I touched his arm. "We have to find Cecily," I said, and quickly told him what I had just learned from Herschel. "She can't kick him out into the cold like this."

"I agree that he can't leave tonight. I don't think even Cecily would demand that if she took a moment to think about it. The weather is terrible." He paused. "But if she insists that he has to go, he can just stay anyway. This is a big place. He can just hide out in the lodge until morning. It's not like there aren't a lot of vacant rooms to sleep in. This place cleared out like it was under a police raid."

"I still think we should try to talk to her about him. Should she really be firing anyone right now when she's signing the papers to sell the lodge in a matter of hours? Shouldn't she just leave that to the new owner?"

"I see your point, but I can guarantee Cecily won't. She is technically still in charge of the lodge, so she can hire and fire whoever she pleases."

I knew that was true, but to kick Herschel, and Tiny for that matter, into such a terrible night seemed to be downright, well, *cold.*

Tate put a hand on my shoulder. "I can tell you're still not convinced. Let's go find Cecily and see if we can make her understand how unkind she is being."

Tate and I found Cecily in the restaurant. It was eerie how quiet the place was with most of the staff and guests gone.

Every barstool stood empty. Cecily sat at one of the tables with John Paul, the bartender I had met earlier. He noticed Tate and me first and smiled. "Can I grab you both a drink? We have plenty of food, too. The chef prepared for a full house this evening."

I shook my head. "Not right now, but thank you."

Tate said the same.

Cecily frowned at us, then turned to the bartender. "Can you give us a moment?"

John Paul nodded and seemed to be visibly relieved to be getting away from Cecily and whatever documents she was reviewing with him.

She picked up her papers and neatened the stack in front of her. "Have you found the person who killed my husband yet? Your Detective Caster is breathing down my neck. I have deals that need to be made, so I can go back to New York tomorrow."

I stared at her. Her husband had died yesterday. Yesterday. And she was already over hearing not only about his death, but about him. It was unbelievable.

Tate sat in the bartender's vacant seat, and I perched in a chair between Tate and Cecily.

"We haven't caught your husband's killer yet, but we will," Tate said with full confidence.

Cecily barked a laugh. "And how exactly are you going to do that? All of the suspects have left." She reached into her bag, pulled out an envelope, and set the envelope in front of Tate.

Tate looked at it. "What's this?"

"Your money for the case. You didn't solve it. We still don't know who sent those notes, but I felt obligated to pay you and to put an end to this."

"An end to what?" I asked.

Cecily's eyes slid in my direction. "This case. I realized now it doesn't matter who sent those notes. My husband is dead. Now is the time for me to concentrate on keeping the company he left behind afloat."

Tate looked as if he wasn't going to take the money. His hand hovered over it.

I, on the other hand, didn't have the same qualms, and picked up the envelope. We had come here to do a job and deserved payment for it. Yes, the case went off the rails when Dr. Madd was killed, but that wasn't our fault. Had Cecily been more forthcoming with the threatening notes from the beginning, we might have been able to find the culprit before they had a chance to kill.

Cecily smiled at me. "I see you are the more practical of the two." She gathered up her papers and started to put them in her bag. "If that's all, I think we're done here. I suggest that you leave as soon as the weather breaks in the morning."

"That's not all," I said. "We still have the problem with Herschel."

She raised her eyebrows at me. "I don't see a problem with him. I fired him. I told him to pack up his things so he could leave. We won't need his services here at Garden Peak any longer."

"He can't leave until the morning. The weather is too bad," I said.

"He will just have to risk it. I will not abide disloyalty."

"How is telling you that he doesn't want you to sell the lodge disloyal?" Tate asked.

It was a question I had wanted to ask myself.

She scowled at Tate. "Because I'm the boss, and

I make the decisions. As long as he works for me—which he no longer does—he has to respect my decision, even if that choice is to sell the lodge."

The windows rattled, and there was a bang outside. I winced.

"It's just the lawn furniture getting thrown around in the wind. The staff should have secured it," Cecily complained.

"You let most of the staff go home. The few who are left are doing the best they can."

She wrinkled her nose as if she did not agree. Another deck chair flew by the window.

Tate pointed at it. "You can't send a man out in that."

She glowered at him. "Fine. Herschel can stay, but as soon as the weather breaks, I want him out of here. If he doesn't leave promptly after the storm, I'll hold you accountable." She stood up. "Now that that's settled, we need to do something to get through this night, so I have planned a little dinner party for everyone who is still here. The bartender and I were just going over the drinks menu, and I have already met with the chef. It'll be a small party. There are only nine of us staying at the lodge at the moment, plus a handful of staff."

"Does that include Herschel?" I asked.

"I suppose it must, but you keep him away from me." She picked up her bag and marched into the kitchen.

I didn't think that would be too hard. I couldn't imagine Herschel wanting to speak to her after the way she'd treated him. I'd be surprised if he agreed to come to the dinner.

Chapter Twenty Six

*I*N A PLACE AS LARGE as Garden Peak Lodge, it wasn't until the dinner party that I realized who had stayed behind. I had to admit I was surprised by the people who decided to stay. Frederick Hume was among them. Maybe he was still holding onto hope that Cecily would buy Miracle Smooth for Maddly-Care, or maybe he couldn't afford to make reservations somewhere else, since his stay at the lodge was free.

Benny B was there, acting as server. He'd stayed until the last moment, hoping to get that big story that would give him the break he needed to jump from covering celebrities in the Finger Lakes to bigger and more exciting beats.

He winked at me when he placed my drink on the table. It was a hot coffee. I was going to need my wits about me if I was going to survive this night and solve the case. Though I supposed that solving the case wasn't my job anymore, since Cecily had already given Tate and me our fee. She had paid us, and thanks to modern technology and my smartphone, I had already deposited her check into our business account. Fortunately, the storm hadn't knocked out the closest cell phone tower yet.

Tate said I was paranoid for depositing the check as soon as I got back to my suite, but at least I was paranoid with some money in the bank.

Cecily entered the dining room in a form-fitting dress and her hair and makeup on point. I had guessed correctly that she wanted her guests to dress up for the occasion.

I had only brought one dress to the lodge, and I had worn it to the New Year's Eve party, but I had a pair of black, wide-legged slacks and a silver silk blouse that I had packed just in case. Now I was glad I had, even if the clothes were a little wrinkled. I hoped that the dim lighting would hide that.

Everyone at the table had dressed up. Tate, who sat across from me, had even worn a suit. Until this weekend, I had never seen him in anything other than jeans and T-shirts.

As I sipped my coffee, I studied the faces at the table. In addition to Cecily, Frederick, Tate, and myself, Herschel was to my right, with Tiny sitting behind his chair. Edwin and Pierce were also there. I wished my friends had gotten off the mountain when they could. Between Tate and Cecily sat the winery owner Jeremy Stone, who was looking quite pleased with himself. On the other side of Herschel was Heather Madd, Dr. Madd's ex-wife. I couldn't for the life of me decide why she was still here. Why hadn't she left like the rest of the guests?

I leaned across the table to Pierce and Edwin.

"What are the two of you doing here? Why didn't you leave?"

Edwin wiggled his eyebrows. "I don't want to miss all the drama."

Pierce shook his head. "Edwin loves drama, but when Tate told us that the two of you were staying, we decided to stay too. Besides, we've lived in the Finger Lakes all our lives. A bad winter storm doesn't scare us."

"Speak for yourself," his fiancé said. "I'm a little scared, but the drama is worth it. Besides, how many people can say they've been invited to a fancy dinner party with Cecily Madd? Let's all take a photo later!"

Cecily clapped her hands when all the guests were seated. "As this is our last night at the lodge, and due to this dreadful storm, I thought it was important for us to enjoy one last meal. For me, it will be my very last here. My beloved husband Garret and I decided to host this New Year's celebration here at Garden Peak Lodge to share the Finger Lakes with our friends and skincare community.

"Also, I came here to decide what to do with the lodge itself. It had been left to me by my father. It was a precious gift because I knew how much this place meant to him. It has been special to me, in particular, because my parents divorced when I was a baby. My relationship with my father was nonexistent through most of my life. I believe leaving this place to me was his way of apologizing for that, and consequently, I kept the lodge for sentimental reasons."

Herschel was seated next to me, and I could feel his body tense. Tiny sensed it too and put a calming paw on his lap.

"However." Cecily's voice was firm. "Sentiment has no place in business, and I have to consider what will be the best business move going forward. As I will now be in charge of MaddlyCare as the CEO, I need to remove other responsibilities from my list. That includes the lodge."

Heather picked up her glass of wine. "You can't make too many changes to MaddlyCare without the approval of the shareholders." There was a slight lilt to her voice, and I wondered if Heather might have had a few glasses of wine before coming down to dinner.

Cecily scowled. "I own eighty percent of the company. I can do whatever I want with it. Your measly ten isn't even a blip on the radar."

Heather held her glass out to Cecily. "Garret held eighty percent. You have nothing."

"I'm his heir."

Heather took a big gulp of wine and then said, "Are you sure about that? I wouldn't be making statements like that before I saw the will with my own eyes."

Cecily glared. "I checked it before we left."

The room was quiet. Had Cecily just said she checked Garret's will *before* they left, so she was concerned before they left NYC for this weekend in the Finger Lakes that he might die?

Across the table, Tate's brows knit together into a frown. I guessed any remaining fondness he had for Cecily had finally dissolved.

Cecily plastered a smile onto her face. "As I was saying, I'm very pleased to announce that Jeremy Stone of Stone Vineyards, right here in the Finger Lakes, will be the new owner of Garden Peak Lodge. I believe he is the perfect person to continue the legacy of this place. If my father were alive, I'm certain he would agree."

Stone, who sat to Cecily's right, smiled. "It will be a great pleasure to take over the lodge. It has so much potential, and I know that my team and I will guide it into the next phase of success. I'm going to start by making some much-needed updates."

The lights went out. I pushed back from the table as if to be ready to spring into action. Someone squealed. I thought it might be Herschel. Everyone started talking at once.

"Don't worry," the chef said. "Just stay where you are. The generators will bring the light back on in a matter of minutes."

I sat back down. The time ticked by. It could have been three minutes, or it could have been ninety minutes. My eyes adjusted to the dark with the help of the yellow emergency lights peeking in through the cracks around the swinging kitchen door.

Several people turned on their cell phone flashlights. As I was about to get up because I couldn't take it anymore, there was a hum, and the lights came on.

Cecily clapped. "See, we're fine. The generators will stay on through the night."

I hoped she was right. Garden Peak Lodge wasn't a place I wanted to be in the dark.

"They don't power everything," Herschel warned. "They will keep the kitchen going because of the freezers and refrigerator. They also support the water pump for the well and the furnace. The generators are for the essentials. The emergency lights in your rooms will work for a time, but some of the outlets will not."

"Well," Stone said. "Since we're in a remote location on the side of the mountain, this could be a problem. Cecily, we need to discuss this before we sign the final documents for the sale."

Cecily looked like she wanted to jump across the table and strangle Herschel.

"Of course," she said in a steely voice. "We can discuss it after the meal."

Ridge walked into the dining room just then. He was wearing his usual jeans and brightly colored sweater. "Weren't you going to invite me to dinner, Sis?"

Cecily scowled at him. "I didn't think you would want to come. You have made no effort to speak to me all weekend."

Ridge grabbed a chair from another table and shoved it in between Tate and Frederick Hume. Frederick looked like he wanted to run, although that might not have anything to do with Ridge. From what I could tell, he always appeared to be ready to bolt.

With eyes bright with glee, Benny B quickly made up a place setting for Ridge as Tate and Frederick scooted their chairs farther apart to make more room for Ridge.

"What would you like to drink, sir?" Benny B asked in his best waiter voice.

I wondered if I was the only one who could hear the anticipation in his voice. Benny B was thrilled about Ridge's arrival. I bet he'd also taken mental notes on the argument between Heather and Cecily. He was going to have one whopper of an article to sell.

While Ridge settled into his seat, Benny B brought out the first course, a winter squash soup that smelled heavenly on such a cold night.

Glasses of water and wine were refilled. I noted that all the wine on the table was from Stone Wineries. Not by accident, I was sure. Cecily very much wanted this deal to go through. I supposed nothing was stopping her, not even her husband's death, since he had no claim to the lodge. The lodge was hers and hers alone. Yet I wondered at the logic of selling it before they had settled her husband's estate. Heather was right that Cecily might be acting too soon. Even if she was named the sole heir in the will, wills could be contested. Did she really want to give up the only property that wasn't also attached to her husband? With as much money as Dr. Madd had, I thought she was foolish to believe no one would contest his will.

Jeremy Stone smiled at me. "It's nice to see you again. I'm surprised you decided to wait out the storm here when you had a chance to leave the mountain."

I set my water glass back on the table. "I could say the same about you."

He smiled. "I'm here for the business, of course. Also," he added in a low voice, "it doesn't hurt to see how the lodge weathers this blizzard before I make anything official. You can never be too careful with real estate."

"I'll remember that," I said. "What makes you want to purchase the lodge?"

"I'm branching out and trying to build my empire, as it were, around Seneca Lake. This isn't the only property I'm buying this year. It is the most expensive, though; Cecily is making sure of that."

I glanced down the table and saw Cecily was having a conversation with Heather. It looked tense, at
best, but at least it was keeping her occupied for the
moment.

"Are you concerned about the recent events at the
lodge?"

"If you mean Dr. Madd's death, no. That has nothing to do with me or with the purchase of the lodge.
Cecily and I have been talking about this a long time
before this weekend. I even have a team in place,
ready to come in and make Garden Peak Lodge live
up to its potential."

I raised my brows when he said team. That didn't
bode well for Herschel and the other employees at the
lodge. "How long had you been talking to Cecily about
buying this place, if you don't mind my asking?"

"At least a year. Maybe two. I have had my eye on
this place for a while."

I frowned. If Cecily had wanted to sell the lodge for
so long, what had caused her to wait? Her husband?
Did she have to remove him to sell it?

Chapter Twenty Seven

ʜᴇ ɴᴇxᴛ ᴄᴏᴜʀsᴇ ᴡᴀs ᴀ choice between lobster or steak. I went with the lobster. It seemed that Cecily was hosting this blizzard dinner to impress Stone. I think the chef knew it, too. He peeked into the dining room now and again, looking increasingly nervous with each course that arrived on the table. He also seemed to pay special attention to Stone's reaction. Like every employee at the lodge, the chef must have wondered how the change in ownership would impact his position at the lodge. Stone had said his "team" would come in. Did that mean he planned to replace everyone? I wasn't surprised if the entire staff was concerned about that. I knew I would be if I were in their place.

The meal continued through dessert. Cecily spent most of the time having a whispered conversation with Stone. Maybe she was trying to salvage her deal, since he wasn't happy with the generator power in place at the lodge.

Next to me, Frederick picked up his water glass with a shaky hand. The liquid splashed out onto his blue button-down shirt as he tried to bring it to his lips.

Directly across the table from Frederick, Ridge glared at his sister. If looks could kill, I'd be worried for Cecily. She had given her husband the same deadly expression when he had announced that Kiera Bellworthy would replace her as the face of MaddlyCare. It was at that moment that I saw the family resemblance.

"Frederick," I said just above a whisper. "Is everything all right?"

"Yes." He set his water glass down as if giving up on it. He had never managed to take a drink. "Yes. Why wouldn't everything be all right?"

"You seem to be a bit tightly wound."

He licked his lips. "Did you give Cecily Miracle Smooth samples?"

I shook my head. "I haven't. I'm sorry. It completely slipped my mind when the storm hit. I'll give it to her after dinner, but are you sure you don't want to be the one to give it to her?"

He looked at Cecily and appeared to turn green. "I couldn't."

Across the table, Pierce was sipping his after-dinner cappuccino. Edwin had two empty mousse dishes in front of him. Pierce didn't do sweets.

"Pierce, have you tried Frederick's eye cream yet?"

Pierce's face lit up. "I have. It's amazing. I swear one of the laugh lines under my eyes completely disappeared."

Edwin set his spoon in one of the empty dishes. "He's right. His eyes have never looked better."

"I'm glad you brought this up, Darby, because

Frederick, you and I should talk after dinner." He glanced down the table to Cecily, and seeing that she was still in deep conversation with Stone, he went on to say, "I think we can work together on this. I have friends at other companies who might be more much pleasant to work with than MaddlyCare. I'd like to help you."

"You would?" Frederick smiled and looked, for a brief moment, genuinely happy. "I'm just a scientist. I don't know how to handle the business side."

"And I'm a businessman, not a scientist. This is what will make this work," Pierce said.

"I'm okay with this, as long as I get free samples of your eye cream for life," Edwin chimed in."

"If we can forge a partnership, you certainly can," Frederick said.

The lights flickered off and then came back on.

"What is going on with the generators?" Cecily directed this question to Herschel.

Herschel took a spoonful of mousse and studied it before answering her. "I suppose it doesn't matter what I know. I don't work here any longer, do I?"

Tate arched his eyebrows at me. It seemed that Herschel had grown a backbone since he was fired. He knew there was nothing she could do to him anymore.

"I would think that out of respect for my father, you would want to make sure the lodge was well-protected," Cecily said. "You told me he was your friend."

Ridge snorted. "What respect did you have for our father, Cecily? You lived just down the mountain and never came to see him. Despite that, he gave you this place. You know he did that to punish me, not to award you."

Cecily glared at her brother. "I will not talk to you about this at the table."

"You won't talk to me about it ever. Instead, you plan to sell the lodge out from under me out of spite."

She looked down her nose at him. "Maybe you shouldn't have done things to anger our father and put your security in jeopardy. That has nothing to do with me."

Ridge clenched his jaw and appeared to be holding himself in place so he wouldn't jump across the table and strangle his sister.

Cecily stood. "I suggest that we all turn in for the night. I think, like many of you, I plan to make an early start so I can leave the lodge in the morning." She smiled at Stone. "Just after we finish our final paperwork."

Stone didn't smile back. Did the winery owner regret his decision to buy the lodge already?

The table broke up. Pierce and Edwin took Frederick under their wing, and I let out a sigh of relief. Even from the start, that partnership was much better than any Frederick Hume could have hoped to have with MaddlyCare.

"What are you smiling for?"

I looked up and found Tate smiling at me.

"I think Frederick is going to be okay, and I'm happy about that. I feel sorry for the guy. He has a good product, but he's too afraid of his own shadow to share it. Pierce will help him with that."

"Have you been using his eye cream? Your eyes are looking extra sparkly tonight."

"What kind of line is that?" I groaned. "It's a wonder you ever have a date."

He sighed. "It's true. I haven't had a date since moving back to Herrington."

"Really?" This was news to me. I'd assumed Tate was out and about when we weren't on a case. He was a handsome and charming guy. It was a bit hard for me to imagine him just sitting at home eating Flamin' Hot Cheetos.

"I just haven't seen anyone who sparked my interest," he said casually.

There was a tiny pang in my chest. He hadn't seen anyone who interested him?

"At least I haven't seen anyone I'm interested in who's also interested in me."

What did that mean? Who was he talking about?

I followed Tate out of the restaurant.

The great chandelier in the lodge lobby wasn't lit. Apparently, it wasn't powered by the backup generator. Cecily and Stone walked around the lobby; he pointed at things and she frowned. I guessed Stone was cataloging what was on and off during the storm, and every time he saw something off, he mentally deducted from the purchase price of the lodge. Which I had to admit wasn't fair to Cecily. Winter storms couldn't be helped, especially not in the Finger Lakes.

The fire from the large fireplace gave off light and much-needed warmth in the drafty lobby. I found Frederick shivering in front of the fireplace.

"What are you doing here alone?" I asked. "I thought you were meeting with Pierce and Edwin."

He jumped. When he looked over his shoulder and saw it was only me, he relaxed just a tad.

"Are you okay?" I asked.

"Yes, I'm just waiting for Pierce and Edwin. They ran up to their room to get a notebook and some files. They seem to be very serious about helping me sell my eye cream." He clasped his hands in front of him.

I smiled. "You couldn't work with a nicer pair of guys."

He nodded. "I should have spoken to them much earlier. It would have saved me a lot of grief this weekend."

"So was it worth coming out here after all?"

"I think so, and now, I'm ready to get off the mountain."

"I think most of us are."

He looked around the lobby. Benny B came out of the restaurant with a large grin on his face. What was he smiling about?

Frederick visibly relaxed when he saw him.

"Frederick, are you worried about seeing someone?"

His hands fluttered on his lap. "Worried about seeing someone? No—why would you ask that?"

"Every time someone comes out the restaurant, you jump."

Ridge came out of the restaurant then. He was scowling. With that expression on his face, I could see the family resemblance between him and Cecily. They both had a sour disposition.

Instead of relaxing when he saw it was Ridge, Frederick froze. His body was tense, and he was as stiff as a board.

Ridge strode across the lobby and out the back door into the snow. Did he really think he could walk back to his cabin with no problem in this foul weather?

"Why are you afraid of Ridge Tragger?" I asked.

"I—I'm not afraid of him."

I cocked my head. "You froze up when he came out of the restaurant."

Frederick looked as if he might be ill.

"Tell me," I insisted.

"He was on the mountain that morning Dr. Madd was killed," Frederick said, barely above a whisper.

I wasn't really surprised to hear that. Ridge was the ski instructor for the lodge, and he had a cabin not far from the ski house. "Ridge has been here all weekend. He lives here."

Frederick's Adam's apple bobbed up and down. "He was carrying a crossbow."

My heart sank to my feet.

I couldn't think of a single reason why Ridge would need a crossbow on New Year's Day morning. Archery classes only took place in the summer, according to Herschel. Hunting season was long over. The archery shed where Ridge must have gotten the crossbow was way on the other side of the property; I knew that because I had walked there in the snow with Tiny and Tate. There really was no reason for Ridge to be carrying a crossbow. None at all.

"Why didn't you come forward?" I asked. "The police need to know about this."

"After I heard about Dr. Madd's murder, I spent most of my time hiding in my room. Hiding from Ridge, maybe. Hiding from having to talk to anyone. I'm not proud of it." He wouldn't look at me. "I know I have a good product. I do, but I have severe anxiety. The people who know me back home would be shocked that I worked up the nerve to even come out here. I went to the New Year's Eve party. It was hard for me, but I did it. I thought—I thought—that I was finally conquering this disease that has controlled me for so much of my life."

My heart went out to him. Everyone dealt with some level of anxiety, but it sounded like Frederick's case was extreme. And from what I had observed of him, he was constantly on edge. I could see him finding a large, confident athlete like Ridge intimidating.

"I can see that you're nervous, but you came to dinner today."

He nodded. "It took everything I had to do it, especially with the storm going on outside. Every time the window rattles or the wind howls, I jump. It's hard to explain how I feel. It's this vibration in my body. It's like a thrum that won't stop. Every muscle is tense and ready to run. It took all my physical, mental, and emotional strength to make that dinner tonight. I knew it was my very last chance to get my eye cream in front of Cecily Madd." He dropped his head. "And I blew it, but I'm glad, in a way. I wouldn't be working with Pierce and Edwin had things gone differently. It can be difficult for me to share my ideas with people."

"You shared them with me right away," I said.

He turned to look at me. "You're different. I don't feel like I'm being judged by you."

I internally winced, because I had not always had kind thoughts about Frederick. I had wondered why he didn't get on with it and pitch his idea to the Madds. I was happy to learn that my internal criticism of him didn't show through. "Do you want me to wait here with you until Pierce and Edwin come back?"

"You don't have to," he said, as the elevator doors opened and my two friends came out. They were smiling and Pierce carried a briefcase. It seemed to me like they were very serious about working with Frederick, and that warmed my heart.

"Darby, perfect. You stay here and we can try the eye cream on you."

"Nope, nope," I said. "I have to go find Tate." I jumped out of my seat.

Edwin made clucking chicken sounds behind my back

Chapter Twenty Eight

IN THE MEANTIME, I NEEDED to decide what to do about Ridge. Was he the killer? When he left the lodge after dinner, I assumed that he went back to his cabin, but I didn't know for sure.

I had to admit he looked good for the murder. He had means, motive, and opportunity. Then, I thought about his motive. Was it a good one? If Cecily had been the one who was shot, I wouldn't doubt Ridge was behind the murder for a second. She was selling his home right out from under him.

At the sole legal owner of the property, she had the right to, but I couldn't imagine that sat well with Ridge. He had made it clear at dinner that he was angry with his sister. Would he kill his brother-in-law for revenge? It seemed farfetched, and if that was the case, it had backfired horribly. She'd sold the lodge anyway, perhaps even faster than she would have otherwise.

I walked around the lobby and stared out the large window that looked onto the patio. When the sun shone, and skies were clear, I could see the slope and the ski house from where I stood. Beyond that was Ridge's cabin.

I started to open the door, just to feel how bad the weather was. Without even setting a toe outside, my breath was sucked out of me, and I was pummeled with snow.

I was about to close the door when hands appeared and slammed it shut for me.

"What are you doing?" Tate asked, frowning at me. "You can't go out in that."

I dusted the snow off my blouse. "I wasn't planning to go out in it. I was just seeing what it was like."

"It's cold, wet, and miserable. What else do you need to know?"

"I need to know if Ridge went to his cabin or is still lurking around the lodge. This is a big place."

"I don't think even Ridge would have taken the risk to walk back to his cabin. It would be too easy to get lost in the snow. He could go ten feet from the back door and lose his way."

I shivered when I thought of that. I imagined that the same would be true for me if I went in search of his cabin. It was even more likely I would get lost, since I didn't know the terrain as well as Ridge did. "I saw him go out the back door after dinner."

Tate shook his head. "Then he's crazier than I thought. Why are you looking for Ridge?"

As quickly and quietly as I could, I told him about my conversation with Frederick.

His eyes went wide. "You can't go out there looking for him. You can't even see your hand in front of your face."

"What if he tries to hurt Frederick?"

"Does he know Frederick saw him on the day of the murder?"

"I don't know. Frederick didn't say either way if Ridge saw him that morning."

"I think it would be more prudent to keep an eye on Frederick rather than look for Ridge. If Ridge suspects Frederick saw him, and Ridge is the killer, he'll go looking for the witness."

I shivered. "I left Frederick at the lobby fireplace with Edwin and Pierce."

Tate and I found Edwin and Pierce sitting by the fireplace looking bewildered.

"Where's Frederick?" I asked.

"That's a good question," Pierce said. "He said he was going to be right back, and we haven't seen him since."

"Did something happen?"

Edwin shook his head. "No. I mean, the front door opened and Ridge came into the lodge. He said he couldn't make it to his cabin tonight and would stay here until the weather broke."

"Frederick took off right after that." Pierce frowned. "No matter how good his eye cream might be, I'm not sure we should work with him if he blows us off like this."

"He's just nervous," I said. "Or maybe he felt sick and didn't want to admit it. Tate and I will track him down. Why don't you two go to bed?"

Edwin nodded. "I'm pretty tired. Let's discuss the eye cream in the morning."

"Fair enough," Pierce said.

After they left, Tate asked me, "Why didn't you tell them about Ridge?"

"I don't want to involve them more than they already are."

He nodded.

"Let's find Frederick and make sure he's okay."

"What's his room number?"

I shrugged. "Herschel would know. His apartment is behind the reception desk." Without waiting for Tate, I walked across the lobby again. The door behind the reception desk was closed. I knocked on it. I heard Tiny give a friendly woof on the other side of the door. Herschel was in there.

"Herschel, it's Darby and Tate."

There was a shuffling sound on the other side of the door. When the door opened, Herschel stood on the other side in his pajamas. Around him, there were open suitcases and boxes. He was in the process of packing up his life at Garden Peak Lodge. After so many years at the lodge, there was a lot to pack.

He stepped back from the door and let us inside. "You will have to forgive the mess and my appearance. I'm trying to decide what to take and what to leave behind with instructions to donate. It's hard to believe I've accumulated so many possessions in this studio apartment." He looked at the ground.

"Can you tell us Frederick Hume's room number? I'm worried about him," I said. "I just want to check that he's okay."

"He did seem rather nervous at dinner," Herschel said. "I can't look him up on the computer system. For one, the computers are not supported by the generators. For two, Cecily changed all the passwords on the registration system after she fired me." He shook his head. "I have to hand it to her: When she decides to get rid of a person, she does not play nice. She goes for the jugular. She knows how this job has been my whole life, so she took it from me." Tears gathered in his eyes. "I don't know what else there is for me to do in this life."

"Whoa," Tate said. "Don't sell yourself short. The Finger Lakes are a massive vacation destination. I'm sure there will be plenty of resorts and hotels that will want to hire you."

Herschel sighed. "I suppose. I have to find something else. I do want to feel useful again. I haven't felt that here in the last few years. Everything—well, until Cecily showed up—ran so smoothly here at the lodge. There was very little for me to manage. Sure, the occasional upset or overly demanding guest, but there were no big changes that needed implementing, not since Cecily and Ridge's father died. God rest his soul. He was a good man, even if he was harsh.

"I think Cecily takes after him in a lot of ways. When Mr. Tragger made up his mind about you, that was it. There was no redeeming yourself. His son is the perfect example of that. When Ridge fell in with the wrong crowd after failing to make the Olympic team, and got into all that trouble, that was it. Mr. Tragger would never kick his child out in the cold, but he certainly wasn't going to leave his lodge to Ridge after seeing what poor choices he made."

"So he left it to Cecily instead," I said. "It strikes me as odd, since he wasn't that involved in her growing-up years."

"That had to do with Cecily's mother more than anything. Their marriage broke up on terrible terms, and Mr. Tragger never really recovered from it. He effectively cut his first wife out of his life, and since Cecily was her daughter, he cut her off too, until she was an adult. Then Mr. Tragger let her in. But I wouldn't say they were close. I do think he left the lodge to Cecily to punish Ridge— just as Ridge said at dinner." He took a breath. "When you think about someone's will, it really is their last statement to the world. They make a point of telling everyone who or what is most important to them. They also, like Mr. Tragger, can use it as a last recourse of discipline." He scratched Tiny's head. "Tiny here, a dog he'd only had one year before he died, did better off in Mr. Tragger's will than his son did. I think we all need to remember that."

I could feel my heart beating against my ribcage. Ridge could very well be the killer. I could see him being angry enough to take another life. That made me even more worried for Frederick Hume. If Ridge realized he had seen him that morning with the crossbow, Frederick could be in real danger.

"If you can't access the computers to get Frederick's room number, how do we get it? He might be in danger."

"Oh, it's 213."

"213?" Tate asked.

"Yes, I might not be able to access the computers, but I have the room numbers for all the guests memorized. I always do. It's just part of being a manager."

"How many rooms are in the lodge?" I asked.

"Seventy-three."

"And when the lodge is full, you can remember seventy-three room numbers as guests come and go?" I asked in disbelief.

"Yes." He looked confused. "Should that be difficult?"

Chapter Twenty Nine

ATE AND I TOOK THE grand staircase to the second floor. Room 213 was at the very end of the hallway. Before we were halfway down the corridor, I could see the door was at least partway open. I broke into a run.

"Darby!" Tate called after me.

I don't know what I expected to see when I stepped into the room. Ridge holding Frederick by the throat, maybe? What I found was nothing. The room was empty. The bed was made, and there weren't any personal belongings in the bedroom or bathroom. Frederick's room was not a large suite like the ones Tate and I had, so there were only two small rooms. There was nowhere to hide. I even checked the closet.

When Tate came into the room, I glanced over my shoulder. "He's not here."

"I can see that," Tate said.

"Could Herschel have the room number wrong? A lot of guests checked out today. He might have confused Frederick's room with another."

"I don't know," Tate said. "He seemed pretty

confident about the number, and he can remember seventy-three of them, you know."

I sighed. "Frederick couldn't have left the hotel. If he did, he'll be dead before Ridge ever finds him."

"Do you think Ridge would hurt him?"

"I don't know," I said. "But it's not worth taking the chance."

"Okay," Tate said. "Let's see if we can find him or Ridge."

Tate and I spent the next two hours searching the lodge, but had no luck finding either man. It was a massive place. There were many places to hide.

"We will have to try and look for them in the morning," Tate said. "It's after midnight. We are both exhausted. Everyone else has long since gone to bed."

I nodded, feeling defeated. I couldn't help but think I'd let Frederick Hume down.

The next morning, I was up at five. It didn't matter that I had gone to bed so late the night before. It was the time I always woke up to get my run in before work. It was still dark out, but the lights were back on at the ski house. I glanced at the clock on the bedside table. The numerals blinked bright green. Power had returned to Garden Peak, and it was not just from the generators. I took that as a good sign.

In the lights around the back patio and the ambient light from the nearly full moon, I could see the storm had passed. In its wake was a blanket of fresh snow that lay perfectly untouched on the side of the mountain. The snow fringed everything from the deck furniture and the roofs of the buildings to the tree limbs in the woods. It was beautifully peaceful. One would never know that the snow had made such a violent entrance from the heavens by looking at it.

I glanced at my cell phone. It was now five-ten. Despite the early hour, I made a phone call.

Austin picked up on the first ring. "Darby, are you okay?"

"Yes," I said.

"How many people stayed on the mountain last night?"

"Ten, maybe eleven or twelve. I'm not sure if I saw all the lodge staff who stayed behind."

"But you're okay?"

"Yes, I'm fine. Exhausted, but fine."

"I couldn't sleep at all last night, knowing you were up on the mountain. I was such an idiot to leave. I should have let my officers escort guests off the mountain and stayed behind."

"As far as I know, everyone at the lodge is all right, but I do have some information I have to share with you." I quickly told him about my conversation with Frederick Hume and what he had seen the morning of the murder.

"So Ridge is the killer."

"Probably. Last night, Tate and I tried to find Frederick and Ridge, but couldn't. I like to think Frederick is hiding someplace in the lodge until he can leave."

"And Ridge?"

"He's somewhere in the lodge too, or now that the weather has cleared, he might be in his cabin again.

The weather was too bad last night to make it to the cabin safely."

"I wish I could be up there with you."

"You're not coming back to the resort?"

"I am, but not until the mountain road is opened. Several trees fell across the road in the storm, and it's going to take some time to clear," Austin said. "I called the county and told them it was top priority to clear the road to the lodge, so we can get back up there. I'll call again. We will be there as soon as we can. Don't take any risks."

I didn't say anything.

"Darby, did you hear me?"

"I have to find Frederick and make sure he's okay. And if Ridge is the killer, you don't want him getting away, do you?"

"He's probably already left. I'd rather he escapes than you go chasing after him."

There was a knock on the door that divided my suite from Tate's.

"Who's that?" Austin wanted to know.

"It's Tate."

There was silence on the other end of the line for a long beat. "Of course it is," Austin muttered. "I'm going to call the road crew again and will text you when the roadwork is underway. Don't do anything stupid."

"I would never."

He snorted and ended the call.

I pulled on a sweatshirt over my pajamas and opened the door for Tate.

Tate, who was in a white T-shirt and gym shorts, scratched the back of his head. "That was Austin."

"How did you know?" I asked.

"I could feel the exasperation through the call when you said my name."

"He's trying to get a road crew to clear the road. Several trees are blocking the plows. As soon as he does, we can leave. In the meantime, we need to find Frederick. I'm worried about him."

"What time is it?"

"Five-twenty."

Tate yawned.

"Get dressed. The power is back on. We have to find Frederick before Ridge does."

Tate went back into his room without another word. For once, he was taking me seriously.

Chapter Thirty

 HAD DECIDED THAT ONE OF the easiest ways to
find Frederick was to call his cell phone. I dug
through my small suitcase until I found the sample
of eye cream that he had given me. Tate came out of
his bedroom just then. "You're finally going to give the
eye cream a try? You don't need it, in my opinion. You
don't look a day over five."

I peered at him. "Are you trying to butter me up
for some reason?"

"I would never."

The sky was beginning to lighten outside, but the
sun wouldn't fully be up for another hour. That was
just too bad. I had to find Frederick now.

I called the number on the bottle. It went directly
to Frederick's voicemail. Either his phone was off or
not charged. I wasn't completely surprised, but was
disappointed nonetheless. I saved the number in my
phone to try again later.

"Maybe Herschel knows something," I said. "Let's
go."

"Yes, ma'am," Tate said, with a salute.

When we entered the lobby, I walked straight to Herschel's door behind the front desk. The desk was empty. I supposed with so little staff on hand it wasn't prudent to staff it twenty-four hours a day.

I knocked on Herschel's door. Tiny barked on the other side of it. To my surprise, when Herschel opened the door, he was fully dressed. I peeked into his small apartment and saw a pile of neatly labeled boxes and three suitcases all ready to be moved out.

He took note of my nosiness. "I couldn't sleep, and with the power out, there wasn't much else I could do but pack up my things to move." He looked from Tate to me and back again. "Did you find Frederick last night?"

"No. That's why we're here now. Do you have a universal key that we can borrow?"

He wrinkled his nose. "I do, but I shouldn't give it out."

"You don't even technically work here any longer," Tate said. "What difference does it make to you?"

Herschel seemed to consider this. He then walked over to a desk against the wall, opened a drawer, and removed a key card. He handed it to me. "You're right. I don't owe this place anything. Here." He cleared his throat. "Why do you want to find Frederick so badly?"

"We think he witnessed the murder," Tate said.

I wanted to kick him for saying that. The fewer people who knew what Frederick had seen, the better.

Herschel paled. "Why didn't he say anything before?"

"He was afraid," Tate said. "Ridge is pretty intimidating."

"Ridge!" Herschel said. "You think Ridge is the killer?"

I frowned at Tate. "We don't know, but he's a good suspect. His motive is difficult to pin down, though."

"If Cecily had been killed, there would be no debate. Ridge hates his sister," Tate said.

"Oh, oh," Herschel said. "Th—that's awful. I've known Ridge since he was a boy. He's gone through some difficult things, but I can't believe this. Do you know where he is?"

I shook my head. "We haven't been out to the cabin yet. My guess is he went back home when the weather cleared."

He nodded.

"In any case, I'm more concerned about finding Frederick. As soon as the road leading to the lodge opens, the police will come up the mountain and find Ridge. We just have to keep Frederick safe until then."

Herschel pulled at his collar. "You think they will arrest Ridge?"

"They will question him again, that's for sure. It doesn't look good for Ridge. If I were him, I'd be working on my story now, and might be even thinking of someone else to blame," Tate said.

"Oh." Herschel paled. "Well, I'll let you two go look for him."

Tate and I left Herschel's apartment.

"How are we going to find Frederick?" Tate wanted to know.

It was a good question. I removed my cell phone from my pocket and called Frederick's number again. This time the phone rang. On the other end, there was a tentative hello.

"Frederick!"

"Who's this?"

"It's Darby. Are you okay?"

There was silence on the other end of the line.

"Frederick?"

"I'm okay."

"Where are you?"

"I'd rather not say. I'm just waiting for the road to open so I can leave the mountain."

Leaving Garden Peak was really what we all wanted to do.

"I don't want Ridge to find me." His voice quavered.

"Has he been looking for you?" I asked.

"I don't know. I'm not going to take a chance on coming out, if he is."

"Okay," I said. "Stay where you are, and I'll call you when the road is open, and you can leave. Please keep your phone on."

"Okay." He ended the call.

Tate raised his eyebrows at me.

"He's hiding. My guess is he's barricaded himself in one of the guest rooms," I said.

"It's not a terrible idea. I mean, if Ridge is the killer and catches up to Frederick, the chemist doesn't stand much of a chance."

"As long as he's safe. I know Austin is trying to get here as quickly as possible."

As I said this, Herschel and Tiny came out of his apartment. Herschel was all bundled up. He waved at us. "Just taking Tiny out," he said in an unusually high-pitched voice.

"What going on with him?" Tate asked.

"Maybe he's just sad about leaving the lodge."

I thought about following him, but the elevator binged, and Cecily strode out of it. Even though it was still early morning, she looked completely ready for her day, with perfect hair, coordinated outfit, and matching ski boots.

"I was hoping I would see the two of you this morning," she said. "The road will be cleared within the hour. A tree fell across the road halfway up the mountain, causing the delay. The storm stopped close to three, I believe. As soon as it opens, Jeremy Stone and I are leaving." She patted her smooth hair. "I'm pleased Stone and I were able to agree about the lodge. It's one less thing for me to worry about as I have to clean up the mess my husband left behind in MaddlyCare. I'm up for the task. Work has always been the way I dealt with difficult situations. I don't believe grief will be any different."

It was interesting that she mentioned grief because, from what I had observed, she experienced none of it. I knew very well that everyone dealt with death differently, but Cecily was an extreme case.

"Have you seen your brother recently?" I asked.

"Ridge?" She sniffed. "No, I don't really have anything to say to him. He's made this sale process with Stone more difficult than it had to be. Ridge and I barely had a relationship before, but now that I've sold the lodge, I can see us going our separate ways. I think that's for the best. We are very different people."

I glanced at Tate, and he gave a slight nod. "A witness saw Ridge carrying a crossbow on the mountain the morning of your husband's murder."

"What witness?" she asked.

"I can't say until the police have a chance to speak to the witness."

She glared at me. "I don't care what your witness

saw. My brother didn't have anything to do with Garret's death. And your opinion doesn't matter. You're not on the case anymore."

"Cecily, I think you need to consider the possibility," Tate said.

Cecily gave an incredulous laugh. "You think my brother killed my husband? You have lost your minds."

"He's not happy about your selling the lodge. He's going to lose his job and home."

She snorted. "No, he's not. Stone promised me that Ridge would always have a place here. He's a great ski instructor. He has a cabin he maintains himself. There's no reason for Stone not to keep him on. It costs next to nothing for Stone to have Ridge work and live here. Also, it doesn't hurt to have someone living on the property full-time. Things come up at all hours with guests, and Ridge can be here for those things."

I pressed my lips together. Stone might have given her his word to keep a place at the lodge for her brother, but he wasn't legally obligated to do that, not like Cecily had been due to her father's will. Ridge wasn't the nicest person in the world. I could see Stone growing tired of his antics and kicking him out. At that point, Cecily and Ridge would have no recourse to make Stone do anything.

As Tate and I walked away, he asked, "What are you thinking?"

"Huh?" I blinked at him.

"I know that look. The wheels are spinning overtime in your brain."

I sighed. "I'm glad Frederick is safe, but I'm uneasy not knowing where Ridge is. Cecily might believe she is appeasing her brother by having Stone promise he won't kick Ridge out, but I don't think Ridge is going to believe that Stone will keep that promise. To be honest, I worry about what he might do."

"Well, there's only one way to put your mind at ease, then," Tate said.

I looked at him expectantly.

"That's to find Ridge."

"I was hoping you'd say that."

It made the most sense to start looking for Ridge at his cabin. Tate and I went up to our rooms and bundled up for a hike across the slope to the lone cabin on the property, then went down and exited through the back door. Despite the seriousness of our mission, I couldn't miss the beauty around us as we trudged through the deep snow. Everything was fringed with white, from the tiniest branch on a pine tree to the roof of the ski house. The snow on the top of the ski house draped so perfectly over the eaves that it looked more like frosting than snow.

"You know," Tate said, as he matched his stride with my much shorter one. "Your purple snow suit is kind of cute. It's growing on me."

I gave him a look. "Sure it is."

"No, really. You'd look adorable in anything. Even a Barney costume." He looked into my eyes, and all I saw was sincerity.

My face felt like it was heating to a thousand degrees. What did Tate think he was doing? We were partners; business partners. The only kind of partners we could be if the agency was going to work.

"There's the cabin," I said, not even trying to hide

the relief in my voice when it came into view. I quick-ened my pace. We needed to catch a killer before I could overanalyze what Tate meant by that compli-ment.

I knocked on the door, but there was no answer. I tried the handle and it gave. "Hello! Ridge?"

There was no answer.

Tate stepped around me. "Let me go in first."

I gave him a look.

"I know you're tough, but I was in the Army. I know how to search a cabin for an assailant."

I stepped back. "Go for it."

Tate went inside, and I could hear him moving around the cabin. A few minutes later, he reappeared in the doorway. "No one's home."

I followed him inside the small building. The first thing I noticed was how clean the cabin was. There wasn't even a stray coffee mug on the kitchen coun-ter. A blanket was neatly folded and draped over the arm of the sofa.

"If I didn't know better, I would say that Ridge was former military, too, just by looking around," Tate said. "I don't see a smoking crossbow, do you?"

"No," I said with audible disappointment, but then something caught my eye. In the middle of the rug, there was a large paw print. It was much bigger than that of a normal dog.

"Tiny was here," Tate said.

"Looks like it." I had an uneasy feeling in the pit of my stomach.

What I didn't know was why seeing Tiny's paw print was making me feel that way.

Chapter Thirty One

ʙY EIGHT IN THE MORNING, we saw a plow coming up the long driveway leading to the lodge's front door. I stood with Tate at the front door. It was time to get off this mountain. This came as both a relief and a disappointment. I didn't like the idea of leaving Garden Peak Lodge with unfinished business.

Two police cars and Austin's SUV pulled into the driveway. It seemed that they had followed the plow up the mountain.

Austin jumped out of the SUV and walked toward us. "Where's Ridge?"

Tate shook his head. "We don't know. We checked his cabin a little while ago, and no one was home."

"We'll find him," Austin said. "There's only one road in and out of the resort. Where could he have gone?"

I wasn't sure it would be that easy. Ridge had lived on the mountain most of his life. He knew every inch of it. I was willing to bet he was a competent outdoorsman too. He might be able to stay one or two steps ahead of the police, at least for a while. I watched as Austin's officers went around the side of the building.

Cecily came out of the lodge, and Herschel followed close behind with her bags. It seemed that even though he'd been fired, he still felt obliged to help guests check in and out of the lodge.

"Thank God you're finally here," Cecily said to Austin. "I'm ready to leave this place and get back to my real life in Manhattan."

Austin nodded and followed his officers around the side of the building.

Stone drove up to the front, got out of his SUV, and took Cecily's bags from Herschel. He put Cecily's suitcases into the back of his SUV. "We should be at the Syracuse airport in less than three hours."

"I can't wait," she said. "It's time to get back to civilization." She smiled at him. "It's so very kind of you to drive me to the airport, Stone."

"It's the least I can do after you sold me this place. I'll take good care of it. I promise."

She smiled even wider.

Herschel looked as if he might faint, and his eyes dashed back and forth around the snow-covered lawn as if he expected someone to jump out from the trees at any moment. Tiny pressed up against his owner's leg, as if he sensed Herschel's nerves.

Frederick Hume stepped out of the lodge with a lone suitcase.

All the color drained from Herschel's face when he saw him.

Tate must have noticed too, because he asked, "Herschel, is everything okay?"

"Okay?" He blinked at Tate.

Stone smiled at Frederick. "Where are you headed?"

"I called a car service. I can wait," Frederick said.

Stone waved his hand. "Don't be silly. There is plenty of room in my car for you and your suitcase, even with all of Cecily's luggage. Ride with us."

Frederick hesitated.

"Why waste your money when I can take you there for free?" Stone asked.

Frederick nodded, as if more to himself than to Stone. "You're right. I would appreciate the ride. Thank you."

Stone started to put the suitcase in the trunk of his car.

Herschel ran down the steps. "No, wait. I don't think Cecily would want to ride all the way to the airport with Frederick. She might be uncomfortable."

Stone cocked his head. "She'll be fine. She's not that delicate."

Cecily threw open the door of Stone's car. "Let's go. I don't want to miss my flight."

"We're going to give Frederick a lift to the airport too," Stone said.

"Fine. I don't care. I just want to leave." She slammed her door shut with such force that all the snow fell from the closest shrub to the ground.

Herschel stepped back from the car. He was almost shaking.

Frederick got into the back seat, and Stone sat behind the wheel. I let out a breath as they drove down the driveway. Austin and another police officer came around the side of the lodge as the SUV went out of the gate. By their posture, I guessed they hadn't found Ridge yet.

Benny B came out of the lodge. He was no longer in his uniform.

I crossed my arms. "Taking off?"

"Sure am. What a scoop. I will be writing about this place and MaddlyCare for weeks." He sighed. "I really was counting on you, Darby, to solve the murder to give my articles that extra punch. You might be losing your touch."

I narrowed my eyes at him.

"Benny, if I were you," Tate said. "I would just go."

Benny looked at the dark expression on my face and his eyes widened. "I didn't mean anything by it."

I uncrossed my arms. "Speaking of unsolved mysteries, where were you the morning that Dr. Madd was killed?"

His eyes went even wider. "I told you. I was in bed sleeping after a late night."

"I know that's what you told me, but I don't believe you. You were lying."

He sighed. "If you really must know, I was doing yoga. It keeps me centered."

"Why didn't you just say that?"

"I don't know. It's not something I want broadcast around the world."

"I really don't think anyone cares if you do yoga or not, Benny B," Tate said.

"I've made enemies in this business, you know. They're just waiting to get back at me. Maybe you can practice solving your homicide cases by trying to find the people who don't like me, Darby. You might need the practice after this flop."

I scowled at him.

He waved his hands. "Okay, okay, I'm leaving. I'll see you on the next case, Darby. Whether you solve them or not, you find some interesting stories for me to write about."

After Benny B went back into the lodge, to pack up his things, I guessed, I shook my head and sighed.

"What do we do now?" I asked Tate.

"Chalk it up to experience."

I gave him a look.

"What? You can't win them all. Have you solved every case that came across your desk?"

"No." I put my hands on my hips.

"That's exactly my point."

"This time is different. A man is dead."

"And we're pretty close to certain that Ridge is the killer. The police will catch up with him eventually. He's never wanted to leave this mountain. He'll be back. When he is, they'll arrest him."

It wasn't that I thought Ridge would get away with murder. I agreed he would eventually get caught because he would want to return to the lodge. But anyone who shoots an unarmed man in the back with a crossbow must be more than a little unstable. I was more worried he would hurt someone else before they caught him. That was why I was glad Frederick was getting out of Herrington while he could.

Herschel and Tiny stood on the lodge steps. Herschel looked so small and scared standing next to his giant dog.

Tiny ran over to us and asked for a head scratch. I obliged. All the while, I worried about his owner.

"Let's get our stuff and get off this mountain, too," Tate said.

We started toward the lodge, when there was a massive bang. I froze. "What was that?"

"It sounded like a car crash," Tate said.

Tiny's Saint Bernard instincts kicked in, and he ran off down the road.

"Tiny!" Herschel called.

We shared a look. Then Tate took off for one of the two snowmobiles parked next to the lodge. I ran after him. He jumped onto the snowmobile, and I hopped on behind him. He thrust a helmet at me. "Put it on."

"There's just one. You should wear it."

"Put it on." His tone left no room for argument.

I was still tightening the strap when the snowmobile flew through the entrance gate.

The road down the mountain was slick. Even though it had been plowed, the accumulation of snow was so great that a layer of snow and ice was packed down on the road, which was good for the snowmobile. Maybe not so good for Stone's car.

I looked over my shoulder and saw Austin and another police officer following us in Austin's SUV. I hoped they had snow tires.

"Oh, no," I said, as we came around a curve in the mountain road.

The SUV lay on its roof, caught between two large trees. The impact into the trees was what had caused the sound we heard at the lodge. Tiny pawed at the windows and barked.

Tate stopped the snowmobile a few yards away. I was off the machine before he even had a chance to cut the engine. I knelt by the driver's side window.

Condensation clouded the front windows. I couldn't see a thing. I moved to the back of the car and saw what had caused the crash. There was an arrow in the rear tire.

"Tate!" I called, just as I heard a bang. Now there was another arrow sticking out of the car's fender just to my right.

Tate ran over to me. "What was that?"

"Someone is shooting at the car." I pointed at the tire. "I'll give you three guesses who it might be."

"I don't need three," Tate said. "I see him right over there."

I spun around and saw Ridge standing at the tree line, holding a crossbow. I swallowed. He stared at us but made no attempt to hide or run away. He didn't care if we knew he was the one who had attacked Stone's car. He wanted us to know.

Tate ran in that direction.

"Tate!"

I was about to get up and follow him, until I heard a voice in the car calling for help.

Austin and the officer appeared at my side. The three of us got the back car door open. Frederick, who had been in the back seat, lay on the roof of the car. He groaned, but was able to crawl out.

The officer was on the radio with an ambulance. I prayed it could make it up the mountain.

I helped Frederick to a tree and leaned him against it. There was a bloody gash on his forehead, but other than that, he looked all right. "What's your name?"

"Frederick Hume," he said.

"What day is it?"

"January third."

I let out a breath. "Stay here a second."

Tiny sat with him.

By the time I got back to the car, Austin and the officer had gotten Stone and Cecily out.

Stone held his arm like it was broken, and Cecily had a small cut on her left hand from glass. But it could have been worse. It was a miracle they weren't more seriously injured.

"Where's Tate?" Cecily asked.

"He went after Ridge, who shot your car. Do you still think your brother is innocent?"

She paled. "I never thought he would try to hurt me. I would have never..."

"You would have never what?" I asked, and studied her face.

The mask that she constantly wore crumpled slightly. Maybe the accident had shaken her up more than I thought. But just when I thought she might crack completely, her mask slid back into place.

"The EMTs will be here as soon as they can, but with the road the way it is, it will take them at least an hour to get from town up the side of the mountain," Austin said.

"Maybe it would be best to take them back to the lodge then," I said. "I mean, as long as no one is seriously hurt. It might be better to get everyone in from the cold."

"I'm not going to miss my flight!" Cecily said.

"You were just in a major car accident, Mrs. Madd. I don't think it's wise for you to get on a plane," Austin said.

Tate returned. "I think I know where he's headed." He ran to the snowmobile.

I jumped to my feet. "You can't go after him," I said.

"Sure I can," Tate said as he climbed onto the snowmobile.

"Not without me." I jumped on the back of the snowmobile.

Austin waved his arms. "Wait!"

"We can't wait. He'll get away again," Tate said.

I wrapped my arms around Tate's waist just as the snowmobile jerked forward. The snow hit the shield on my helmet. Tate turned off the road into the trees. We were going uphill.

"Where are we going?" I shouted in his ear.

"I'm going to get ahead of him. He's heading back to his cabin."

"To do what?"

"Have the last stand? I don't know." He grabbed my hand from his waist and put it on the handlebar. "Switch places with me."

"Are you crazy? The snowmobile is in motion."

"It's easy." He stood up and swung his right leg behind me. The next thing I knew, I was seated in front of him and driving the machine.

Just behind us, another snowmobile burst out of the trees. Ridge was on it. His crossbow lay across the handlebars. He was heading straight for us.

I glanced over my shoulder for a split second. "What now?"

"Slow down," Tate said in a calm voice.

"Slow down? If I slow down, he'll catch us."

"That's what we want."

"You want him to catch us?"

"I want you to pull alongside him. I'm going to jump on him," Tate shouted into my ear.

"You're going to what?" I cried. It took all my strength to control the machine going up the mountain.

"Get next to him. I'll take care of the rest."

"It's too dangerous."

"Darby, trust me. I know what I'm doing."

I looked over my shoulder at Ridge heading straight for us. When he was just shy of my bumper, I jerked the controls to the right and we were next to him. Before Ridge knew what was happening, Tate leaped from my snowmobile to Ridge's, knocking Ridge out of his seat. Both Tate and Ridge fell in the snow and rolled downhill in a tangle of arms and legs.

Ridge's snowmobile continued up the mountain. A crash echoed as the machine ran into a tree.

Tate ripped off the man's ski mask. Ridge's red face glared at us. Tate straddled him with a knee on either arm, pinning Ridge's arms to the ground.

"Get off me," Ridge said.

"I don't think so. You tried to kill your sister and us."

Ridge tried to roll back and forth in the snow, but it was no use. Tate had him pinned in place. I wonder if the knee hold was something he had learned in the military.

The crossbow stuck out of the snow a few feet away. I picked it up and pointed it at Ridge.

"Why did you kill Dr. Madd?" I asked.

He glanced at me from his spot on the ground. "You're not going to be a danger to anyone holding the crossbow like that. Your finger isn't even close to the trigger."

"It would still hurt if I threw it at you," I said. "Again, why did you kill Dr. Madd?"

"Because I had a deal."

"A deal with who?"

"Who do you think?"

"Cecily," Tate said. "She sent the notes to lay the groundwork."

"Cecily?" Ridge scoffed. "No, it wasn't my sister."

Tate's face fell. "Then who?"

My heart sank. "It was Herschel, wasn't it?"

Ridge's dark eyes darted in my direction. "It seems she is better at detection than you are," he said to Tate.

Tate looked at us. "But why?"

"The lodge," I said. "Herschel didn't want her to sell the lodge."

"Then why not kill Cecily?" Tate was still confused. "Why kill Dr. Madd?"

"If my sister died, the lodge would still go to a new owner, because it said in my father's will it would have to be sold and the money donated to charity. My father did everything he could to punish me, even rob me of my inheritance. Herschel thought if Cecily had to deal with her husband's death, she'd go back to New York City and forget about our little lodge for a while."

I shook my head. "Did Herschel ask you specifically to kill Dr. Madd?"

"Not directly, but I knew what he wanted. He told me as long as he was in charge of the lodge, I would have it easy here. I wouldn't even have to teach ski lessons any longer if she would just leave. What he said made sense to me. I knew that if I eliminated Dr. Madd, my sister would get his company. At that point, she would have no reason to want this place. She could give it to me, and we'd both have what we wanted."

"But that's not the way it worked out," I said.

He scowled at me. "No, that's not the way it worked out. My sister had been married to Garret Madd for too long. She learned all his manipulative ways to make money—to steal money—from the people working around him. My sister knew Stone had been interested in buying the lodge, so when she knew she was going to be rich from her husband's death, she wanted more."

"I think that's enough," a cold voice said.

I turned around to see Cecily holding a gun and pointing it at Tate and Ridge.

"There is no need to continue to bore Tate and Darby with our family drama."

"There wouldn't be any family drama if it weren't for you," Ridge spat. "You're the one who caused all of this."

She chuckled. "You caused your own pain, brother. You were always Dad's favorite. Your mother was the one he loved, and you're the child he raised. But you threw that all away to party and get in trouble time and time again. Is it any wonder why he wrote you off in his will and put me in your place? He might not have loved me as well, but he knew I wouldn't be an embarrassment."

Ridge's face flamed bright red. "Your husband

didn't love you either. That seems to be a pattern for you. You're replaceable."

Cecily moved the gun, so it was pointed more at her brother. "Do you really think I didn't know about his plan to replace me? There's nothing that happens at MaddlyCare that I don't know about. My husband thought he was sneaky by keeping his ideas in another place. He didn't trust me." She laughed. "The joke was on him, because I didn't trust him either. I won't be replaced."

"So you wrote the notes," I said in disbelief. It was so calculated, even for Cecily.

"I didn't have a financial stake in the company. He always promised to give me some stocks or assets, but he never did. I realize now that was one of the ways he controlled me. He promised things that he never delivered. Then I learned that he planned to replace me as the face of MaddlyCare. That wasn't feasible. I wrote the notes to scare him and stop him from doing that, but he ignored them. Ridge did me a favor by killing him. I wouldn't have eighty percent of the company otherwise."

"You didn't divorce him because of the prenup," I said.

"Very good, detective."

"Why hire us?" Tate asked.

She smiled at him. "Even though I haven't seen you in so long, Tate, I knew you, and I knew you'd never solve the case of the notes. Why would I hire someone to find the author of the notes when I had written them myself? It was so crazy it just might work. I will confess to the notes, yes, but I had nothing to do with my husband's death. From what I've heard, that was my brother and Herschel. I knew Herschel was trouble."

"I wouldn't have been trouble if you didn't force me to be."

We all looked in the direction of the voice and found Herschel standing at the tree line with another crossbow.

Tate groaned. "Does anyone else want to come out of the woods with weapons?"

I adjusted the crossbow—which I didn't know how to use—in my hands. "Let me get this straight. You, Cecily, sent those notes, to scare your own husband. Herschel, you put it in Ridge's head that if Dr. Madd was killed, Cecily would leave and everyone at the lodge could go back to life as it was before. And you, Ridge, acting on that, killed Dr. Madd. You're all culpable in some way."

Cecily pointed her gun at Herschel. "That might be so, but I don't have blood on my hands like these two. Herschel is the one to blame for that."

"Ridge made a choice," Herschel said. "Putting an idea in his head doesn't mean he had to act on it."

"Of course it does," Ridge said. "And you'll know that as well as I do when the police arrest us both. You won't last half a day in prison."

Herschel's face paled as white as the snow.

During the conversation, Tate's hold on Ridge must have weakened, because suddenly, Ridge threw him off his chest. Tate landed in the snow like an overturned turtle. Ridge grabbed the gun from his sister's hand and pointed it at Herschel. "Since you won't last in prison, I might as well finish you off now."

"Put the gun down!" It was Austin who shouted this. He and his police officers had finally caught up with us.

My finger quivered by the crossbow's trigger. I knew I wouldn't be able to pull it. Just as I was trying to decide what to do, a giant beast came crashing through the forest. Tiny leaped into the air and landed squarely on Ridge's chest. The gun flew out of his hand.

I kicked the gun away from him, and Tate picked it up.

A long line of drool dripped on Ridge's face.

I can still hear his horrified scream.

Epilogue

ATE WALKED INTO MY OFFICE a month after our adventure at the ski lodge. "Well, we started this year off with a bang."

I looked up from my desk, where I was making a list of cases and clients I needed to follow up with. The list was much longer than it had been before the tumultuous holiday weekend. I wasn't sure I could chalk that all up to the publicity the agency had received for solving Dr. Madd's murder, and the flurry of exposés and articles Benny B had written about it. It seemed like every week he published a new article about "The Murder at the Lodge," or so he called it. He'd written an article on all three culpable people in the crime: Cecily, Herschel, and Ridge.

He was very appreciative that Tate and I had solved the case. He'd sent me flowers with a note that said his readers loved the story. I was sure they did. I personally didn't read any of Benny B's write-ups about the New Year's Eve weekend. I knew I would become too irritated about the liberties he would surely have taken with the facts.

Even though Cecily wasn't involved in the murder, the news of the threatening notes she'd written had been leaked to the press—thanks to Benny B, I was sure—and MaddlyCare was reeling from the death of its founder and the vindictiveness of his wife. It was hard to say if the skincare company would be able to come back from this.

Ridge was in prison facing trial for the murder of Dr. Madd and the attempted murders of Frederick Hume, Jeremy Stone, and Cecily. It seemed fair to say that he would be in prison for a long while after his confession on the mountain.

And Herschel was in for a long prison stay too. Even though he hadn't pulled the trigger on the crossbow, he had talked Ridge into the crime, and bribed him with a cushy position at the lodge. He had been arrested for conspiracy to commit murder.

The only person to really come out on top from the weekend was Kiera Bellworthy. She made rounds in the press to share about her harrowing experience at Garden Peak Lodge. From that, she'd landed a role on a reality TV show for celebrities who had fallen from grace. It wasn't a Hollywood blockbuster, but it was a place to start from to rebuild her career.

Gumshoe slept in the chair across from my desk. It had taken a whole week for him to be willing to be around me after my stay at the ski resort. The smell of Saint Bernard was hard to shake, and Gumshoe wanted me to remember that. He was less than pleased that Tiny was now a fixture at the agency.

After his arrest, Herschel had asked Tate and me to make sure the dog had a good home.

Tate leaned on the doorframe. Tiny forced himself

past my partner into the small office and went right up to Gumshoe.

The cat sat up in his seat and arched his back. He let out the most awful hiss I had ever heard. Tiny's tail wagged, and he grinned at Gumshoe like he had been reunited with his long-lost brother.

"I knew they would get along," Tate said.

Gumshoe let out another warning hiss.

"Yep, they're doing great." I shook my head.

Tate laughed and rubbed the side of his beard. "I need to talk to you about something."

I set my list aside. "What's up?"

"I've got a big case." His eyes shone.

I grimaced. "In the last big case, we were almost killed."

He wiggled his eyebrows. "True."

"Right, so don't be surprised that I'm not jumping out of my seat ready to hear about this one."

"Aww, come on. I thought we agreed to trust each other on that mountain."

I rolled my eyes. "I trust you to help me avoid being killed by an assailant. I don't trust your ability to pick a worthwhile case."

"How am I going to learn if I don't get a chance to try?"

"Fine. What is it?"

"What do you think about going undercover as brother and sister pastry chefs—"

I groaned.

The End

Goat Cheese Phyllo Puffs

A Hallmark Original Recipe

In *Frozen Detective*, private eye Darby Piper pretends to be Tate Porter's date for a fancy party at a mountain lodge. The two are secretly investigating a case, and most of the guests are dressed to kill. Every detail of the event is elegant, from the décor to the appetizers, including these Goat Cheese Phyllo Puffs. They're simple to make, and like Darby, you might not be able to eat just one!

Prep Time: 30 minutes
Cook Time: 20 minutes
Serves: 16

INGREDIENTS

- 3 ounces (3/4 stick) butter, unsalted, melted

- 16 - 9" x 14" phyllo sheets, thawed if frozen
- 1-pound chevre (goat cheese), mild

PREPARATION

1. Preheat oven to 375F.
2. Scoop chevre into 24 - 1 tablespoon portions and reserve on wax paper.
3. Gently unwrap phyllo dough from packaging and unfold. Cover stack of phyllo sheets with plastic wrap followed by a damp kitchen towel. Remove one sheet of phyllo and re-cover the stack. Lay the phyllo on a work surface with the short side in front of you.
4. Brush with melted butter. Lay a second sheet of phyllo on top of the buttered phyllo. Brush with more butter. Cut the stacked phyllo from short side to short side into 3 even (3" x 14") strips.
5. Place 1 scoop of cheese near the corner of a phyllo strip on the end closest to you, then fold over to enclose filling and form a triangle. Continue to fold the strip like a flag, keeping the triangle shape. Lay pastry on a baking sheet, seam side down. Brush top with butter.
6. Repeat until all the phyllo has been used. Recipe may be prepared up to three days in advance at this point – simply wrap in plastic and store in the freezer).
7. Bake 20 minutes or until golden brown, rotating the pan once to ensure even browning. Cool slightly before serving.

Turn the page for a free sample of

MURDER
BY PAGE
ONE

A PEACH COAST LIBRARY MYSTERY
FROM HALLMARK PUBLISHING

OLIVIA MATTHEWS

Chapter One

"I WAS PROMISED CHOCOLATE."

I directed the reminder toward my new best friend, Jolene Gomez, after entering the bookstore. I threw my gaze into every visible nook and cranny of To Be Read in search of chocolate-covered pecan clusters.

Jo owned To Be Read, an independent bookstore on the southeast side of Peach Coast, Georgia. It wasn't that I needed the food bribe to come to her bookstore—or any bookstore—especially when a bunch of authors were signing their books. It was just that, well...promises had been made.

"Marvey." The tattooed businesswoman's tan features warmed with a welcoming smile. Her coffee-colored eyes shifted to my right. "Spence. I'm glad you both made it."

Jo seemed relieved, as though she'd worried we wouldn't come. Why would she have thought that? I kept my promises, especially those made to another book fanatic. Jo and I had bonded over our love of books, our newcomer status—she was from Florida and I was from New York—and chocolates, which reminded me today's stash was still conspicuously absent.

"Of course we came. We're readers. On top of that, we're here supporting our friend." I nudged Jo's shoulder with my own.

"The others are on their way," Spence said, referring to the members of the Peach Coast Library Book Club.

Spence and I had walked over from the library after our Saturday afternoon meeting. It was about a fifteenminute walk, and the weather on this May Day had been comfortably warm. As geographically challenged as I was, I'd been glad to have Spence with me. On my own, I probably would've still been circling the library's parking lot.

Spencer Holt was a local celebrity, although he'd deny it. The Holts were the richest family in Peach Coast and one of the wealthiest in Camden County. They owned a bed and breakfast, a hotel, a local bank, and the town's daily newspaper, *The Peach Coast Crier*. It was considered required reading among the residents, and Spence was the publisher and editor-in-chief.

The family was also philanthropic: Peach Coast's answer to Gotham City's Wayne Foundation. Spence's mother, for example, served on the board of directors for the Peach Coast Library—which technically made her my boss.

For all his money, prestige, power, and good looks—think Bruce Wayne with a slow Southern drawl—Spence was very humble. He was more interested in listening than talking about himself, and he seemed to prefer comfort over fashion. I once again noted his brown loafers, faded blue jeans, and the ruby-red polo shirt that showed off his biceps and complimented his warm sienna skin.

Spence shifted his midnight gaze to mine. "If you want pecan clusters, we can get some at the coffee shop after the signing."

After the signing? "It wouldn't be the same." Translation: that would be too late. Far too late. I continued scanning the store, my mind rejecting the truth my eyes had confirmed.

"I haven't put the chocolates out yet, but I'll get you some in a minute." Jo waved a hand as though the treats weren't important. The right sleeve of her citrusorange knit sweater, which she'd coupled with leafgreen jeans, slipped to reveal the University of Florida Gators logo inked onto the inside of her small wrist. Jo was a proud alumna. "First, let me introduce you to Zelda Taylor. She's the president of Coastal Fiction Writers. The authors who're signing today are members of her group. Zelda, you know Spence."

"Ms. Zelda, it's nice to see you again." Spence's greeting rumbled in his Barry White voice.

"Mr. Spence, it's always such a pleasure," the redhead gushed. Her porcelain cheeks glowed pink. "How is your mama?"

"She's very well, ma'am. I'll tell her you asked after her." Spence's smile went up a watt. The poor woman seemed dazed.

I tossed Spence a laughing look. "Is there anyone in this town you don't know?"

Spence's smooth forehead creased as he pretended to consider my question. "Well, nearly one thousand people reside in Peach Coast. I'm sure I've yet to meet one or two of them."

Jo gestured toward me. "Zelda, this is Marvella Harris. She moved here from New York—the city—four months ago. She's the library's new director of community engagement."

Zelda tugged her attention from Spence. Her appearance was flawless: well-manicured nails, perfect makeup, and salon-styled hair. She was camera-ready for a photo spread in a Southern homes magazine.

"Oh, yes. I read the article about you in the Crier a couple of months back." Her voice was now imposing, as though she were reading a town proclamation. "Welcome to Camden County. What brings you all this way, Ms. Marvella?"

Referring to the county of residence instead of the town was taking some getting used to. I supposed it was like New Yorkers saying we were from Brooklyn, The Bronx, Queens, or Staten Island. Only people from Manhattan said they were from "the city."

"Just Marvey, please." The Southern custom of adding a title to a person's name was charming, but it was a lot to say before getting to the point. "I want to help the library increase its outreach and services. Do you have a library card?"

Zelda's eyes widened. "Why, yes." Her commanding tone had faded. "Yes, I do."

Although suspicious of her response, I gave her the benefit of the doubt. "Excellent. I look forward to seeing you at the library. You should join our book club. We meet the first Saturday of each month."

"Oh. That sounds nice." Zelda smoothed her silver cotton dress in a nervous gesture. I sensed her casting about for a believable excuse to get out of the meetings.

Spence offered an incentive. "Marvey serves Georgia Bourbon Pecan Pie and sweet tea after every meeting—but you have to stay till the end of the meeting for the refreshments."

Panic receded from Zelda's eyes to be replaced by interest. "Oh, well, now. That would be nice indeed."

I turned my attention from Zelda to survey To Be Read. I loved the store. It was like a giant welcoming foyer, flooded with natural light. Closing my eyes briefly, I drew in the scent of crisp new paper from thousands of books and magazines. Fluffy furnishings in pale earth tones popped up at the end of aisles and in quiet nooks. A multitude of blond wood bookcases stuffed with stories offered the promise of adventures and the thrill of knowledge. A couple of Jo's employees were setting up for the book signing. They'd already arranged the wooden chairs and matching tables. The twenty-somethings transferred books from wheeled metal carts to each author's assigned table. Jo's third employee processed purchases at a checkout counter while engaging each customer in conversation as though they were lifelong friends. Every now and then, a burst of warm laughter rolled across the store.

But there still wasn't a single chocolate-covered pecan cluster in sight.

"I'm sorry I missed the meeting." Jo's gaze swung between Spence and me, twinkling with curiosity. "How was it?"

"It was great," Spence said. Slipping his hands

into the front pockets of his jeans, he turned to me. "I'm impressed you were able to get the club up and running so quickly, within a month of your arrival."

"We librarians are known for our efficiency." It was a struggle to keep the smugness from my tone.

Spence's compliment filled me with a massive sense of achievement—and relief. Even though it was only our third meeting, I'd known the book club would be a success. We'd already attracted twenty-five book lovers, all from diverse backgrounds and each strengthening our argument for a bigger budget. *That* continued to be my motivation.

Leaving my parents and older brother in Brooklyn to relocate to Peach Coast with my cat had been hard. My roots were in Brooklyn. I'd lived my entire twenty-eight years in the New York borough, but I'd grown increasingly frustrated by my lack of opportunities to shine in my public library system. There, I was just one of many small fishes in a very big pond. I couldn't generate any waves. Not even a ripple. But I'd been confident that, if given a chance, my ideas for growing the community's interest in and support of the library could make a big splash. Here, in this small town, I'd finally be able to try. The library's success would make at least some of my homesickness worth it.

Jo grinned. "So who came in costume, and what did they wear?"

Spence ran a hand over his close-cropped hair. His voice was devoid of inflection. "Mortimer painted himself blue and called himself Aquarius."

This month's member-selected read was the latest paranormal fiction release by Bernadine Cecile. I loved paranormal stories. This one featured a world in which meta-humans used the power of their zodiac signs to defeat villains—hence Mortimer's costume. He wasn't the only one who'd gotten carried away. Most of the members hadn't wanted to read *Born Sign*, but the first rule of book club was to keep an open mind. To my relief, the novel had been a hit.

Zelda spoke over Jo's laughter. "Marvey, if you don't mind my saying, that's a lovely pendant." Her gaze had dropped to my sapphire cotton T-shirt, which I wore with cream khakis and matching canvas shoes.

"Thank you." I touched the glass pendant. I'd suspended it from a long antique silver chain. It held a silver-and-black illustration of the cover of Lorraine Hansberry's *A Raisin in the Sun*, the version depicting the Younger family's dream home.

Jo inclined her head toward me. Her long raven ponytail bounced behind her narrow shoulders. "Marvey makes those herself. And the matching hair barrette. She draws the pictures and puts them in the pendants and barrettes."

Zelda glanced at my shoulder-length, dark brown hair, but she couldn't have seen my barrette, which gathered my hair behind my head.

"You're very talented." Her eyes glinted with admiration— and longing. "Do you sell them?"

This question came up a lot. Each time, I stood firm. "No, it's just a hobby. I'd like to keep it that way."

I'd been making those pendants and barrettes since high school. The craft fed my love of art and jewelry making, and allowed me to pay homage to great works of literature. It was the kind of activity

I could do while listening to an audiobook. Although I often gifted sets to family and friends for birthdays and holidays, the hobby was something I did for enjoyment, not for money. If I mass-produced them, it wouldn't be fun anymore.

Jo's dark eyes twinkled with mischief. "With all the interest people have shown in your pendants, you may have to break that rule."

Spence flashed his silver-screen smile. His perfect white teeth were a dentist's dream. "Maybe you should give a class. That way, you can teach people how to make their own pendants."

"That's a great idea. The course could be a fundraiser for the library." New books. Updated software. Additional periodical subscriptions. Every little bit would help. I shelved the idea to consider in depth later.

"Ready for another great idea?" Spence's lips twitched with humor. "Run the Cobbler Crawl with me."

The man was relentless. I responded to his winning smile with a chiding look. "For the fourth time, no, I will not."

The Peach Coast Cobbler Crawl was an annual three-and-a-half-mile race to raise money for the local hospital. Each two-member team had to stop and eat a large, heaping spoonful of peach cobbler at the one-, two-, and three-mile points. The first team to cross the finish line together won.

"I can't enter the Cobbler Crawl without a running partner." Spence had been trying to convince me to form a team with him almost since the day we'd met.

I was running out of ways to say no. "Why don't we

both just give a donation and watch the event from the sidelines?"

Jo laughed. "You should do it, Marvey. You run six miles every day. Three and a half miles will feel like nothing."

Now they were ganging up on me. "If we only had to run, I wouldn't hesitate. But I don't think I can run *and* keep down the cobbler." I shuddered to think of the consequences.

Zelda came out of her spell, dragging her attention from my pendant. "I'm the exact opposite. I could eat the cobbler, no problem. But I couldn't run a mile in a month of Sundays."

Determined to change the subject, I turned to Zelda. "How many members of the Coastal Fiction Writers are published?"

"We're a small group, but we're growing. At the moment, there are twelve of us. Four of our members are published."

"Five." Jo lifted the requisite number of fingers. "I ordered books for five members. I think you're missing Fiona." She addressed Spence and me. "Fiona Lyle- Hayes just released her first book, *In Death Do We Part*. It's a mystery, and it's gotten great advance reviews."

Spence sent me a look before switching his attention to our companions. I could tell he wasn't giving up on the Cobbler Crawl. "We ran a piece about her book in the *Crier*."

"Oh, yes. How could I have forgotten Fiona?" Zelda clutched her pearl necklace. Her smile seemed fake. That was curious.

"Fiona helped coordinate the signing." Jo glanced

at her employees who were setting out the books before returning her attention to Spence and me. "She's also the writing group's treasurer."

"Yes, Fiona manages our money. She's good at that." Zelda flashed another tight smile, then looked away. Tension was rolling off her in waves. I really hoped it didn't bubble over and ruin Jo's event.

I glanced toward the entrance again to see more of our book club members arriving, as well as quite a few strangers—each one a potential new library cardholder. Four of the newcomers made a beeline for Jo, who identified them as the local authors who were signing today. I concentrated on the introductions, but keeping names and connections straight strained my brain. Of course, Spence knew all of them. I resolved to stick to him like gum on his shoe.

The authors dressed up their displays with promotional postcards and trinkets. Jo's employees put the finishing touches on the arrangements, which included the bowls of the long-promised-but-seemingly-forgotten chocolate-covered pecan clusters. Jo and I had only been friends for four months, but I'd known she wouldn't let me down. I began drifting toward the signing area—and the chocolates—when Jo's voice stopped me.

"I wonder what's taking Fiona so long?" Jo checked her silver-and-orange wristwatch. A frown cast a shadow over her round face. "The signing starts in ten minutes. I thought she'd have her books out long before now."

Zelda scanned the store. "Fiona left our writers' meeting early, saying she needed to get ready. Where is she?"

Jo jerked her head toward the back of the store, sending her ponytail swinging. "She's been in the storage room. She wanted to examine her books and bring them out herself."

Weird. "Why?"

Jo shrugged nonchalantly, but I saw the aggravation in her eyes. "She didn't say, but I suspect it's because she thought my staff and I would damage her books."

Zelda's smile didn't reach her eyes. "Fiona can be a pain in the tush. Bless her heart."

Bless her heart. That was a Southern phrase I'd heard before. It didn't mean anything good.

Read the rest! *Murder by Page One* is available now!

Thanks so much for reading
Frozen Detective. We hope you enjoyed it!

You might like these other books
from Hallmark Publishing:

Dead-End Detective
Murder by Page One
Out of the Picture
Behind the Frame
Still Life and Death

For information about our new releases and
exclusive offers, sign up for our free newsletter at
hallmarkchannel.com/hallmark-
publishing-newsletter

You can also connect with us here:

Facebook.com/HallmarkPublishing

Twitter.com/HallmarkPublish